ACCOLADES

A Stone's Throw is a superbly crafted and emotionally told Young Adult coming-of-age story about a girl named Maggie Stone after her life pivots in an unanticipated direction from San Francisco to Montana's ranch country. On reading, I realized a different theme. When a dark cloud covers your world, look for the silver lining. Maggie is instantly likable and seems to be a bit of every girl. I enjoyed *A Stone's Throw* and highly recommend this very satisfying read to not only the YA crowd but to adults of all ages. I can easily visualize a TV series based on this wonderful storyline.

~Jeff Bailey, author of the highly
acclaimed *Sing Family Conspiracies*

Through skillful storytelling, Wayne Edwards delicately intertwines the innocence of youth with the depth of his protagonist's intelligence as we watch her navigate distressing life circumstances. *A Stone's Throw* tenderly captures the odyssey of growing up, offering a heartwarming narrative that would make an invaluable addition to any educational curriculum.

~Naomi Roberson, The Word Count

A Stone's Throw

A heartwarming story of a city girl and her rancher grandfather turning adversity into love and community.

WAYNE EDWARDS

QUANTUM SHIFT
PUBLISHING

For information about special discounts for bulk purchases, please contact wayno_wce@yahoo.com

Cover Art by Don Greytak
Cover and Interior Design by Quantum Shift Media

ISBN: 978-955533-26-3 (print)
ISBN: 978-1-955533-27-0 (e-book)
Library of Congress Control Number: 2024906712

Printed in the United States of America

First Edition

Denver, Colorado

DEDICATION

I dedicate this book to a special friend and my writing mentor, Linda Hassinger.

Mrs. H, as she was known to her students during her tenure as an English and drama instructor at Denton Schools, strongly encouraged me to write during my retirement years. Linda was my unofficial beta reader, reviewer, and content editor for my first two books, *Pacer Coulee Chronicles*, and *Buster the Bridger Mountain Bear*, and was actively providing counsel in the early stages of the story development of this novel.

Unfortunately, Linda passed away before *A Stone's Throw* could be completed and published. I will be forever grateful for her help and support throughout my writing projects and will dearly miss her sharp mind and clever wit.

ACKNOWLEDGMENTS

I would first like to thank my fifteen-year-old granddaughter, Rylee Bigelow, for being my source of inspiration in writing "A Stone's Throw." The strong grandfather-granddaughter bond we share in real life provided the vision to develop the fictional storyline of this novel, where the relationship journey begins under a cloud of unknowns and mistrust.

As in my previous two books, I would like to extend a special thanks to my wife, Lorinda, and my three daughters—Sara, Kelley and Katie—for constantly being asked to review and critique the seemingly endless manuscript changes that were made along the way. Your patience and counsel was invaluable in eventually being able to submit a final rough draft manuscript to the editor.

I want to again thank my sister, Colleen Murphy, for her continued contributions in getting my stories to the finish line. As a former high school English instructor, her input in creating this novel was meaningful and appreciated.

I would also like to thank Sue Poser and Wanda Lucas, both longtime, now retired elementary/middle-school teachers in my hometown of Denton, for taking the time to read and review this manuscript as it was approaching the final draft stages. Since both educators have a lengthy history of leadership roles in various youth reading councils and organizations, their critique and feedback was most relevant and useful toward the ultimate goal of targeting the young adult audience.

I would be remiss if I didn't recognize the many contributions of Keren Kilgore of Quantum Shift Media, the editor and publisher I worked with to bring *A Stone's Throw* from the rough draft stage to the final product. Her astute and experienced guidance throughout the entire project process was of the utmost value.

I would like to give a shout out to Dr. Dick Rath, my old Lewistown, Montana veterinarian friend, for kindly agreeing to be my animal research source and having the patience to answer all the "what would be the treatment protocol in the 1960s for when a (insert type of animal) suffers this (insert injury/disease/condition)" questions.

I would also like to extend a special thank you to Montana's nationally known and highly regarded pencil sketch artist, Don Greytak, for creating the art on the book cover and in some of the chapters. The likeness of the girl on the book cover to my granddaughter Rylee is uncanny, and his attention to the detail of the era-specific farm machinery in all the drawings is remarkable. Readers will also especially enjoy the real-life look of the sketches of the dog's encounters with a skunk and a rattlesnake!

Chapter 1

A TRIP TO THE EMERGENCY ROOM

I won't lie—I was a really scared twelve-year-old girl the afternoon I found myself in a San Francisco hospital Emergency Room. I sat on an old wooden bench squeezing hands with my best friend, Cho Jeong on one side, and her mother, Sun-Ju on the other. I was happy to have my bestie Cho with me, but even more grateful to have Sun-Ju around to help explain to the admitting nurse why my mom was brought to the hospital in an ambulance. It's not that I wasn't familiar with my mom's medical condition, but it was reassuring to have an adult present who was also aware.

It seemed like we had been in the waiting room for a long time, but a glance at the half-hidden clock on the grumpy receptionist's desk showed we had only been waiting for a little over two hours. All three of us had been anxiously watching the steady flow of patients, nurses, and doctors through the revolving door that led to the treatment area where a nurse or doctor would frequently call out to a patient's family members.

Finally, it was our turn. "Lillian Stone? Family of Lillian Stone?" shouted a disheveled-looking man in a white coat who suddenly appeared from the treatment area entrance door.

"Over here!" exclaimed Sun-Ju, all three of us jumping up in anticipation. Pointing to me, she said, "This is Lillian's daughter, Maggie. I am Sun-Ju Jeong, and this is my daughter Cho. We're family friends."

"I'm Dr. Canfield," the frazzled-looking doctor said as he approached. "We've done all that we can to ensure Ms. Stone is as comfortable as possible for the moment, but I just want to go over a few of the things you told the nurse when Lillian was admitted."

"Sure, okay," I replied, ready and willing to answer any questions that might help the doctor treat her condition.

"So, the nurse said you indicated your mom has had these kinds of, shall we say, trance-like blackouts before?" Dr. Canfield asked, looking directly at me.

Glancing at Sun-Ju for support and reassurance, I replied. "Yes, what you called trance-like blackouts, well, I call them *spells*. She's been having them a couple of times a month for a long time, but it's been more often than that lately. The spells last longer than they used to, but never for more than half a day. This is the first time it's ever lasted this long."

"Okay, thanks for confirming that. Since this appears to be related to a brain or nervous system disorder, we're going to move her to the neurology floor where she will spend the night. She needs to see a specialist, so we have called for a neurological evaluation. Ms. Stone, ah, I mean you, the family of Ms. Stone, have an appointment tomorrow at 2:00 p.m. to see Dr. Kakarla. He's one of the top doctors in our Neurology

Department and has already started taking X-rays and running some diagnostic tests."

"Ca-can I see her now?" I suddenly burst out, fighting back the tears about to spill from my eyes. "Can I sleep with my mom tonight? I mean, I always sleep next to her, especially wh-when she's having ah-ah—a spell!"

"I'm sorry, but your mother needs complete quiet and bed rest right now. She won't be able to receive any visitors, at least not until Dr. Karkarla examines her and permits visitation," the doctor explained.

Looking at Sun-Ju, the doctor asked, "Does Maggie have any family here, or will you be the one bringing Maggie to her appointment tomorrow?"

"No, Maggie doesn't have any other family here. I guess you could say I will be caring for her until Lillian is released from the hospital, and they can return to their home. So yes, I will be responsible for getting Maggie here tomorrow and for any further appointments," Sun-Ju replied.

"Very well then. Dr. Kakarla's office is directly above us on the fourth floor—the neurology floor. He will explain his exam findings to you then," Dr. Canfield stated as he disappeared as quickly as he had entered through the revolving treatment room door.

"That means a brain doctor will look at her, right?" I asked Sun-Ju as we drove out of the bustling Emergency Room parking lot. "I mean, I've always figured that my mom's spells must have something to do with her brain not working the way it's supposed to, right?"

"Yes, Maggie," replied Sun-Ju as Cho continued to clasp my hand comfortingly. "A neurologist is trained in matters of the mind and brain, so I think that's exactly what your mom needs right now. And don't you worry about tonight or any other night. You can stay with us until your mom comes out of this spell and you are able to move back into your apartment. But for now, let's swing by your place and pick up some clothes and your personal items."

"I can miss some school and come with you tomorrow to hear what the brain doctor says about my mom, right?" I asked anxiously, relieved I could stay with the Jeongs in my mom's absence.

"Yes, yes, of course, you can come," answered Sun-Ju before quickly adding, "And no, Miss Cho, you will not be missing school to come with us." Despite the severe nature of my mom's medical situation, Cho and I couldn't help but share a smile over Sun-Ju answering the question we all knew Cho was about to ask.

Chapter 2

A VISIT TO THE NEUROLOGY FLOOR

I'm not kidding when I tell you I was nervous as a cat when Cho's mom and I sat in the neurology reception room waiting to see what Dr. Karkarla had to say about my mom's condition. It seemed like we had to wait a long time again, so to stop constantly looking at the Tuesday, April 15, 1969, 2 pm appointment card or repeating my nervous habit of rolling and unrolling my long brown hair ponytail into a ball to help pass the time, I grabbed the latest issue of *Sport* from the magazine rack.

I flipped to an article about San Francisco Warriors' forward Jerry Lucas. I'm a big sports fan, so I already knew he was a great NBA basketball player. What I learned that morning while waiting for the doctor was that he had a photographic memory and had developed a memory system to help remember all kinds of things: names, numbers, shopping lists—stuff like that. Even though I thought I had a pretty good memory, I made a note to try some of his techniques to remember the names of new kids at school.

I read every article in *Sport* and was rooting through the shelf for another magazine when an older lady in a white nurse uniform entered the room. "Lillian Stone? Family of Lillian Stone?"

"Yes, we're here for Lillian Stone," said Sun-Ju as we leaped from our chairs in unison. "This is Lillian's daughter, Maggie, and I'm Sun-Ju Jeong, a family friend."

"I'm Carla Yates, one of Dr. Kakarla's nurses—please follow me," she said, motioning us with a hand gesture as she hurriedly swept us from the reception room to a busy hallway.

After negotiating several bends in the corridor and weaving our way past nurses, doctors, and what I assumed were other visitors like us, Nurse Yates deposited us in a small, cluttered office that had "Dr. Aditya Kakarla, Neurology" stenciled on the upper glass panel of the door.

"Please have a seat," ordered Nurse Yates, pointing to the only two chairs in the small reception room. "Dr. Kakarla and Dr. Drummond will be in shortly to visit with you."

Before Nurse Yates could slip back into the hallway, I anxiously blurted out, "Has my mom come out of her spell yet? I mean, she must be awake now, right? She's never been in a spell for this long before—please tell me she's awake."

"I'm sorry. I'm so sorry," said the nurse as Sun-Ju wrapped a comforting arm around me. "Her, ah, her condition, unfortunately, hasn't changed. That's why you need to visit with the doctors, as they can explain her situation much better than I can."

Nurse Yates left the room before I thought to ask why we were seeing two doctors now, so I asked Sun-Ju. "They didn't tell us yesterday that we would be seeing two doctors, did they? Does this mean something awful is going on with my mom?"

"Whoa, Maggie. Let's not get too far ahead and start worrying about things needlessly. Let's just settle down and wait for the doctors to explain their findings," Sun-Ju said supportively.

"You must be Sun-Ju Jeong and Maggie Stone?" asked the first of the two doctors who entered the room. I thought he must be from India because he looked a lot like my classmate Devi's dad. After we both confirmed our identities with a nod, the short and stocky, brown-skinned man stated, "I'm Dr. Kakarla, the neurologist who has examined Lillian Stone, ah, your mother. And this is Dr. Drummond, our Chief of Psychiatry here at San Francisco General. I called him in to consult on your mother's case."

"Hello, nice to meet you both," mumbled the much older psychiatrist. "Let's go downstairs to my private office, where we'll have a bit more room and can speak more comfortably, shall we?"

We all followed the stooped, shuffling doctor into the elevator, where he asked me to push the button for floor three. His office was only a few doors down, and as he sat behind his desk he motioned Sun-Ju and me to sit on the couch. As Dr. Kakarla pulled up a chair to sit directly across from us, I couldn't help but wonder if Dr. Drummond made his patients lie down on the couch where we were sitting—you know, like you see in the movies or on TV.

"Okay, I'm sure having all these doctors examining your mother is confusing to you," stated Dr. Kakarla, including both Sun-Ju and me in his eye contact. "Let me explain. I'm a doctor of neurology, meaning that my medical specialty is diagnosing and treating disorders that affect the brain and spinal cord. I've done a thorough examination of Ms. Stone, including neuro tests for seizures and X-rays to check for tumors. Those are the two most likely physical conditions that might cause this comatose-like state—or spell—as you call it. Upon review of the results from these initial X-rays and tests, we are not finding any evidence of either tumor or seizure activity, nor any other nervous system disease or abnormality that might be a causative factor."

We were learning a little about the skeletal, muscular, and nervous systems in science class this quarter, but all this talk about seizures and brain tumors was far beyond the scope of that class. *No tumor,* I thought excitedly! That had to be good news, right? Then the doctor continued, and I knew what he really wanted to say wasn't what I wanted to hear.

"Now, while that is good news, I must warn you that we doctors and researchers still don't know a great deal about the brain and how it functions," Dr. Kakarla continued. "In addition, we have a long way to go in developing the X-ray capability to provide images of detailed quality and clarity. For example, currently, we lack the X-ray capacity to detect small tumors or even somewhat larger growths that may be deeply embedded in the brain. So, simply put, there is the possibility that a small, slow-growing tumor may be present but not yet detectable on the X-ray. But again, there is no evidence of that at this point."

"Now, that brings us to why I included Dr. Drummond in our meeting today," Dr. Kakarla offered, regaining my attention while pointing to the older gentleman with the kindly eyes behind the thick-lens oval glasses perched on the far end of his nose. "Dr. Drummond is a psychiatrist, meaning that he also deals with matters of the brain and nervous system, but his focus is on diagnosing and treating mental and behavioral disorders. Often, neurological and psychological conditions overlap. Do you understand what I'm getting at?"

"Yes, I think so," I said hesitantly, not really knowing if I totally understood the avalanche of neurology and psychiatry information that was roaring through my brain. "Do you mean that even though you're pretty sure my mom doesn't have anything like tumors or seizures in her brain, her spells might be caused by her mind being, well, you know, her mind kind of being mixed up?"

"That's exactly right, Maggie. I'll bet you're a good math and science student," said Dr. Kakarla with a look of approval washing through his expression. "Let's see if we can't make things even clearer for you," suggested Dr. Karkarla. "But first, could we confirm some of the information you gave the admitting doctor in the Emergency Room yesterday? That will help us complete our diagnosis and treatment plan for your mother. Dr. Drummond will take it from here."

"Fine, fine, yes, indeed," began the psychiatrist in a soft, almost hypnotic voice. "Okay, let me go over some details just so I have everything straight," he said, thumbing through the pages of the treatment chart he held in his lap. Turning to me with large eyes magnified through thick lenses, he continued. "You are Margaret, ah, Maggie Stone, daughter of Lillian Stone, right?"

"Yes, doctor, that's right," I said nervously.

"Fine, fine, and you would be Sun-Ju Jeong, a family friend, and Maggie's acting guardian?" he asked, turning his gaze from his notes to Sun-Ju.

"Well, not officially her guardian, but in the absence of other family members nearby, my husband and I will be taking Maggie under our care for a while, hopefully until her mom can return home," Sun-Ju explained.

I won't lie—for my age, I'm an independent, strong-minded kid who usually doesn't cry easily, but I started to tear up at the word *guardian*. Not only was my mother still in a spell, but I guess I now had guardians—even if they were unofficial.

I reached for a Kleenex, and everyone stopped talking and looked at me. After blowing my nose, I reassured the doctors I was okay to continue answering questions.

Dr. Drummond continued, "Now, Maggie, according to the Emergency Room notes, your mom went into this spell early on Monday morning—is that correct?

"Y-yes, that's right. I couldn't wake her up to go to her early morning breakfast shift at Del's—she's a waitress there—so I had to call her in sick. This has happened quite a few times before. I went ahead and got ready for school and left around 8 am. She's usually out of her morning spells by the time I get home from school, but this time she wasn't." I paused for a few seconds, thinking back to finding her still in her pink pajamas, lying in the same curled-up position I had left her in. Her hair was matted.

"She had drooled a little bit and felt warm," I continued, "so I cleaned up the spittle and wiped her face and forehead with a cool rag. I checked to make sure she was breathing okay, just like Sun-Ju had taught me. Her breaths seemed really shallow compared to her other spells, and that scared me. I gently shook her to try and wake her, but her body just stayed limp. She didn't open her eyes or respond at all. I started to freak out—that's when I called Sun-Ju for help."

"I see, I see," the psychiatrist said as he scribbled in his chart. "When did you start noticing her having these trance-like blackouts? How often do they occur, and how long do they usually last?"

"I-I think I was about eight or nine when I first noticed that these spells were different from just a deep sleep," I began, my voice still shaking a little from feeling overwhelmed with all that had happened over the last few days. "She didn't have them very often back then, maybe once a month or something like that. And they didn't last very long either, maybe just a couple of hours at first. Then, one time, she had a spell that lasted way longer than the others. I got really scared and started crying. I knew I needed to get help. That's when I called Sun-Ju. She came right over and stayed with me until my mom woke up."

"I see, I see," he repeated, writing the information in my mom's chart. "Now tell me, Maggie, what happens to your mom after she enters a *spell*? You mentioned a deep sleep—is it like she's in a deep sleep?"

"Yes, I would say so," I answered. "You can't wake her up when she's in a spell, no matter how hard you try."

"Does she ever speak when she's in a spell?"

"No, she never speaks," I replied.

"Does she ever display any kind of emotion? What I mean is, does her facial expression ever indicate that she might feel happy, sad, anxious, or troubled? Does she ever have a big emotional outbreak, such as loud laughing or crying out like she's scared or angry?"

"Well, sometimes I think she looks sad," I replied after taking a long pause to think over his questions carefully. "And sometimes I think she looks like she's scared. I don't think she's ever laughed or cried out like she was angry, mad, or anything like that. I don't know—it's like her normal mind just gets up and goes out the front door to somewhere else for a while."

"Yes, Maggie is exactly right," interrupted Sun-Ju, turning her attention from me to speak directly to the doctors. "If I may, although I haven't witnessed many recently, I've seen quite a few spells over the past years. I've seen both sadness and fear on her face. It seems she just withdraws from the outside world for a while like she has to take a break from reality."

"Thank you, thank you. This is most helpful information. Now, has Lillian ever seen a doctor about these spells—I mean, before now?" asked Dr. Drummond.

"She never wanted to go to the doctor. She said she didn't have the money," explained Sun-Ju, hanging her head, embarrassed for being neglectful. "Not that she ever talked about it much, but she once told me she thought she could manage these blackouts on her own. Even so, I should have insisted she see a doctor before now, before she ended up in a long spell like this one."

Pausing to jot down notes in the chart, Dr. Drummond turned back to me and asked, "Can you think of any specific thing or event that might trigger her to lapse into one of these spells? You know, like talking to a certain person or something from work that might cause her undue stress or anxiety?"

I thought about that for a few moments and answered, "No, I've kind of wondered about that too, but I can't think of any person or thing that might cause it. It seems like it just happens. No one thing sets it off, or at least not that I can tell."

"Well," said Sun-Ju hesitantly, glancing at me apologetically as if she was about to say something that would upset me, "I can think of one thing that might be a trigger. I think she has some issues from her past that are disturbing to her. She is the type of person who keeps to herself, but I think some deep-seated memories from her youth contribute to her withdrawing into herself and falling under these spells."

"It's okay, Sun-Ju, you can tell him," I said, having a good idea of what she would say about my mom's bad memories.

"Well, Lillian never talked much about it, but I do know she became pregnant with Maggie when she was in high school—at age fifteen or sixteen, I believe. The pregnancy situation didn't sit well with her parents, particularly her father. Their relationship deteriorated until Lillian eventually ran away from her Montana home. Maggie was born here in San Francisco."

"I see, I see," Dr. Drummond repeated. "That's very helpful information. Here's the plain English version of what Dr. Kakarla and I feel is happening with Lillian, ah your mother. While it certainly isn't common, I have seen a few cases similar to Lillian's at my office over the years. Without getting into complicated medical mumbo-jumbo, we really don't know what causes the brain, or the mind to escape from the present and wrap itself away in a protective cocoon. As Dr. Karkarla explained earlier, sometimes a brain tumor or a seizure disorder can cause this type of condition. But since we don't see any evidence of that yet, we are inclined to think it might be a withdrawal mechanism to deal with some type of recent or past stressful or traumatic event. And the high school pregnancy situation you just described certainly fits the bill. It is encouraging news, at least up to now, that your mother has always come out of her spells in a reasonably short time. While we are hopeful that will again be the case, I must stress that there is no way to predict if or when she will return to a state of normal consciousness."

Questions started racing through my mind. *What if my mom were to stay in this spell for weeks, or maybe even months? What will happen to our apartment? How long will I be able to stay with the Jeongs, and who would take care of me if I couldn't continue to stay there?* Too many questions and too few answers. I didn't even try to hide the river of tears that began to flow down my cheeks.

Chapter 3

LIFE IN SAN FRANCISCO

I want to tell you the story of my mom and our life in San Francisco. We lived in a tiny, one-bedroom apartment on the second floor of a five-story apartment complex. My mom always said that we lived in a working-class neighborhood. I wasn't really sure what that meant—didn't most people, except for old, retired folks, live in neighborhoods where everyone worked? Later, I realized what she meant was that people in our area didn't have jobs that paid a lot of money. There weren't any fancy homes, ritzy stores, or expensive restaurants where we lived. The houses were old and very close together. We didn't live in a slum, but it wasn't a very nice part of the city either.

There were some pretty rough kids who roamed the streets, and a lot of them were looking for trouble. Let's just say there was more than one street corner that my best friend Cho and I avoided when we were walking to school or out and about playing in the streets. And it wasn't at all unusual to hear police sirens blaring day or night.

My mom made me aware at a young age that we had to spend what little money she made carefully. She would always tell me that paying the rent, utilities, and groceries used up most of the monthly income, and that there wasn't much left over for things like clothes, presents, and stuff like that.

San Francisco Golden Gate Bridge near Maggie and
Lillian's apartment

But don't get me wrong. The reason we didn't have much money certainly wasn't because my mom didn't work hard. She waitressed during both of the morning and evening shifts four days a week down the street at Del's Corner Diner. And then every Friday and Saturday night, you could find my mom at Gable's Tavern directly across the street from Del's.

The Tavern was a long and narrow building, with the bar at one end and a stage and big dance floor on the opposite side. A bunch of pool tables sat in the middle. You see, my mom was a singer in a band. *Sterling Saint and the Satin Slippers* was the name. Don't even ask me where they got it! The band consisted of my mom and three guys, not one of which had "Sterling" or "Saint" as a first or last name. As far as I knew, none of them wore satin slippers either, at least my mom sure as heck didn't. Cho had this band name thing figured out as well as anybody. She said it was cool for bands to have goofy names—the goofier the better. Why else, she would always say, would anyone name their band *Three Dog Night* or *The Funky Railroad*?

Sun-Ju worked at Del's Diner too. My mom tells the story about being so nervous on her first day of work that she dropped an armful of dirty dishes, shattering them all over the floor in front of a table of customers. She stood frozen in place, expecting the boss to stomp out from the kitchen and fire her on the spot. But Sun-Ju, who had already been working there for a long time, took the blame and saved Lillian's job. That's how she and my mom met and became friends.

We didn't do it during the school year, but this past summer Cho and I even started working a few shifts at Del's. The Jeong's lived just a couple of blocks from us, and our apartment was only another few blocks from the diner. Since I lived closer to Del's, Cho would usually walk down to my apartment before our shifts. We would do our hair and put on a little of the makeup that we swiped from my mom's bathroom cabinet.

"Here's Mutt and Jeff," Del would always say when we walked arm-in-arm through the door. I guess we did look kind of funny together, me being tall and slender with long, dirty-blond hair, and Cho being eight inches shorter with closely-cropped jet black hair. We didn't waitress or anything important like that, but we bused tables—you know, clearing the dirty tables and preparing them for the next customer. We always joked that I was the Ketchup and Mustard Queen, and Cho was the Butter and Jam Queen, because we made sure each table had a full complement of those items.

Even though table-bussers work behind the scenes and usually don't get tips, we were always glad when Mr. Spika came through the door. He was a nice old man who came in every day for a late breakfast. He liked lots of strawberry jam with his toast, so we quickly learned that if we made a big fuss over making sure he had extra packets at his table, he would give each of us a quarter.

Anyway, on the weekends, Cho and I used to sneak down to the Tavern to listen to my mom's band. Of course, they wouldn't let kids inside the bar, but on the warm summer nights they would leave the back door by the stage open to let some air in. That door opened into the alley, and that's where Cho and I would hang out and dance to the music—right next to the garbage dumpsters.

By the way, my mom is a really good singer. I think maybe her best talent is that she can change her voice to sound almost exactly like the real artist. I'm not kidding—she can sound like Mama Cass, Cher, Loretta Lynn, Patsy Cline, even Tina Turner or Diana Ross. Unfortunately, my mom didn't pass her great singing gene down to me. I'm definitely a better dancer than I am a singer. In fact, Cho and I could dance the socks off most of the people on that dance floor. One of the guys in the band used to call us "the alley-dumpster dancers!"

If it sounds like Cho and I are always together, you've got that right. I go to her house a lot after school on the days my mom is working. Since we are in the same class at school, we go to her house to get our homework done before going out to play or roam the neighborhood. Cho is the oldest of five siblings, so it's always pretty hectic around her place. Like my mom, Sun-Ju works several jobs, and her dad works long hours managing a

Korean restaurant. As a result, Cho often has the responsibility of babysitting her brothers and sisters after school. I usually stay around to help, especially with the two youngest sisters.

Although their work schedules prevent my mom and Sun-Ju from getting together outside of their waitressing at Del's, I think my mom would consider Sun-Ju to be her best friend. I've heard my mom thank her for letting me hang around their place all the time, and I'm always happy to hear Sun-Ju reply, "we think of her as just another one of our kids." Anyway, I'm pretty sure Sun-Ju understands my mother better than any other adult. She has watched over both of us, and I don't know what I would have done without her coming over to help me when my mom started to have longer and more frequent spells.

Now, let me explain something. My mom is pretty much a typical mom, when she isn't having a spell, that is. Or at least she was before the spells began to happen more frequently.

I think I was about seven when every now and again I couldn't wake her up in the morning or after a nap. That was when I first realized that something was wrong with her. I remember getting really scared one morning when I couldn't arouse her, and I hightailed it two blocks down the street to get Sun-Ju to come help me. Fortunately, Mr. Jeong was home to take care of their family, so Sun-Ju and I hurried back to our apartment. She sat with me for what seemed like hours before my mom finally awakened. I remember hearing Sun-Ju talking to Mom and strongly suggesting she see a doctor. But my mom insisted there was nothing wrong except being overly tired from work.

After that episode, Sun-Ju left her home and Del's Diner phone numbers scotch taped to the olive-green rotary phone that was mounted on the narrow wall next to the fridge. She had me call her every time my mom went into a spell. Whenever she could, Sun-Ju would stay with me until my mom woke up. She taught me what to do—to stay calm and talk to my mom like everything was normal. Even though she would say nothing back, Sun-Ju said it was important to talk to someone during a spell. She said there were true reports of a person coming out of a coma and remembering what people had said or read to them.

But sometimes, before my mom would wake up, Sun-Ju would have to leave for work or home to take care of her own family. I won't lie, as a seven- or eight-year-old, I was scared to death to be left alone with a mother lying lifelessly on the bed, even if it was only for a few hours. I vividly remember crying and clutching her dress when Sun-Ju had to leave early, but I always tried to quit sobbing and start talking to my mom again after she had left.

"Okay Mom, it's time for you to wake up. Your shift starts at 4:00, that's only a few hours from now, so you need to get up and get going. You know, Sun-Ju works a lot, and she won't be able to run over here every time you have one of these longer spells. And how do you expect me to take care of you when I'm supposed to be in school? How am I supposed to do my homework when I have to watch over you?"

By the time I was nine or ten, I was getting old enough to understand that my mom had a serious medical issue. And while dealing with her spells never became easy, I did finally get to the point where I rarely had to call for Sun-Ju's help. At least my mom was becoming aware enough of her medical condition that she continued to teach me how to care for myself and our house. It was like she knew she'd have to become dependent on me to be the adult in the family, even if I was just a kid.

Looking back, she must have worried that her spells were going to start lasting longer and become more frequent, as she began teaching me how to do all the tasks around the house. I started going down to our apartment's creepy basement laundry room (we called it the "dungeon") by myself to do our laundry. I started doing most of the grocery shopping and cooking. My mom started showing me how to handle our finances by putting a list of our monthly bills and the day of the month they were due on the fridge. She taught me how to write out the checks and balance the checking account. "You're getting to be quite the little banker!" she would proudly tell me.

I should tell you I pretty much already knew how to cook—well, sort of. Our idea of a typical dinner was to grill up a toasted cheese sandwich and dip it in a bowl of Campbell's Chicken Noodle soup. Or if we really wanted a fancy dinner, we'd throw a hamburger or a pork chop in the frying pan. My mom used her tip money from waitressing (hidden in an envelope in her pajama drawer) to buy groceries, so I would take some cash and go down the street to Bert's Grocery Mart to do our shopping. I'd buy milk, bread (Wonder Bread—because Bert said it didn't get moldy as fast as the other brands), Skippy's peanut butter, jelly, Velveeta cheese, lunch meat, and a box of Cheerios and Frosted Flakes. I pretty much lived on peanut butter and jelly sandwiches and cereal, especially during a spell. If I wanted a special treat, I would grill a toasted ham and cheese sandwich in a frying pan and heat a can of soup. And, oh yeah, I always made sure to keep back enough change to buy a bag of my favorite oatmeal-raisin cookies for dessert.

I won't lie, as much as I worried about my mom when she was in a spell, I started to get angry with her as I got older, and the episodes became more frequent. I remember having a conversation with her about this very thing one day.

"Mom, you are having more spells than ever—and they are lasting longer, too. Do you realize what happens when you do this? I have to get up and get ready for school all by myself. I have to worry about whether you will be awake when I get home. And if you're not awake when I get home and I get scared and need Sun-Ju, I have to worry if she's at work and can't get away. And if she is home, I have to worry whether Mr. Jeong is off work so he can look after the kids. Can't you see how hard this is on everyone? Especially me?"

"Oh honey, I'm so sorry!" Mom cried, reaching out and grabbing me by the arm. "It's not like I want to go into these spells. I promise I'll try really hard not to have as many. I know it's tough on you and I don't mean to burden you with all this responsibility at such a young age."

"Well, that's what you're doing," I snapped back at her. "None of the other kids my age has to do all the grocery shopping, cooking, cleaning, and bill paying. It's just not fair that I have to be an adult when I'm still a kid. What if you keep having more spells and start missing more work shifts and there isn't enough money to pay the bills!" I screamed. "What do I do then?"

Then my mom would start sobbing hysterically and I would feel bad for bawling her out. I'd give in and we'd hug forever. I'd pat her on the back and tell her everything would be all right, even though I knew it wouldn't be.

Here's another thing that I hadn't given much thought to until Dr. Kakarla started asking questions about how often my mom had spells: I suddenly realized she never had a spell on a Friday or Saturday. Why was that? The only thing I can think of is that she loved to sing with the band on the weekends so much that she wouldn't let her brain take a vacation when they were scheduled to play at Gable's.

I won't lie, it hurt my feelings when I realized she only has spells when with me, but never while performing with the band.

I guess that means she'd rather be with the band than with me. It kind of makes me mad that I have to be the grown-up at an age when I should just be playing with my friends instead of shopping, cooking, doing laundry, and paying bills.

And about the spells? I don't know what to tell you other than eventually my mom would just come out of it. I'm sure it sounds crazy, but whether she was coming off a two-hour or a six-hour spell, that's honestly what would happen. You know how a hypnotist snaps their fingers, and the subject comes back to real life? It was just like that.

Until now, at least my mom had always come out of her spells within a matter of hours. I guess it took her lying in a hospital bed for several days for me to realize a spell could last much longer. So, I was surprised—no, make that shocked—when my mom experienced a spell she couldn't snap out of.

Chapter 4

ST. PETER'S ORPHANAGE

Standing in front of an iron gate that led to a double wood door entrance to a fortress made of brick and stone, I again found myself holding hands with Sun-Ju and Cho.

"It will be alright, Maggie," Sun-Ju said, trying to be convincing as we waited for the door to open. Soon all three of us were in the direct line of the icy stare of an older, imposing-looking woman dressed in full nun-habit attire.

In a raspy, high-pitched voice that didn't seem to match its maker, she identified herself as Sister Mary Francis, Mother Superior of the St. Peter's Orphanage.

"Which of you is Margaret Stone?" she barked. I usually always tell people that I go by Maggie instead of Margaret, but I didn't have the nerve to do anything more than meekly raise my hand to confirm that I was their next orphan.

Okay, so I'm getting a little ahead of myself. Do you remember when I told you about Sun-Ju telling me and the doctors that I could stay with the Jeong's during the time my mom was in the hospital, at least "for a while"? Well, before I knew it, "for a while" had quickly turned into a month. Sun-Ju would go to the hospital to see my mom every Sunday. I couldn't go because they had a stupid rule that you had to be at least fourteen in order to visit a patient's room. Sun-Ju would return with a sad look on her face, and I would know there had been no change in my mom's condition.

I've already mentioned that my mom's recurring spells frequently required me to buy groceries and pay the bills at an age far younger than most kids even learn of such things. So, I knew what it cost to run our household, and I was well aware that taking me on as an additional house guest would be a burden on the Jeong family budget.

To make matters even worse, I had only been staying at Cho's house for a couple of weeks when Mr. Jeong suggested I check my mom's mail to make sure we weren't getting behind on any bills. *Oh no,* I thought, my heart pounding. I'd been so preoccupied with my mom's lengthy spell and hospital stay that I'd forgotten all about keeping up on the rent and utility bills!

"Oh honey," said Mr. Jeong after I showed him the letter from Greenwood Apartments with a big red RENT PAST DUE stamped on the front and back of the envelope. And to make matters worse, I had to explain to him that there was only enough cash and money in our checking account to pay the utility bills and about half of the past due rent. "I'm sorry, Maggie, that I haven't paid closer attention to your finances. I guess we've all hoped that your mother would snap out of her spell and return home and to work. I didn't think about bills piling up."

"Well, it's my fault for not remembering to pay the bills, Mr. Jeong," I said, shaking my head in embarrassment. "Because of my mom having more and more spells, she's been teaching me how to do all the things parents usually do. I've been pretty much paying all the bills for the last year, so I know how much money is in the bank account and how much tip money we have. I know what bills need to be paid and when they're due. I guess with all that's happened, I forgot to pay attention to it all."

"I wish we could help pay your rent and other household bills until your mom can come home, but Sun-Ju and I can barely pay the expenses on our own place," Mr. Jeong said reluctantly. "What I can do is go with you to visit the manager of your apartment complex. Hopefully, after explaining your mom's extended hospitalization situation, he will accept the partial rent payment in exchange for you moving out of the apartment immediately."

The realization that we were about to lose the only home I have ever known hit me like a ton of bricks when he added, "I'm afraid it's either that or the landlord will evict you from your apartment and confiscate whatever belongings are remaining.

"And not to add fuel to the fire, but the hospital bills are starting to mount. Since Sun-Ju and I are acting as you and your mom's temporary custodians and guardians, we received a letter from the hospital today requesting your mom's financial information. They need to determine who is responsible for paying for your mom's care, so do I have your permission to go to your bank and request an accounting of your mom's finances to take to the hospital?"

"Ah-ah, yes, I guess so," I stammered, my stomach beginning to churn at the thought of how to pay hospital bills. "How are we going to pay the hospital bills when we don't even have enough money to pay rent?"

"Don't worry, Maggie. I know you don't have any money, and you'll have even less with Lillian being in the hospital and not able to work. There's a new program that President Johnson signed into law a few years back; it's called Medicare and Medicaid. Medicare is a healthcare program for senior citizens, and Medicaid is a healthcare program for low-income people. I'll take your financial information into the hospital, and I'm sure your mom will qualify for Medicaid coverage."

"So you mean Medicaid will pay her hospital bills? Really?"

"Yes, honey. I think they will. I'll go to the bank and the hospital tomorrow and find out for sure."

"Alright Mom, this has gone on long enough," I said angrily under my breath as I carried a sack of her clothes out of the apartment. "Just look at this. Because you won't wake up, we've just lost our apartment and the Jeong's are having to help me move all our belongings to the loft in their garage. I hope you know we have absolutely no money, and I probably won't be able to stay at Cho's house much longer because they don't have enough money to take care of me either. We're lucky the hospital bills are covered by some program called Medicaid, or we'd be up a creek without a paddle on those bills, too. So I'm telling you right now—it's time for you to snap out of this spell and come back home and go to work!"

And then several weeks later, just as I was wrapping my head around the fact that my mom and I no longer had a home, Mr. Jeong cleared his throat one morning and suggested the four of us gather around the dining room table. From the suspicious glance he exchanged with Sun-Ju as we sat down, I had a sinking feeling my "for a while" stay was about to end. Even worse, I had also been avoiding thinking about the next obvious question that lay lurking like a black storm cloud over my head: If I wasn't to live with the Jeongs, then where would I go? And with whom?

"Maggie, Maggie honey," Sun-Ju hesitantly started after exchanging another worried glance with Mr. Jeong. She reached across the table to take my hand. "I wish I could say that you can stay with us for however long it takes for your mom to get better. Both Mr. Jeong and I consider you to be part of our family, but again, we barely make enough money between us to feed, house, and clothe the six children we already have."

"But Mom," interrupted Cho tearfully, "where is Maggie going to go? Remember, we're both going to work at Del's again this summer, and maybe we could get even more hours at Dantoni's or O'Malley's. I'm sure they need help with washing dishes and busing tables. Please Mom, could Maggie stay if we get enough jobs? I promise-promise we'd give you everything we make to help out with groceries and the other bills. Pretty please?"

I glanced at Cho and then Sun-Ju and Mr. Jeong. Everybody looked sad. "It's okay, I understand," I told them. It really wasn't okay, but deep down, I knew this day might come if my mom didn't snap out of her spell. Trying to remain calm while my stomach churned like I'd swallowed an Oklahoma tornado twister, I reluctantly repeated Cho's question. "Where will I go? Do you know where I can stay until my mom gets better?"

Looking back to her husband as if searching for support, Sun-Ju said, "Well Maggie, when we started to run out of money and your mother wasn't showing any sign of snapping out of her spell, Mr. Jeong and I visited with Father Piquette down at our church. As you might already know, St. Peter's is more than just a church and cathedral. They have an orphanage there, and they also house a private K-12 Catholic school."

It took me a second to fully grasp where Sun-Ju was heading with this: *You're sending me to an orphanage? You're sending me to an orphanage school? You would really do that to me?*

"I know that you're a very good student, Maggie, and the kids at the orphanage go to St. Peter's school—both the school and orphanage come highly recommended. They have all the necessary funding to support you and the other students. We should all stay positive in thinking that your mom will be back with you soon, but until that day comes, we think the orphanage is the best place for you."

Before I could recover or even react to the news that I was now apparently an orphan, Cho jumped up and screamed at her parents, "I can't believe you would pull my best friend from our school and send her to an orphanage! I hate you, I hate you!" She raced out of the room and slammed the door.

"She doesn't mean that," I said softly and lowered my head as the tears began streaming down my face. When I looked up, I saw tears in their eyes, too. Although I wasn't feeling it at all, I did my best to put on my brave face and tried to be strong, even though I suddenly felt like I was going to throw up all over the kitchen table.

"It's okay, I understand," I lied. "I know how hard it has been to take me on, you know, the extra money you have had to spend to take care of me. You've been very nice to let me stay this long. St. Peter's is no doubt the best place for me to go until my mom gets better. Ah-ah, when will I, you know, when do I go?"

"I'm so sorry, Maggie, but they have a slot opening up on May 12th—this next Monday. We'll move you in that morning. I've already spoken to your teachers and the administration at your school. They've been in contact with St. Peter's, and we've been assured all your classes and credits will transfer. I wish we didn't have to change schools with only three or four weeks before summer vacation, but we had to move quickly or we would have lost the spot."

"I understand," I lied again. "And I won't even be there that long—she'll come out of that spell, and we'll be back home in no time, you'll see."

I won't kid you—I was really scared. I mean, I truly was thankful that the Jeongs let me stay with them for as long as they did, but sending me off to an orphanage? Despite feeling like I had just been abandoned and sentenced to life in Alcatraz, I didn't have the heart to tell them that St. Peter's Orphanage was the last place in the world I wanted to go.

Chapter 5

WHERE AM I?

You know how it's weird when you wake up somewhere different from what you're used to, and it takes a minute to figure out where you're at? I had just started getting used to opening my eyes from my mattress on the floor in the crowded confines of Jeong's kids bedroom when I was greeted by the few weak rays of morning sunlight that were able to squeeze their way through the opaque window blocks above my orphanage bed. My new sleeping assignment was on the top bunk of one of the multiple beds that filled the crowded quarters of the girls dormitory. It only took a glance at the thin bed sheet and the faded yellow, paper-thin blanket to explain why I was shivering.

Even though our old apartment was now becoming just a memory, it was the only home I had ever known. That occupied my thoughts, dreaming almost every night that it would still be available for us to move back into as soon as my mom snapped out of her spell and came home from the hospital. I remember every nook and cranny of the tiny space, like the crack in the wall above the bedroom window my mom tried to hide by hanging those curtains with giant sunflowers. The thought of how close together the apartment buildings were in our neighborhood. I mean, from our bathroom, you could almost reach out and open our neighbor's bathroom window.

It took me a couple of weeks waking up at the orphanage to get accustomed to the routine of yet another new place to call home. The boys' and girls' dorms each contained seven bunk beds, separated only by a razor-thin wall. The bathroom and shower stalls for each were at the far end of the dormitory, also adjoined by another flimsy wall. Every night you could easily hear the boys talking and rough housing before one of the Sisters called for lights out. The kids at the orphanage were a pretty rowdy bunch, and I quickly learned which boys and girls to keep your distance from.

Fourteen-year-old Anna Cleery and sixteen-year-old Walter Brubaker were the two who scared me the most. They hated each other and started their bickering the first thing in the morning. I'm an early riser and was always awake by the time Anna and Walter started their morning ritual.

At precisely 5:30 a.m., Walter would make his way out of bed and into the boys' bathroom. I don't think I have to spell out to you the loud and disgusting noises that boys can make in the bathroom, especially when they think it's funny that everybody can hear them. He would carry on with his antics until Anna Cleery would shout out from her bunk, "You are such a pig, Walter! Can't you be quieter, you moron?"

"Stuff it, Cleery," he would shout back, although most of the time they both used nastier language than that. Everyone but Anna seemed to know he did it just to get under her skin, but all of us girls were too afraid of her to say it.

It also took some time to figure out how things really worked at the orphanage. You see, not everybody that went to St. Peter's school lived at the orphanage. Only twenty-eight of the seventy students were actual full-time resident orphans. Of those twenty-eight, Sandi Thompson (my one friend in the whole place) and I were the only orphans among the fifteen students in our sixth-grade class.

Remember when I told you that Sun-Ju said that St. Peter's had this great K-12 private school and made it sound like a place where parents would pay good money to enroll their academically gifted children? Well, according to Sandi, Sun-Ju's portrayal of the school wasn't anywhere close to accurate. Most of the non-resident attendees weren't top students. In fact, the majority were troublemakers who had been expelled from their former schools because of poor grades, bad behavior, or frequent run-ins with the police. In other words, they were sent to St. Peter's because they needed a strict and disciplined school environment. Well, they sure found that at St. Peter's!

Unfortunately, it didn't take me long to learn that the teachers could deliver a double dose of discipline and punishment in the blink-of-an-eye. I had a rude awakening from the very first day at my new school, as both of my sixth-grade homeroom teachers, Sister Mary Ellen (Math and Science) and Sister Grace Evina (English and History), ran the classroom with an iron fist. Have you ever heard the old saying, "spare the rod and spoil the child?" I think it means you'll spoil an unruly child if you don't spank them. Anyway, it must have been the nuns' motto, as they were both quick to firmly swat the hand of a misbehaving student with their rulers. And if that didn't do the trick, they weren't the least bit shy about bending the offender over the desk and making use of the wooden paddle that was hung in plain sight next to the blackboard. I was never one to get in trouble at school, but believe you me, I tried to be extra careful to stay on the good side of the nuns.

I hadn't been in school for much more than a week before I found myself in a no-win situation. I was off by myself shooting baskets in the recreation yard during lunch one day when Anna Cleery and two of her mean friends surrounded me on the court. Anna was big—big like an older boy. Not fat, but broad shouldered and muscular. I tried not to look at her face, as the widespread angry-looking red pimples and deep pockmarks made her even more mean-looking.

"So Stone, we hear your old lady is a nut-job," began Anna in a nasty, taunting tone. "In fact, we hear she's crazier than a loon. She's probably howling at the moon from the psych ward as we speak, ain't she?"

I just ignored them at first, continuing to shoot as I tried to figure out how on earth Anna Cleery would know my mom was in the psych ward. It didn't take much pondering, as Sandi Thompson was the only person I had shared such information with. We had exchanged our orphan stories, she telling me that her parents abandoned her to run off to some hippie commune, and me divulging I'd never met my father and that my mom was in a coma in the psych ward. Cho would have never thought of telling my family secrets to anyone, but apparently Sandi couldn't wait to blab to the entire orphanage and schoolyard. It made me miss my old home and my best friend Cho more than ever.

"What do you have to say about that, Stone?" Cleery sneered. "We also heard you don't even know who your old man is, is that right, Stone? Can't blame the guy for not wanting a little goody-two-shoes like you around, can you girls?"

I tried to ignore them and just keep shooting, but one of Cleery's sidekicks streaked in to grab the rebound and whipped the ball to Anna. She wound up like a baseball pitcher and threw the ball as hard as she could at my face. Luckily, I blocked the ball before it smashed into my head but couldn't recover in time to prevent Anna from stepping in and connecting with a wicked roundhouse slap to the side of my face.

Now I'm certainly no one that goes around looking for fights, but remember, I grew up in a tough neighborhood and this wasn't my first rodeo—or scuffle, shall we say. Plus, I wasn't about to take this kind of crap from anybody, even if it was three-against-one and Cleery having several years and thirty pounds on me. I was counting on my tall, lean build to deceive the bullies into thinking I was skinny and weak. I am stronger than I look and had the advantage of being much quicker than any of the three, so I was able to slip in a good slap or two in before Anna's sidekicks closed in to secure my arms. I was wishing I had buzz cut my shoulder-length hair when big Anna grabbed my ponytail and jerked me to the ground. With my arms still pinned down and Cleery straddling me, I was helpless to defend the rain of blows to the face that were about to be launched. Fortunately, Cleery was only able to land a couple of punches before the recreation monitors, Sister Mary Ellen and Sister Evelyn Marie, pulled the three girls off me and marched us all to the Mother Superior's office.

"This little snot started the fight," lied Anna Cleery as we walked in the door. "We were just minding our own business, and she came running over and hit me for no reason!"

"Somehow, I highly doubt that's what actually happened, Miss Cleery. But you girls know the rules; fighting is not tolerated regardless of who instigated the fracas," scolded the Mother

Superior as she pulled out an imposing-looking wooden paddle from the closet and handed it to Sister Mary Ellen. "You're up first," she said to Anna Cleery, who bent over the desk like she'd done this drill before. "This is the third time you've been in my office for fighting in the last month, Miss Cleery, so Sister Mary Ellen, swat her three times."

The other two girls in Anna Cleery's gang must have only been involved in two of the other fights, as they received two whacks each. All three girls yelped and screamed like hyena's with each successive strike and stood by the door bawling and holding their bottoms with both hands when their punishment was over.

Motioning that it was my turn, the Mother Superior barked, "All right, young lady, bend over."

I couldn't believe this was actually happening to me but was relieved when Sister Mary Ellen was informed that this was my first fight and was instructed to deliver only one powerful spank to my backside. I was determined not to cry and wail like Anna Cleery and her bandits did, so I set my jaw and prepared myself for the blow. The sting of the paddle against my bottom brought tears to my eyes, but I didn't utter a peep. *No way I'm gonna act like the Cleery gang,* I thought to myself as the two nuns marched us back to our respective homerooms.

After the horrifying and humiliating experience of getting spanked for a fight I didn't even start, I climbed into bed that night, pulled the covers over my head, and cried myself to sleep.

Thankfully, that was the only real trouble that found me during the four weeks I was there, but the entire stay was anything but pleasant. I know *hate* is a strong word, but that about sums up my experience at St. Peter's Orphanage and School.

Little did I know I was about to be moved again, and that my new living arrangement would make my time at St. Peter's look like a walk in the park.

Chapter 6

MEETING IRA

I was eating lunch in the cafeteria when Sister Mary Ellen tapped me on the shoulder and motioned me to follow her out to the hall. I broke out in a cold sweat when we took the dreaded turn in the hallway that led to the Mother Superior's office. A vision of a wooden paddle colliding with my backside came roaring back.

Since I hadn't been in another fight, I racked my brain to remember if I'd violated any other major rule that would warrant a trip to the office of the Mother Superior.

I felt a great sense of relief when Sister Mary Ellen whispered over her shoulder, "Don't worry, you're not in trouble."

If I'm not in trouble, maybe this is good news, I thought. *Could my mom have finally come out of her two-month spell?"*

Thank you, Sister Mary Ellen," said Sister Mary Francis, dismissing the nun with a nod when we reached her office door. "Please come in, Miss Stone."

I came to an abrupt halt after the first couple of steps into the room, as I realized the Sister and I had company.

A thickly built, older-looking man stood up from his chair, holding a tan cowboy hat across his stomach and nervously shifting his weight from one foot to the other. His wrinkled, dark brown suit fit a bit too snug, and a recent boot polish couldn't hide the fact that his cowboy boots were well-used. A belt with a large silver buckle held up his pants. I thought his tie looked funny. Unlike the usual neckties worn in San Francisco, this tie had a single braided cord coming from each side of his shirt collar. The two cords were then joined and secured by a buffalo skull clasp. I would later learn it was called a Bolo tie, usually worn by ranchers and cowboys when they dressed up to go into town or to church.

But it didn't take long for my eyes to lock onto his face. I knew it wasn't good manners to stare, but I couldn't help myself. His face was broad and square, deeply tanned, and leathery. This man had obviously spent a lot of time out in the sun and wind. Unlike most of the older men that I had seen, he had a thick stand of hair that he wore in a high buzz cut. His hair color was somewhere between gray and pure white, and it looked like he'd used some type of butch wax to make it stand up. The full circle around his head where his hair was mashed down from the rim of his cowboy hat looked kind of silly, I thought. He had white, bushy eyebrows that framed his sharp blue eyes. I wouldn't say his eyes were cold; cool would maybe be a better term—stern and alert, for sure. His eye color was a deep blue. I had only been over the Golden Gate Bridge a few times, but his eyes reminded me of the blue water in the bay.

But the most distinguishing feature I couldn't peel my eyes from was the deep, crevice-like scar on the right side of his face. It started at the corner of his mouth and extended to the lower part of the ear. As I looked closer, I realized that whatever had made the wound had also removed that little thing-a-ma-jig that hangs at the bottom of the ear—you know, the lower part of the earlobe. He had a hearing aid sticking out of that ear too, which the ear doctors did a lousy job of color matching.

"Maggie," said Sister Mary Francis, interrupting my rude staring. "This gentleman here in front of you is Mr. Ira Stone. He is your grandfather, and he tells me you have never met. Mr. Stone, this is your granddaughter, Maggie Stone."

You've heard the expression about getting a lump in your throat, right? Well, this wasn't just a normal-sized lump—this was like trying to swallow a watermelon compared to a grape! I won't lie, until my grandpa came up in the conversation with the doctors at the hospital, I hadn't thought about him for quite some time. I wonder about my dad way more often than I do my grandfather.

Now, I should explain that my mom would clam up whenever I brought up either of them. When I was younger, I would ask, "What's my dad's name? Did he go to your school? Were you two girlfriend and boyfriend?" She would never answer my specific questions, and would only say, "He's not a nice man. You're better off not knowing anything about him."

My mom would always answer questions about my grandma, but I ran into the brick wall again when asking about my grandpa. "Didn't he like you? Did he get mad at you when you got pregnant with me? Did he kick you out of the house because of that? Why doesn't he ever call or come to see us? Does he not like me?" I would repeatedly ask when I was younger.

But just like when inquiring about my dad, I would get the same dismissive answer. "Both your grandfather and I are stubborn and set in our ways. It's for the best that we parted ways, and that's all I'm going to say. I'm sorry that you don't have a father or grandparents in your life, but that's just the way it is. Worrying about people you've never known is a waste of time."

As thoughts of conversations with my mom raced through my head, I made an effort to swallow that watermelon lump in my throat and softly whispered, "Hello, sir."

I continued to stare at his scar before finally forcing myself to look into his eyes instead. He appeared to be as frightened as I was, nervously glancing back and forth between me and Sister Mary Francis before replying, "Hello there, young lady." His voice was deep and scary.

"Mr. Stone has come to take you to live with him at his ranch in, where is it you are located, Mr. Stone? Ah, yes—it's in Montana, correct?" inquired the Sister, then continuing in a tone that was kinder than usual when my grandpa confirmed with a nod. "You see, Maggie, you came to us because your mother got sick and could not take care of you. When no other family or friends came forward to petition to be your guardian, we accepted you into our St. Peter's Orphanage. But now, with your next-of-kin grandfather presenting, he has the right and legal authority to take you from here to live with him. Do you understand what I am saying?"

For the entire month I had been at the orphanage, I had dreamed of only one person coming to take me home—my mother. I just knew she would snap out of her spell, and we'd find a new apartment, and everything would return to just as it was before. I never wanted or expected anyone else to come and take me from the orphanage—certainly not this spooky-looking grandfather whom I had never met. And definitely not this man who never liked my mom or me enough to come and see us. I mean, he didn't even care enough to write us a letter or make a phone call. Nope, I didn't like how this situation was shaping up—not one bit.

"Yes, Sister," I answered, fully understanding but not liking what she was saying. I hated living at the orphanage, but at least it was in San Francisco and close to the hospital and to Cho, even though I only saw her occasionally since coming to St. Peter's. The thought of being suddenly uprooted and sent to Montana to live with a grandfather I had never even met was freaking me out. Heck, I wasn't even sure where Montana was, but remembered from Social Studies that it was a big state up by Canada, full of mountains, elk, moose, and bears. Wherever Montana was, I didn't want to go there. Not with this man, anyway.

Sister Mary Francis told my grandfather to stay in her office while she walked me to my bunk bed in the dormitory. The bottom two drawers of the chest that sat next to my bed were mine, and the Sister helped me pack my clothes and underwear into a garbage sack. I didn't have a suitcase.

The Sister then walked me and my grandpa out to his car, an older model, pea-green colored Ford that was shaped like a square box. Since I didn't think the Mother Superior even liked me, I was a little surprised when she gave me a hug and told Mr. Stone how lucky he was to be getting a girl as well-behaved and smart as I was.

I was even more surprised when she pulled me to the side as Mr. Stone was getting in his car and whispered, "Just so you know, I'm sorry I had to discipline you for fighting. I know Miss Cleery and those other two started the whole thing, and you were just defending yourself. But I had to apply the rules against fighting equally to all involved."

With that surprise admission, I reluctantly climbed into the passenger seat and Mr. Stone drove me away from the St. Peter's

Orphanage and the hospital where my mother lay under the worst spell ever.

We had driven a few blocks in silence before I finally worked up enough nerve to speak. "Mr. Stone? What should I call you?"

"Well, young lady," he replied after a lengthy pause. "I guess you can call me Ira. That's what most folks back home in Montana call me. Yep, I reckon Ira will do just fine."

"Okay, Ira," I quickly replied. "Can we stop and see my mom before we leave?"

"Ahh, I stopped by the hospital to see her before I picked you up. I'm sorry, young lady, but she isn't well enough to see visitors."

I let that news sink in for a few minutes before turning back to face Ira. "Did you see her? Can she talk? She doesn't ever talk if she's still in one of her spells."

There was another long, uncomfortable pause before Ira finally responded. "No, no, she didn't speak. The doctor said it's like she's in a trance or something like that. They really don't seem to know what ails her and don't have any idea when she's gonna snap out of it, either. They just don't seem to have any answers—not now, anyway."

See what you've done? I scolded my mother silently as we passed within blocks of my old school and our apartment, then past Del's, Gable's and a park where Cho and I had played for hours on end. It hit me as suddenly as Sister Mary Ellen's paddle that those cherished visions of my old life with my mom were vanishing as quickly as the scenery from the window of Ira's Ford. *Please Mom, please wake up and tell this man with the scar to bring me back to you, bring me back home!*

"Can we stop at Cho's house, then?" I asked anxiously. "She's my best friend and she'll wonder where I've gone if I don't say goodbye."

"A-ahh," he stuttered, "I'm afraid we can't make any stops like that. I'm a-needin' to hit the road and get back to the ranch," Ira said. "It's a 24-hour drive back to Montana and I can't be expectin' the neighbors to do my chores forever."

I curled up my knees and snuggled so close to the passenger door that my cheek was pressed against the window. I pretended like I was napping, but I was too angry at this man—my so-called grandfather—to actually go to sleep. Tears began to slide down my cheeks. *So chores are more important than seeing my mom or my best friend? If not now, when will I get to see them again?* I also had a few thoughts for Ira. *Why now? Where have you been the last twelve years? What are you going to tell my mom when she wakes up and learns you've kidnapped me to your dumb ranch?*

We had been driving for what must have been a couple of hours and were well outside of San Francisco before I broke the uncomfortable silence. "Ira, we'll keep checking on my mom, right? I mean, if she wakes up, I'm sure she will wonder where I am. I'm always there for her when she comes out of her spells. She'll be worried if she doesn't see me when she wakes up."

"I promise I'll keep in touch with the doctors, young lady," the scar-faced man replied.

I won't lie—I wasn't sure if I believed he would. After all, until earlier that day, he hadn't seen my mom since she ran away from home when she was sixteen. I was twelve, and he had just met me for the first time a few hours ago. So no, I wasn't sure I believed him at all.

Chapter 7

THE TRIP TO MONTANA

I didn't know if Ira was quiet by nature or if he didn't like me enough to talk. I'm not one bit shy and I can blab away with the best of them, but there was something about Ira that made me hesitate to try and start a conversation. When he found a radio station and turned it up loud, I took that as a strong hint he wasn't interested in visiting.

With not much else to do in the cab of the truck I kept sneaking looks at Ira. I couldn't stop looking at that scar on the right side of his face. A vision appeared in my mind of someone using a hammer and chisel to carve out a deep cleft from the side of his face. The wound looked like it was made of a white-gray chunk of granite, so it was a far different color than the rest of his leathery, brown-tanned face. I also noticed his face was covered with a stubble of whiskers everywhere except the cleft. There was nary a whisker within the borders of the scar.

Finally, to take my mind off the scar, I risked an attempt to make conversation. "How long will it take us to get to Montana?"

"It's a fair piece, that's for darn sure. We're almost to Nevada and we'll stop at Twin Falls, Idaho tonight. Then another long day tomorrow through Idaho and a good hunk of Montana until we get to the ranch at Sandstone Springs. Like California, Montana is a big state—takes the better part of a day to drive across it."

Even though my mom would rarely talk about her time in Montana, I do remember her mentioning the little town where she went to school—Sandstone Springs.

"Do you have cows on your ranch? Or horses?" I asked.

"Yep."

I waited for him to explain further, but the only one speaking was the weatherman on the radio. I tried again. "So, Ira, is your ranch big? I mean, do you have a lot of land?"

"It's a decent-sized chunk of ground. Not the biggest ranch around—not the smallest neither."

"My mom said she went to school at Sandstone Springs. Is your ranch close to town?" I asked.

"Depends on your definition of close—seven miles away," he responded.

"My mom said it is a really small town," I prompted.

"Yep, sure is," he said with finality.

When Ira turned the radio up even louder, I took the hint and curled back up against the door and watched the miles roll past from the passenger window.

It was also beginning to dawn on me what Ira had mentioned earlier. He said we were going to be spending the night at a motel in Twin Falls; was I going to be sharing a motel room with an old man that was no more familiar to me than the man in the moon? I said a quick prayer in my mind–*please God, tell me I have a separate room!*

I tried to push that worry to the back of my mind, but the thought that popped up next was even worse. *What if my mom doesn't come out of her spell and take me back home to San Francisco? What if I'm imprisoned forever in the middle-of-nowhere Montana with this scar-faced old man that claims he's my grandpa?* I'm not kidding—even St. Peter's Orphanage was looking pretty good to me at this point.

I inwardly groaned when Ira returned from the motel office with only one key in his hand. "They wanted twelve dollars for another room. Should give a guy a discount for getting two rooms, but nope, they said they'd charge the same for a second room. Highway robbery if you ask me, and I won't abide by it," Ira declared as we entered the small room with twin beds. To top it off, the room smelled of decades-old cigarette and cigar smoke, mixed with multiple stains on the carpet that reeked of pet urine. Trust me, it was downright gross!

Despite being nervous about staying in the same room with this man I didn't know, at least he let me use the bathroom first to brush my teeth and put on my pajamas. I scooted to the very outer edge of my tiny bed so that I was as far away from Ira as I could get. Since I was facing a wall with a full-length mirror, I could see Ira's reflection as he carefully hung his shirt, pants, and suit coat on the only two hangers that were in the closet. I don't know if you've ever heard the expression "farmer tan" before, but I almost had to giggle at the stark contrast between Ira's tanned face and forearms to the white shorts, T-shirt, and pearly-white legs that had obviously never met the sun.

Ira didn't bother with any kind of "good-night, sleep-tight" conversation. He crawled into bed, pulled the covers over him, and was snoring away within minutes.

It took me a long, long time to fall asleep. I reflected back on my life's recent whirlwind. Only as a baby could I have been more hopeless and powerless than I'd been over the last two months.

First, my mom abandoned me by burying herself in an eight-week spell. And then, just when I'm getting comfortable staying at my best friend Cho's house, her parents shuttle me off to the worst place I've ever been—an orphanage!

And now? I'm lying in a smelly motel room next to a scary old grandpa who before now never even acknowledged my existence. And when he does finally make an appearance, he kidnaps me off to a middle-of-nowhere ranch a thousand miles away.

Only when I forced my thoughts back to happier times—dancing with Cho in the alley behind Gable's without a care in the world—did I finally slip into a restless sleep.

Chapter 8

THE RANCH HOUSE

*I*t was dark when we arrived at the ranch. I awoke just as we drove down a dirt lane toward a house and some outbuildings and could see from the dim yard-light that a dog was racing toward the car.

"Get down!" Ira growled, as we parked in front of the house, and he opened his door. My mouth widened into a giant yawn. I knew it wasn't polite to yawn and not cover your mouth, but my arm was too tired from the long trip to make it that far.

"Don't worry, Dimwit don't bite—but he will lick your ears off if you let him," Ira said. I opened my door and suddenly had a dog in my lap. And sure enough, I received a good face washing before Ira hollered at him again and he jumped back out.

"It's late and we both could use some shut-eye," Ira remarked. "I'm gonna chain this mutt so we can get our stuff out of the car in peace. You two can get properly introduced in the morning."

After we unloaded the car, Ira led me through a mudroom entryway and through a small kitchen to the base of a steep stairway. "Living room and spare bedroom this-a-way, bathroom and my bedroom over here," he said, pointing first to our left and then to the right. "Your bedroom is straight away at the top of the stairs, but I 'spect you need to use the bathroom first. Ain't no bathroom upstairs, so we'll have to share this one. I cleared out the two drawers on the left side of the sink for you to store your hairbrush and toothbrush and, ah, you know, your personal stuff."

It was good to use an indoor bathroom again. Other than using the restroom at the motel or when stopping to eat or at the gas station, Ira would just pull off the main road to some semi-secluded spot when it was time for a potty-break. I quickly learned that "I need to see a man about a horse" meant you needed to go behind the car to pee!

It turned out I only needed one of the two empty bathroom drawers to store the few toiletries I pulled from my garbage bag. After quickly washing my face and brushing my hair and teeth, I put away my hairbrush, hair ties, toothbrush, and paste. I had to giggle when I remembered I had packed a single tube of lipstick and a few other makeup items that I'd swiped from my mother's cabinet. Not that she ever let me wear lipstick or eye shadow out in public, but she was always a good sport in letting Cho and I experiment with her makeup kit when playing dress up.

After we'd both used the bathroom, Ira grabbed my bag and led the way up the narrow stairway of the old farmhouse to a room at the top of the stairs. "I'll give you a tour of the whole house in the mornin', but this here will be your room," Ira stated, a dim glow from a single lightbulb revealing what would be my third bedroom in the last two months. "Your closet is behind that door—you can use that chest of drawers."

The room was small but immaculately clean. The walls were pale yellow and gave off a fresh paint smell. With an ornately carved wood border, the mirror atop the chest resembled an antique. The bedspread and pillowcase were color-faded, perhaps from too many years of sun exposure through the east-facing window. Someone neatly made the bed.

"Was this my mom's room?" I asked hesitantly.

"Nope. There are two more rooms on this floor, and you can check 'em out whenever you like. Your mom's room is at the end of the hall. There might even be some of her old clothes and shoes in there that you could wear. Don't look like you got much in that garbage sack of yours."

Ira was right. After he headed back downstairs with a quick "nite, see ya' in the mornin," it didn't take long for me to unpack my clothes from the half-full sack.

When the bag was empty, I ventured out to the hallway. From the sparse light spilling out from my bedroom door, I could see a chain extending from a single hallway ceiling light bulb. I figured the bulb had long since burned out, as several tugs on the chain only resulted in continued darkness. Curiosity got the best of me, and I slowly turned the creaky doorknob and entered the first of the two rooms in the hallway. This time, a tug on the chain was successful, as the lonesome bulb flickered its weak rays of light a couple of times before finally holding steady.

This room appeared to be my grandma's sewing and knick-knack room. A large sewing machine contraption, the likes of which I'd never seen, was up against one wall. The sewing machine had a neatly stacked pile of doll clothes next to it, and a yellow flower-pattern dress was hanging from a clothes hanger on the wall. I suspected that my grandma Audrey made both the doll clothes and the teenaged-size dress on that sewing machine.

A workbench ran the full length of the opposite wall, where plaster casts of little hands and feet and several different sized bird-feeders were carefully placed. The passage of time had faded the once colorful knick-knacks that were no doubt painted by my mother when she was just a child. I was surprised to see that all the cute little projects were scribed in a Kindergarten-like writing style as being created by *LILLY*. I had never heard anyone call my mom Lilly—only Lillian.

I won't lie—it was just downright weird when I went farther down the hall to my mom's old bedroom. A pull on the chain illuminated a room that wasn't anything like I had imagined it would be. The entire room was neat as a pin; a frilly white and pink laced bedspread with matching pillow covers adorned the bed, while what looked like a well-handled teddy bear and two matching ragdolls were neatly placed and resting against the pillows. I smiled while looking at the coveralls worn by the teddy bear, guessing that my grandma had sewn those and the matching dresses on the ragdolls. It struck me that Ira hadn't been in the sewing room or my mom's bedroom in a long time, as unlike my bedroom, all the furniture and fixtures appeared to be covered by a thin, even layer of dust.

I looked in the closet and went through the chest that sat against the opposite wall. A quick eye test of what few clothes I found—a couple of blouses, a pair of jeans, one nice dress, and a poodle skirt—revealed they would be way too small for me. An even more apparent size discrepancy was the lone pair of black saddle shoes on the shoe rack on the closet floor. I was surprised when I could barely get my big toe into the shoe. Was my mom that much smaller when she was fifteen, or have I grown that much in the two months since I last saw her? Either way, it frightened me that my memory was blurry as to exactly when I surpassed my mother in terms of height and weight.

Standing in the room where my mom had slept for some fifteen years of her life, I felt a tear slide down my cheek as a cascade of sadness and loneliness swept over me. Even though I hadn't slept with a doll or a special blanket since I was a third grader, I felt the need to have something of my mother's close to me to help me through this first night in a strange house. I don't really know why, but I chose the teddy bear over the rag dolls as I reluctantly marched down the hall and climbed into bed in my new room. I'm not a kid who cries very much, but I quietly wept as I felt my mom's presence from just two doors down. I pulled the teddy bear in close to me under the covers and finally drifted off to sleep, imagining my mom being snuggled next to me—just like she used to be back in our little apartment bedroom.

When I started to stir, the sun was just beginning to shoot some early morning rays into my second-story bedroom window. It took me a minute to figure out where I was. Over the last three days, I had awakened in an orphanage, a motel room, and now, ah, *what the heck, where am I?* Oh yeah, the second floor of an old ranch house in the middle-of-nowhere Montana. My stomach did a flip-flop when it suddenly dawned on me that my so-called grouchy grandpa with the big spooky scar would be waiting for me downstairs. And who knew what he had in mind for the day ahead!

Instead of getting up to face the music, I nestled further under the covers and pulled Teddy even closer. Ira had opened my window before I went to bed, so I lay back and let the unfamiliar sounds and smells of the Montana prairie wash over me.

I figured the cows and horses must be close by, the pungent smell of livestock overloading my olfactory sense. The sounds were like listening to a foreign language being spoken, with each word being new and unrecognizable. One thing was certain: the sounds and smells rolling through my bedroom window were far different from that of the San Francisco morning rush-hour traffic I was used to.

I heard all kinds of different birds chirping. I would later learn that there were blackbirds, robins, owls, hawks, sparrows, crows, and magpies (Ira hated magpies!), to name just a few. And I would soon discern which kind of chirp came from each. I could hear chickens cackling and roosters crowing. I heard the *moo* of cows and the deeper voiced *moo* of what I assumed were the boy cows—steers or bulls is what I would later find they were called. I would also learn how the bulls became steers, which, by the way, usually happens when the calves are branded and is really, really gross. I mean, I sure wouldn't want to be a boy calf and have that happen to me! If it's all the same to you, let's just leave that story for another day.

Over the next few weeks, I would also be able to tell if the cows were in a pasture close to the barn by how clearly I could hear the sound of their tails swishing the flies away. Later that summer, I was introduced to the *whir-whir* sound of grasshoppers flying about. I would learn to despise the nasty little beasts, as they would destroy every thread of grass and plants in their path, including the contents of Ira's beloved garden. It always gave me the chills when a grasshopper would land on my bare arm or leg. They had little claws that I figured helped them stick to the plant stems—but I certainly didn't appreciate them using their clampers to dig into my skin!

But on that first morning, I continued to lie in bed with my ears tuned to the outdoors. I could hear water running—maybe a river or a stream? I heard the occasional *whinny* of a horse and the *quack-quack* of ducks. I definitely sat up in bed when I heard an eerie howl I recognized from watching westerns on television at Cho's. Was it a coyote? A wolf? For all I knew, wolves still roamed the plains of Montana. Whichever one it was, when the howling reached a crescendo, I knew it wasn't just a one-animal band that was creating such loud music. There had to be a pack of them—at least, I thought that was what you called a bunch of coyotes or wolves. I knew it wasn't a *gaggle* of wolves or coyotes. I was certain that a *gaggle* was reserved for describing a whole gob of geese.

As I soaked in the odd new morning sounds, I thought back to the 1,200-some mile, two-day car trip with a man who was a stranger to me. Even worse, this stranger didn't appear to have much to talk about.

Just as I was trying to convince myself to climb out of bed and go downstairs and face him, I heard a shout from the bottom of the stairs and my lower lip began to tremble.

"Breakfast is ready, young lady. Come and get it." *Don't you dare cry,* I told myself as I quickly dressed and headed down to face the unknowns of my new life in the vast, east-central plains of Montana with an old man I barely knew.

THE LAY OF THE LAND

Hearing Ira's call to come to breakfast, I hurriedly threw on a blouse and a pair of jeans and headed downstairs to the bathroom. After a quick stop there to wash my face and brush my teeth, I entered the warmth of the sunlit kitchen with trepidation. With a spatula in hand and standing in front of the stove, Ira was tending to a skillet of sizzling bacon.

"Good morning there, young lady. Have a seat at the table," came his deep voice, turning his head slightly over his broad shoulder to speak. There were two neatly arranged table settings on the small, round kitchen table, and I chose the chair in front of the one without the coffee cup. "How do you like your eggs? Sunny-side up or poached? I always overcook 'em when I try for over-easy, so that ain't an option."

Since I wasn't sure what a poached egg was, I cleared my throat and muttered, "ah, sunny side up would be fine, thank you."

"So it be," he said, nimbly cracking the shells of two eggs on the edge of the skillet and spilling their contents into the pan.

"Hope you like bacon. I have bacon every morning, except on Sundays, that is. Treat myself to pork sausage instead."

As I glanced at the old, but spotlessly clean white tin kitchen cabinets, the soft breeze coming through the half-opened window above the sink brought the welcomed aroma of bacon, eggs, and toast to my nostrils. *I might be nervous, but I'm also hungry,* I decided, my stomach beginning to rumble. Even though I was seated in my chair, I could see the pointed top of the barn through the window. I had to squint to make out what looked like a metal-shaped rooster on a rod attached to the roof. I figured it was some kind of weathervane contraption to see which way the wind was blowing.

"Here, you can butter your toast however you like. This here's a jar of Annie Whitfield's homemade raspberry jelly—mighty darn tasty. It probably ain't proper manners, but I like to put a big ol' glob of jam on my toast and dip it in the yolk. But, you do as you like."

Wow! That's way more talk out of him than I heard the whole trip from San Francisco, I thought. You know how some people start babbling more than usual when they are nervous about being around someone? I wondered if maybe that was why he was suddenly chatty—perhaps he was as uncomfortable around me as I was with him. Whatever the reason, the breakfast of eggs, bacon, and toast with raspberry jam turned out to be a real treat. I was used to no more than a bowl of oatmeal at the orphanage, or Cheerios or Frosted Flakes when I was with my mom.

"I'll wash, you dry," Ira said, motioning me to clear the table. I thought of telling him about my table-busing experience at Del's, but instead just cleared the breakfast dishes and wiped down the tablecloth like the busing pro I am.

"First off, you need to learn the lay of the land right off the bat, young lady," he exclaimed, pointing to the drying rack next to the sink. I grabbed the wash towel and slid as far from Ira as possible, yet close enough to still pass a dish. "We do things different out here in the country than folks probably do in the city. I don't know what all you were expected to do when you were with Lillian, Sun-Ju, or the orphanage, but round here, we work. Don't matter if you're twelve, twenty, or eighty—everybody pitches in and helps."

As I dried the silverware and watched Dimwit streak past the window in an attempt to catch a squirrel (a gopher, I would later learn) before it dove into its hole, I couldn't help but wonder if Ira helped my grandma with household chores. He must have been reading my mind when he continued, "Your grandma did a bang-up job of doing all the cooking and cleaning around here, and now that she's gone, I do the best I can to live up to her standards. I'll expect no less from you—bed made, and room picked up every morning before breakfast. We'll swap cookin' and doin' the dishes duties, too."

Yikes! I was curious if he used to make my mom clean her room because she sure wasn't very tidy around our apartment. We only made our bed when we changed the sheets and were never in much of a hurry to do the dishes or pick up our apartment. The writing on the wall was suddenly coming into perfect focus: my housekeeping habits were about to change big time.

But then again, cleaning up my room and having to make my bed isn't so bad, I thought while I finished putting the breakfast dishes away. I mean, I had already been doing those chores for the last month at the orphanage. And, I'd already had some practice in cooking, if you can call heating up soup or throwing a toasted cheese sandwich in the frying pan "cooking." What I didn't know was that my chore list was about to grow much larger.

"Okay, now that you know what's-what inside the house," Ira confirmed, "let's head outside and I'll show you what your ranch chores are going to be."

Ranch chores? In case you forgot, I'm a city girl. What in the world would I know about ranch chores? I suddenly started to panic at being thrust into the unknown.

Ira issued a warning before opening the mudroom screen door that led to the front yard. "Watch yourself—Dimwit is going to be just as excited to see you as he was last night. He don't have nothin' for manners, so he'll jump on you first thing." Even though we'd had a brief introduction the night before, I was a little leary of Dimwit. I wasn't used to being around dogs, as we didn't have pets of any kind at our apartment. Cho's family had a big yellow cat named Arthur. We were friendly enough with each other, but he was hardly ever around.

Well, Ira was right; Dimwit picked right up from the night before. He started running in circles, always coming back and leaping at me with his front legs and paws extended. He wasn't a big dog, but he almost knocked me down with the force of his jump.

"Dimwit! Get down!" hollered Ira, grabbing his collar and jerking him back to the ground. "Here, kneel in front of him and hold his collar tight. Talk to him, give him some pets, and he should settle down some. Dang silly ol' dog."

"Good boy—that's a good boy, Dimwit," I said soothingly, not really knowing what else to say to this energetic dog that I'd just met. But that approach seemed to work, as other than receiving another good face wash, he quit being so rambunctious.

"Why did you name him Dimwit?" I asked. *Did I just get brave enough to actually ask the scar-faced man a question?*

"Well, I've always had good cow-dogs on the ranch—Blue Heelers, mostly. They're dang smart dogs, they are. But one day a couple of years ago, ol' Dimwit here showed up on the porch step," Ira explained. "He was skinny, scrawny, and looked like he hadn't eaten in weeks. I fed him, and he just stuck around. Took him into town and tried to find his owner—even put up a sign at the grocery store and the Post Office, but nobody ever claimed him. Anyway, he's just a mutt and don't seem to have any more of a brain than God gave a scarecrow. Totally worthless around the cows, he is. Anyway, Dimwit just seemed to be a right-fittin' name for him."

Dimwit roared ahead of us as I followed Ira across the twenty-some yards of the heavily packed dirt and gravel surface that separated the farmhouse from the barn. The barn was just like the pictures I had seen in books at school: painted red with big, sliding doors trimmed in white. A set of corrals, neatly divided by panels and gates into smaller pens, was attached to the backside of the barn. Beyond was a big pasture where a large herd of cattle grazed on the grass. There must have been more than a hundred of them! I noticed that most of the cows were red with white faces; the others were either pure black or black with white faces.

As we entered the barn, the smell of, well, the smell of cow and horse poop hit me like a ton of bricks. It was way stronger than what was wafting through my bedroom window earlier in the morning.

My only previous experience of being around livestock was when my mom and Sun-Ju took me and Cho to an amusement park when we were about six. We thought we were real cowgirls when we rode ponies that plodded along slowly in a circle, but I also remember that neither of us liked the smell of pony poop.

I'd been swatting flies since we entered the barn, so I figured they must be fans of cow manure.

I followed Ira down a dirt alleyway that divided the first level of the barn. Dimwit charged ahead of us, barking at a yellow cat that was streaking for safety. "That's the milking area," said Ira, pointing to the three stalls to the right of us. "Had milk cows for years—Holsteins mostly. Sold 'em and retired from the milking business a few years back."

Opposite the milking stalls were two open stalls, each filled with some kind of bundled grass. "This here is alfalfa hay," Ira explained, pointing to a pile of green bales. "And the yellow stuff is straw. I feed the hay and mostly use the straw to bed down cows and horses in these here pens or out in the corral, 'specially when it's cold, snowy, or rainy. Use it in the chicken house, too.

"Okay, now that I've given ya' a bit of the lay of the land, are you ready to start tacklin' the chores you're gonna be doing from here on in?"

I was quite certain I didn't have a choice. Ready or not, ranch life, here I come.

Chapter 10

BETSY-LOU
AND THE CHICKENS

After the hay and straw pens, Ira led me to the end of the alleyway, where a funny-looking gadget with a big handle came out of the floor. I figured it was a well pump, or at least something like that. To the left of the pump was the staircase to what Ira said was the hayloft, and to the right, I could see into a room full of saddles and what I assumed to be other horse and cattle stuff. But what really caught my eye and ear was the last stall on the right, where Dimwit was excitedly barking at whatever was in the far pen.

"Go on now—git!" Ira hollered at the dog, who barked a few more times and then bounded up the wooden stairs to the hayloft. I heard something bellow before I saw a white nose sticking through the slats of the pen gate. As we approached the stall, I could see that the owner of the nose and the source of all the racket was a young calf. He (or she—I didn't know which) had a black body and a white face and seemed awfully excited to see us. It kept sticking its nose through the gate like it was expecting something from us and wanting it immediately.

"In addition to feeding and watering Dimwit twice a day, bottle-feeding this here calf is going to be your job. Needs fed morning and evening. You'll need to clean out this stall and put fresh straw down every night," instructed Ira.

Great—just great! I don't even know how to take care of a dog yet, and now I'm supposed to water and feed a calf and clean up its mess?

"Most of my calves are born in March and April, but this little gal's momma ended up calving a month later than the others. And to top it off, she wouldn't take this black baldy calf of hers," Ira explained.

I guess I forgot about my hesitation to ask Ira questions because I blurted out a string of them. "What's a black baldy? What do you mean she wouldn't take her? Didn't she want her baby?"

Ira didn't immediately answer, instead scratching the calf's ears. When that didn't seem to settle the rowdy calf, he then let her hungrily suck on his index finger. *Okay, I get it now,* I thought, *the calf wants breakfast and is trying to nurse.*

"A black baldy has a black body and a white face—it's what you get when you cross a Hereford with a Black Angus. Herefords are the red cows with white faces and bags. And nope, her momma wouldn't let her suck for milk—wouldn't let her anywhere near. It happens sometimes, and if you don't have another mother-cow around that's lost her calf to adopt her, then you must bottle-feed them until they're old enough to eat grass or hay on their own.

"As you can see, this little gal is in need of a meal," Ira said, retrieving his finger from the calf's mouth. We only had to go a few steps to enter the room at the end of the alley. "This here is what's called the tack room. It's where I keep my saddles, bridles, halters, and the like. Also use it to store feed sacks and bags of this calf milk powder," Ira explained.

Reaching into the bag and retrieving a measuring cup, he grabbed a bucket with what looked like a fake cow's teat sticking out from the bottom of the pail. "You put two cups of this powdered milk into this bucket and fill 'er up to this red line with water," he said, as hung the bucket on the water spigot and began to furiously pump the handle. After the first four or five vigorous efforts only produced a few intermittent sputtering spits, the successive pumps of the handle finally resulted in a steady flow of water.

"Okay, you try it," he ordered.

"Me?" I asked, incredulously.

"Yup, you. Don't see anybody else waitin' in line, do ya?"

I nervously grabbed the handle and attempted to work it up and down like Ira did. I soon realized this wasn't for the faint of heart or the weak muscle. "No, no, no, not like that!" barked Ira, sounding as if I had all kinds of experience cranking stubborn well pump handles back in San Francisco. "You gotta pump it a lot harder and faster than that to get the water flowing. Now do it again, and this time give it some muscle."

Although shaken and a bit stunned from getting yelled at for attempting to do something I had never done before, I turned away from him so he couldn't see the tear that I felt sliding down my cheek. I bowed my neck, gritted my teeth, and took another turn aggressively yanking that pump handle. The little trickle of the first five or six pumps finally gave way to a solid stream of water. *Thank goodness!* I thought. I was sure the next desperate pump of the handle would separate my arm from the shoulder socket.

"That's the ticket, young lady, that's how ya' gotta work that handle!" Ira exclaimed as I filled the bucket to the proper level at last. He then showed me how to use a big spatula to stir the powder and water together until it was a smooth mixture. "Okay, now when you got all these powder granules and bubbles worked into a smooth mix, pour a tad bit of the milk into this here bowl for the cat and her kittens," he ordered.

"No, no, no, that's way too much!" Ira hollered when the mama cat and her three kittens scurried hungrily to the pan. "They need to stay hungry enough to be good mousers."

I sat back on my haunches, more than a little bewildered after being scolded for just about everything I'd been asked to do so far. But just as I was wondering if I was supposed to pour some of the milk from the cat's bowl back into the pail, Ira swept the bucket over the fence and hung it from the second rail inside the pen. I watched in amazement as the calf attacked the pail nipple like it hadn't eaten in months.

"You can use that little step ladder to hang that pail. Like I said, a milk pail every morning and evening. Fix 'em up like we just did. I know he acts starved, but better that than bloating him with too much. And don't forget to use that other pail to fill his water trough, you can use that ladder for that job, too. Top that water trough off every feeding, even if it ain't empty."

With my arms still silently screaming in agony, I again started pumping and filled the water pail. I stepped up on the ladder and somehow talked my aching muscles into hoisting the bucket over the gate and emptying the contents into the trough.

Ira just grunted as I stepped down, so I guess that meant I finally passed inspection on something. As I alternately watched the cat, kittens, and calf devour their breakfast, I worked up the nerve to ask grumpy Old Scarface a question. "Do the cats and the calf have names?"

"Well, no, I reckon not. Never been fond of cats. If it wasn't for them controlling the mice population, I wouldn't care to have them around the place. No reason why you couldn't name 'em, though. But let's see, back when I had milk cows, I did give 'em names. Let's see, the last two that I had were Betsy-Lou and Cindy-Sue. You could use one of them names for this calf if you like."

"I think she looks more like a Betsy-Lou," I said.

"Then Betsy-Lou it will be," confirmed Ira. "You think you can mix up this milk and feed Betsy-Lou every morning and evening? I don't have time to be running over here to make sure it's done right."

"I can do it," I said, squeezing my hands and hoping that I really could. I did know I could do it better without him looking over my shoulder and hollering at me.

When the calf had sucked the pail dry, Ira showed me how to rinse it out with water. I had to squeeze the fake cow teat hard enough for the water to come through it so the milk wouldn't dry and clog things up. I figured it was probably what milking a real cow would be like.

"Okay, we're done with the barn chores. Let's head over yonder to the chicken coop. Those eggs we had this morning? Those ain't store-bought—they came from our chickens."

Dear God! Taking care of Dimwit and Betsy-Lou isn't enough for a city girl? Cranking on a pump handle that even Hercules could barely move? I can't wait to see what fun the chickens will bring!

"Make sure this dumb dog is with ya' and the bottom door latch is secure every time you leave the barn," Ira ordered when we exited and took a left turn down the lane. Four structures, two on either side, bordered the dirt pathway.

"That's my quonset shed," Ira explained, pointing to the first building on the left. It was a big, gray-metal shed with a funny-looking rounded roof. "My shop is in there—it's where I fix and repair my equipment. Also use it as a garage to store vehicles and machinery."

"What are those buildings?" I asked, referring to the two structures on the same side of the lane as the house.

"The log one is our old homestead cabin. It's where me and your grandmother lived after we was married. The other is just an old storage shed. Gettin' pretty run down but can't bring myself to tear it down just yet," he said.

Was that a hint of nostalgia I heard in his voice? I thought.

The dirt trail between the furthest buildings took a gentle downward dip, leading to a good-sized pond a couple hundred yards beyond. *So that's where the duck quacking is coming from.* Pointing toward the water, Ira commented. "We'll head down there one of these evenings. It's a good spot to relax and do some fishing after a hard day's work. I've got an old army buddy who owns a fish hatchery over by Lewistown. He brings me a tank full of mostly brook trout 'bout every other year, so it stays pretty well stocked.

I could hear the clucking of the chickens before we ever reached the chicken coop. Dimwit quit chasing a bird and suddenly raced toward the clatter.

"Go on now—git!" Ira snarled at the dog again. "Don't let him in here unless ya' want to start World War III!"

I gagged as we slid through the door. I swear the barn smelled like freshly baked doughnuts compared to the stench of the chicken coop! There must have been twenty-or-so hens in the enclosure, and they were creating quite the raucous. Most were up on the row of nests that sat on a shelf that ran the length of one of the walls. The others were scurrying along the floor or flying back up to the nests. All were cackling and raising a cloud of dust. There were a few big roosters in the room, too, but they quickly scrambled out the little side door and into a fenced outdoor pen.

Pointing to a lidded barrel just inside the door, Ira said, "There's chicken feed in there. You'll need to spread four or five handfuls out each morning, here, just like this."

Well, at least that's easier than pumping that water handle, I thought. Little did I know the worst chore was about to be revealed.

"After you spread out the chicken feed, you'll need to gather the eggs. Plus, the hen house needs to be cleaned about once a week and replaced with fresh straw. Come on, I'll show you how to do all that right now."

Ira instructed me how to use a pitchfork (a long-handled stick with three spikes on the end) to get most of the old straw and chicken poop removed from the wood plank floor. I got bawled out a few more times for not using the pitchfork right to get all the straw in the wheelbarrow. And here's the worst thing: using the pitchfork stirred up a lot of dust and made the smell even worse. Ira got pretty disgusted with me when I had trouble spreading the straw the way he was showing me, but I was determined not to shed any tears.

"Okay, now it's time to gather the eggs. That can be a bit tricky, as most of these old gals are pretty dang ornery when it comes to gettin' off their nest," Ira said. "You right-handed?" When I nodded yes, he slipped a way-to-large canvas glove over my right hand that covered almost up to the elbow. "You gotta push these old hens off the nest in a hurry to avoid gettin' pecked. Here, let me demonstrate on these two over here."

With a quick sweep of his arm, Ira swatted the angry and squawking hens off their nests before collecting the eggs and placing them in a wire basket. "These old roosters are pretty dang disagreeable too, so best to make sure they stay in the outside pen when you're gathering eggs. Okay, your turn."

I was scared to death of these chickens, but I tried not to let Ira know that. Using my glove hand, I attempted a tentative swipe to remove the first hen from her nest. I let out a scream as the madder-than-a-hatter momma chicken simply hopped over my glove and gave me two rapid pecks on the arm. One glanced off my glove, but the other struck my bare elbow. I don't know if the tears came from the surprise of the strike or the resulting pain, but suddenly the tears were flowing.

"No, no, no!" hollered Ira. "Not like that! Only one way to do this, and it's how I just showed ya. Gotta move that glove hard and fast to get 'em off that nest." And as if I wasn't upset enough already, Old Scarface had to top it off with, "And bawling 'bout it ain't gonna be of no help."

Well, I quickly wiped my tears with my ungloved hand, bowed my neck for the second time, and made a promise to myself to get through this ordeal without crying again.

I did better on the next try and better yet on the succeeding attempts. But I can tell you one thing for sure, I wasn't looking forward to having to wrestle those nasty old hens for their eggs every morning or having to keep an eye out for rooster attacks!

Dimwit raced up to give me a friendly greeting after we left the chicken coop. I was already appreciative of our fast-growing friendship, and he gave me a look as if he understood what I was going through. *Don't worry, Maggie. He yells at me all the time too, and I can't do anything right for him either.*

Chapter 11

THE GARDEN
AND OL' SWAYBACK

"Next up is the garden," Ira said, acting like I hadn't just been bawled out for crying after being attacked by an ornery old chicken. "In addition to eating our own eggs, we also raise all kinds of vegetables in this here garden. Let's see, we got some corn, taters, peas, lettuce, carrots, onions, rhubarb, and what-have-ya' out here," he continued, proudly pointing out which row was what. I'd, of course, seen gardens in San Francisco, but Ira's yard was bigger than ten of our neighbors' yards put together. And a good half of the huge yard was used as the garden.

"What we don't eat fresh out of the garden, I store in the root cellar for use when the snow flies. One thing for darn sure happens in these parts—weeds will overtake the vegetables if you don't keep 'em whacked down. So, we'll share the hoeing duties. You can hoe around the potato mounds and down the cornrows, and I'll tend to the rest."

Ira handed me a hoe and gave me a detailed lesson in hoeing technique. Since it was still early in summer, the plants were just coming out of the ground, and it would be easy for a newbie like me to mistake it for a weed. For a man of few words, Ira went to great lengths to explain the difference between the two. I broke out in a cold sweat thinking of how I'd get yelled at if I hoed up the potatoes or corn instead.

"These eastern plains of Montana get hot and dry, 'specially as we get along toward July and August. Won't take long to burn a garden up if you don't properly irrigate," Ira explained while moving the hose and sprinkler head to a different location. "Since we don't have an endless supply of well water on this ranch, a guy's gotta be thrifty in water use. I run the hose in the early morning and late evening to avoid evaporation and preserve as much water as possible. Also, a guy needs to hoe while the ground is still damp from the sprinkler. Otherwise, ya' might as well be slappin' your blade against the pavement."

Just as I was thinking there couldn't possibly be any more chores to add to my already daunting list, Ira added another. "Well, I reckon you better get acquainted with Ol' Swayback there," he said, pointing out to a lone horse in a small pasture beyond the barn. He looked to be rubbing his hind end against the wooden posts on a fence corner.

"It's a bad time of year with mosquitoes, deer flies, horseflies, and the like. He needs to be curried once a day to get rid of the flies and keep up a nice coat. He's too old to ride now, retired him a few years back, but he was a darn good horse to work cattle on. I figure he dang sure earned a little extra tender lovin' care in his golden years."

I figured out what Ira meant by currying when he grabbed a tether rope and a big brush, and we headed out toward Ol' Swayback. With all of the flies and mosquitoes we encountered on our way out to the pasture, I was thinking it would feel good to get "curried" myself.

"Watch yourself—this ol' bridge is a little wobbly," Ira ordered as I tentatively followed him across a footbridge that spanned a small stream. "This here is called Coyote Creek. It flows pretty good in the late spring with the mountain snowmelt but won't be much more than a trickle come late August."

I was a little leary as we approached the old horse, as those amusement park ponies were the only time I'd been near a horse. I hoped he was as gentle as the ponies Cho and I rode back then, even though at the time we were sure they were wild bucking broncos! Ol' Swayback let Ira slip on the bridle without a fuss.

"He's a gentle ol' boy these days, you won't have no trouble brushin' him—he plum likes it," Ira said, softly talking and stroking his top side from mane to tail. It was easy to see there was a strong friendship bond between the two of them.

"So, why do you call him Ol' Swayback," I asked.

"Why don't you take a good look at him and see if you can think of a reason?"

I felt kind of silly when I immediately spotted the obvious. Old Swayback had a, well, a U-shaped back. "He, he's got a big sway in his back," I said sheepishly.

"You've got a sharp eye, young lady," he replied in an almost playful sarcastic tone.

Then, Ira smiled at me for the first time since we met. At least, I thought it was an attempt at a smile. It actually made me sad when I saw that the movement of his lips and face was lopsided, only the left corner of his mouth moved up as he grinned. Nothing on the scarred side of his face moved in the slightest. It was then I realized that half of Ira's face was paralyzed—it didn't work at all.

Chapter 12

DIMWIT'S NEW SLEEPING ARRANGEMENT

I'm not sure what it was that awakened me on my second day at the ranch. It could have been the crowing of the roosters, the deep moo of the cows, or the rustlings of the curtains hanging from my open bedroom window. Whichever it was, I was quickly aware of some serious body-movement issues when I tried to get out of bed.

A deep muscle pain shot down my right shoulder and arm when I tried to simply pull back the covers. *What the heck? What happened to my arm?* It all came back to me as I wiped the sleep from my eyes with my left hand and shook off the cobwebs. Two red and angry hen-peck welts stared back at me from the inside of my right elbow. And the second source of the shoulder and arm pain? Well, no doubt the delayed result of yanking like crazy on that water pump handle. *How am I going to pump that handle again this morning when I can barely raise my arm high enough to change out of my pajamas?*

Once I finally managed to get out of bed, I realized there was more. My left hip and thigh were bruised and sore as the dickens. *What? Why am I sore there?* Then I remembered Betsy-Lou being rambunctious and bumping into me when I was cleaning out her stall. I again began to worry if this city girl was anywhere near up to the task of being a ranch worker.

The first week at the ranch went by both fast and slow. I know that's a contradiction, but it sure seems that way. Since the chores took up a good portion of my waking hours, the days went by quickly. Ira wasn't kidding when he said he didn't have time to be looking over my shoulder every day while I did my appointed tasks. He supervised the evening Betsy-Lou feeding on the first day, but I was otherwise left on my own to tend to Dimwit, Ol' Swayback, the chickens, and the garden. I was mostly glad Old Scarface wasn't lurking about hollering and criticizing my every move. But being left on my own with minimal instruction to care for strange farm animals was overwhelming. *Was I doing every chore exactly the way Ira had shown me? Was I remembering every last detail of his instruction?* It was all so new to me. The teaching lessons were such a blur that I was sure I was forgetting something, and it was probably something important.

The slow part of the day occurred in the late evening after the supper dishes were cleaned and put away. Ira still wasn't much of a talker, and he turned in early. I'd either go outside and play with my new best friend, Dimwit, or go upstairs to my room and get ready for bed. Even though I was tired from doing all my chores, my mind was too busy to go to sleep right away. A few of the nights I quietly slipped down the hall to my mother's room and lay on the bed with the rag dolls. *Did you wake up today, mom? Are you feeling better? Did you get our old apartment back? Are you back at Del's? Are you and the guys playing at the Gable's this weekend? Have you seen Cho, and does she miss me?*

I would eventually sneak back to my room. After being serenaded by crickets and the whir of insects outside my opened window, I would finally drift into a deep slumber, with my old life in San Francisco like sugar plums dancing in my head.

It was toward the end of the first week when one late afternoon, I noticed a huge bank of ominous black clouds moving toward us from the southwest. I only knew where the south and west were because Ira had given me a lesson in directions the day before. When he told me directions were important in order to get my bearings, I nodded like I understood what he meant. But I really didn't, not then, anyway.

"See Buffalo Butte over there?" he asked as we stood by the barn and looked over the pasture of cows toward a lonely peak not too far off in the distance. "That's about half a mile straight south of us, so that would be north," he explained, pointing in the opposite direction. "See those hills that are shaped like a saddle way out there? That would be west."

"And that would be east," I said, pointing my finger in the opposite direction, noting that the horizon to the east was mostly flat without any distinguishing landmarks to follow.

"Yup, that's right, young lady," he said. "If you ever get lost, you can get your bearings and find your way home. Just remember to find Buffalo Butte and head toward that."

Ira was sharpening the sickle on his mower, and I had just finished Betsy-Lou's second bottle-feeding of the day when lightning began to light up the sky, followed by loud bellows of thunder. The stifling heat of the late afternoon was quickly being replaced with the cooler air that the increasing wind seemed to be blowing in.

"We better head for the house," shouted Ira. "This storm will be on us before we know it." I sprinted for the house with Dimwit at my heels and held open the screen door for Ira, who was coming along at a gait that was somewhere between a fast walk and a trot—you know, moving like older people do when they're in a hurry. We had no sooner made it inside the kitchen when the storm hit full force.

Now, I've been in storms in San Francisco before, but they weren't anything like this. The wind was howling, whipping the big tree at the side of the house to and fro until I thought it would be torn from the ground. The rain came in sheets, pounding the roof and side of the house like a fire truck was taking aim with a high-pressure water hose. It seemed to me the whole house was rattling and shaking. I just sat on the kitchen chair with my arms wrapped around my chest.

Ira, however, didn't seem too concerned. He got each of us a glass of lemonade and started glancing through the paper as if storms like this were an everyday occurrence. Dimwit was scared just like me. He cried and scratched at the door between the mudroom and the kitchen.

"Can I let him in?" I asked anxiously, knowing Dimwit wasn't allowed in the main house.

"Nah, he's fine," answered Ira. "He gets a little antsy when these storms hit, but he's okay. This is about over, don't even think we're goin' to get any hail."

I knew from school what hail was, but like snow, I had never actually seen or experienced it before. But I found out about hail later that night—did I ever!

It seemed to me that the storm that hit at dusk lasted forever, but it really passed over fairly quickly. I was upstairs in my room reading a book when the lightning started to flash through my window again. Pretty soon, the thunder was back, and the wind was swirling so fast I could hear the branches of the tree outside my room swishing and swaying. All of a sudden, I saw a wicked bolt of lightning from my window, accompanied by an ear-shattering boom of thunder. I jumped up from the bed when my reading lamp flickered a few times and then went black. The rain that had begun to hammer the house was soon replaced by the *WHACK, WHACK, WHACK* of hail pounding the wood siding. I was afraid to get close to my window in case it would shatter from the hail, but I stepped close enough to peer out. *Yikes,* I thought, when a bolt of lightning lit up the yard, and I could see the hailstones bouncing in the grass.

I was so frightened I didn't know what I was going to do, but I knew I couldn't stay in my room. I wished I could run down the hallway and jump into bed with my mom. I was starting to cry, especially when I opened my door and realized the electricity was out throughout the house. Using the handrail, I felt my way down the stairs, the path intermittently illuminated through the kitchen window by lightning flashes. I was hoping Ira was still up and in his living room rocking chair, but another lightning beam showed an empty rocking chair and a closed bedroom door. I was just about to knock when I heard the soft cries coming from Dimwit; he was super scared, too.

So, I went to the mudroom instead, and Dimwit and I lay together on the floor. I wrapped my arms around him, petting him and trying to use a soothing tone to convince us both that everything was okay, even though it wasn't. Fortunately, the task of comforting the shaking dog sort of helped me forget how scared I was, but I started shuddering just as bad as Dimwit when the next thunder-boom exploded, and the hail strikes resumed in force against the screen door.

The noise of the hail was so loud that I didn't even hear the mudroom door open from the kitchen. "Are you okay, Maggie?" Ira asked softly.

"I th-think so," I stuttered, trying hard not to cry in front of him.

"Are you scared?" he asked.

"Y-yes, a lit-little b-bit," I answered, attempting to sound braver than I really was.

He shuffled his feet and glanced outside when another flash of lightning lit up the room, the white hail beginning to cover the front yard and Ira's garden like a blanket of snow. "How would you feel about ol' Dimwit here bunking upstairs with you? Just during the storms, mind you—rest of the time, he sleeps here like usual."

"Yes, th-that would help a lot. Th-thanks, Ira," I said, relieved.

"Well, take his dog bed upstairs with you, then," he said, as Dimwit, his bed, and I quickly headed for my room. I knew that Ira expected Dimwit to sleep on his doggie bed on the floor, but since I was still plenty nervous about the storm, I lifted him up and onto the bed next to me. He seemed happy to be there and snuggled his cold, wet nose into my neck.

"Am I hearing things?" I whispered into the dog's ear. "I think Ira just called me by my real name for the first time."

I giggled when Dimwit let out a sigh like he had noticed it, too.

Chapter 13

LETTERS TO MOM AND CHO

The morning after the storm was my turn to cook. I worried that I would over or under cook Ira's eggs and bacon, and I had previously found the old toaster to be so touchy that it was easy to burn the toast too. But I must have done okay, as Ira didn't complain when I put his plate in front of him, and he took the first few bites.

"Well, young lady," he said as he spread a hearty spoonful of Annie Whitfield's jam on his toast, "I have to go check and see if my hayfields have any hail damage, so you'll be on your own for your chores. I'm a-thinkin' hail is the good Lord's curse on us farmers and ranchers that live in this godforsaken country. A bad hail storm can totally wipe out a hay crop. And if you don't raise enough hay to get your cows through the winter, then you have to buy it, and boom, there goes your profit. Now, I just run cattle and don't raise any grain—we're in wheat and barley country out here—but those grain farmers can watch their livelihood go up in smoke if they get hailed on.

"Anyway, if we didn't get any rain or hail over there and it's dry enough to mow, I won't be back for lunch, so why don't you make me some ham and cheese sandwiches? I think there's potato chips in the pantry, so throw a couple of bags of those into my lunch pail, too. Also, the hail, wind, and rain from last night kind of wreaked havoc on the yard and garden, so you grab the rake and clean up the branches, leaves, and such that are scattered everywhere. With the soil being moist and soft from the rain, it would be a good time to do your hoeing before things dry out. Obviously, ain't no need to water the garden or the lawn either."

"Okay, I'll take care of that," I said, suddenly realizing this was the first time I would be alone at the ranch for the better part of a day. "Ah-ah, Ira? Can Dimwit stay here with me?"

"Yep—he sure as heck ain't any use to me out on the tractor."

After completing my chores and tidying up the yard and garden, I decided to use my infrequent spare time to write to my mom and Cho. I grabbed a pen and paper and sat down at the kitchen table and wrote to Cho first.

Dear Cho,

How are you? I am fine, I guess. We made it to Montana okay. It was a long trip. Part of Montana is full of mountains and flat where the ranch is at. You can see forever. Hardly any people live where we are at. I haven't been to Sandstone Springs (the nearest town to the ranch) yet, but I guess it's tiny.

Ira is what my grandpa says to call him. He looks scary because he has a big scar on his face. I don't know how he got it, and I'm afraid to ask. He's grouchy and doesn't talk hardly at all. I don't think he likes me. He hollers at me if I don't do things right. I call him Old Scarface (but not to his face!)

I have a dog! His name is Dimwit. We are becoming best friends. It's kind of funny because he likes me better than he does Ira. You can't believe how many chores I have to do! I feed the chickens and gather the eggs. Some of the hens are mean and I got pecked on the arm the first day! I also bottle-feed a calf named Betsy-Lou. I have to get in her pen to clean up her poop. She's really rough and bumps into me all the time. But I think we might be friends once we get used to each other. Her mom won't let her drink milk so I have to feed her twice a day.

Ira has a horse named Old Swayback. He is too old to ride, but I have to curry him. That means brush him. He's really gentle. Do you remember those ponies we rode at that park? He's as gentle as they were. Ira has a huge garden, and I have to hoe the weeds where the potatoes and corn are growing.

I have my own room, but it isn't my mom's old room. Does your mom still go see her every Sunday? I'm going to write her a letter right after I finish this. I'm still mad at her for not waking up and causing me to have to go to that orphanage. And now with Old Scarface. But, I'm going to act like everything is okay so that she doesn't worry about me too much. Okay, I better go. You are my best friend, and I miss you so much! Write me back soon!

Your friend,
Maggie

I guess it's kind of silly to write my mom when she's still in a *spell*, but I figure it won't hurt anything, either. Sun-Ju always told me to talk to her when she was in a trance just in case she might be able to hear me. Well, maybe she can hear me through my letters, too. Since she'll have enough to worry about when she comes out of her spell, I decided not to tell her in the letter that we don't have our apartment anymore, or that Ira hollers at me when I don't do the chores right. If and when she reads this or future letters, I want to make sure it sounds like everything is hunky-dory with Ira and me at the ranch. Now, if only I could convince myself of the same.

Dear Mother,

I hope you are out of your spell and can read this. I sure miss and love you! If you wake up and I am gone, I am with Grandpa Ira, so don't worry about me. We are doing pretty good. I'm helping with chores and also with cooking and washing dishes. Ira likes eggs and bacon. Did he like that when you were little? Did you have to do chores? I have a dog named Dimwit, a cat, and some kittens. What was your dog's name when you were little? I get to feed a calf. She's a girl calf, and her name is Betsy-Lou. I have to gather eggs and brush an old horse named Swayback. I also hoe in the garden. Ira doesn't have a TV.

I saw your room. It is clean, clean, clean! Haha, I'm too big for your old clothes! My room is at the top of the stairs. I saw Grandma's sewing machine. Ira says she was a good sewer. I saw your old record albums. One was Elvis, and the other was Patsy Cline. We had some bad storms. Did you used to get scared when a big storm came through? I admit I was scared when the lightning, thunder, wind, and rain hit! And it even hailed. I was glad when Ira said Dimwit could sleep with me when it storms.

Okay, I better finish this and get it in the mail. Don't worry about me. I am okay here with Ira. Get better soon. I love you, Mom!

Maggie

"Okay, Dimwit," I said as I walked outside. "Let's take a little run to the end of the lane and get these letters in the mailbox, shall we?" I think he is smarter than Ira gives him credit for, because he headed down the lane toward the mailbox like he already knew where I was going.

MEETING THE WHITFIELDS

*I*ra and I were out in his quonset when he had me climb over some neatly stacked irrigation pipes to retrieve an old bicycle from the corner of the shop. One thing I had already noticed about Ira was that everything on the whole ranch was neat and organized. Whether it was the house, barn, or sheds, everything was as neat as a pin.

"Let me tell you something, young lady," Ira had told me shortly after we arrived at the ranch. "I never had nothin' growing up. My older brother Ethan and me came from Ohio to this country in 1913 with no more than the shirts on our backs. We homesteaded this very ground where we are standing right now. Do you know what homesteading means?"

When I shook my head no, he explained. "Well, back in the old days, the government would offer a chunk of the land out here in the west to be settled. If a person would put up some kind of shack on the property and farm or raise livestock on it for a certain length of time, then the land would belong to them. That's how I got started on this here ranch. I met and married your grandma a short time later, and right after we was hitched, I built that little one-room log shack I pointed out to you the other day. We eked out an existence the old-fashioned way—elbow grease and just plain ol' back-breakin' hard work. And we were gosh-darn proud of what we built together, little as it may seem we had to show for it. But, I darn sure learned that money don't grow on them Cottonwood trees over there by the creek, and I learned to appreciate and take good care of what little I do have.

"So, just like I expect you to clean your room and make your bed every morning, I expect you to take pride and keep everything organized and well cared for on this ranch. Just as you're expected to share the duties of cooking and cleaning the house, same goes for the barns, shop, sheds, and other outbuildings. You dad-gum well better pick up after yourself when you do your chores. I won't tolerate leaving things helter-skelter. Always remember this, young lady, if you don't take pride in keeping proper care of what is yours, you can dang sure bet nobody else will either."

I didn't say anything then, but Ira's "money don't grow on trees" statement wasn't lost on me. I know that most nine-, ten-, eleven-, and twelve-year-old kids don't think much about money or where it comes from. They don't know how much a gallon of milk, a dozen eggs, or a loaf of bread costs. They don't know how many hours of work it takes to have those things in the cupboard or the fridge. But I know. I know how long my mom had to work to get enough from her paycheck and tips to get our usual stash of groceries each week. I know because I had to do the shopping when she was having one of her spells and even when she wasn't. I'm not trying to make you feel sorry for me or anything like that, but I'm just telling you that I probably had more awareness of real-life things at a younger age than most kids.

"This bike was your mom's—ain't been ridden since she was 'bout your age," he said with a touch of sadness to his voice. "Let me turn on this air compressor and inflate these flat tires." When he was done and turned off the noisy machine, we realized we had visitors.

"Well, for goodness' sake, Ira! This must be your beautiful granddaughter, Maggie!" exclaimed a short, stocky, and rosy-cheeked lady, bustling through the shop door dressed in a faded green work shirt, jeans, cowboy boots, and a dusty *Green Bay Packers* cap. She took me by surprise when she marched right up to me and pulled me in for a big hug.

"I'm Annie Whitfield, your nearest neighbor. This here is my daughter Whitney, but you can call her Whit. That's what everyone calls her except when she's being bratty—then both her father and I call her Whitney. She's going to be an eighth grader this school year, so if I have my information in order, she's a year ahead of you?"

"Yes, ma'am. I'll be a seventh grader."

"Annie, you can call me Annie. I appreciate your good manners, but I'm not used to answering to ma'am. Hey, Ira, I brought some pie, cookies, and a gallon of lemonade, so let's you and me get that into your kitchen and let these young gals gab a bit and get to know each other," said Annie, grabbing Ira by the crook of his arm and directing him out of the shop.

Whit, who had the same short and blocky build as her mother, was dressed almost exactly like her mom, except she had a *Sandstone Springs Feed Co* cap on her head. She was a lot like her mother in personality, too—friendly and outgoing. Whit explained they lived on the ranch, which was, "as the crow flies," about two miles "over yonder." I had never heard those expressions before but figured "as the crow flies" meant the shortest and the straightest distance between the ranches, and "over yonder" was somewhere in the direction of where she had pointed.

I figured Ira had told Annie about my mom being in the hospital and bringing me to the ranch when she gently touched my arm and said, "I'm sorry about your mom being in the hospital, Maggie. I hope she gets better soon."

Whit then explained that her grandpa, grandma, and family had always been the closest ranch to Ira's and that her grandparents were best friends with Ira and my grandma Audrey. She said that even though her mom, Annie, was four or five years older than my mom, they knew each other growing up. "Heck, Sandstone Springs is so small that everybody knows everybody—age doesn't really matter," she laughed. "Have you been into town yet?"

"No, but Ira said we have to go in soon to pick up supplies," I answered.

"Well, you're in for a surprise," Whit exclaimed, with what I would soon find to be an always-present smile on her face. "San Francisco it ain't, honey, San Francisco it ain't. Sandstone Springs is no bigger than a minute!"

Whit said that her dad and mom had looked in frequently on Ira ever since Audrey had died. "My dad helps him if he needs a hand during haying and calving, stuff like that," she explained. "And mom brings him pies, cakes, and cookies when she comes to visit. She thinks he gets pretty lonely. In return, he brings us corn, peas, potatoes, and other vegetables from his garden. Dad also hires him to drive a combine during harvest. I'm guessin' he's already put you to work in that big ol' garden of his?"

"Yes, that and lots of other chores," I replied with a smile. "I have to feed the chickens and gather the eggs, brush down

Ol' Swayback, and bottle-feed Betsy-Lou—she's an orphan calf, you know."

"Speaking of orphans, were you really in San Francisco and living in an orphanage when Ira came to get you?" Whit asked as she tucked an unruly blond curl underneath her baseball cap.

"Yeah, I lived there for about a month after my mom got sick. It was okay, but some of the older guys and girls that lived there bugged us younger kids. They were like, I don't know, juvenile delinquents. They were always in trouble and were mean to the rest of us."

"You're really tall—how tall are you, anyway?" asked Whit.

"Haven't measured lately, but I think I'm a little over 5'7".

"Wow, I'm like five-foot nothin'! I bet most kids your age didn't give you much guff," Whit stated emphatically. "But it must have been hard to live there, away from your mom and friends and all," she said, squeezing my forearm in a caring and understanding way.

"Well, I'm not as tough as some of the older girls were," I explained, squinting momentarily when the morning sun moved far enough across the sky to throw a few bright rays in our eyes through the open quonset hut doors. "But, I grew up in a pretty rough neighborhood. Don't get me wrong, I sure don't go looking for trouble, but the one thing I did learn from growing up in San Francisco and being in an orphanage was to stand up for myself. If you don't, you'll just get run over."

"Yeah, I can see that," replied Whit thoughtfully. "Hey, let's go to the house and get some cookies and lemonade."

As we were just about to the front porch, Whit made a "hush" sign with a finger to her mouth and quietly led the way until we crawled underneath the open kitchen window where we could hear Ira and Annie's conversation. We both were worried that

Dimwit would bark and give us away, but he fortunately just lay down between us and took a snooze.

"I don't know, Annie—I just don't know what the hell I'm doing," Ira said, his voice thick with worry. "I didn't know what I was doing the first time around with my daughter Lillian, but that's when my Audrey was here to help. I wasn't a good father then, so how in the world can I ever be a good grandfather to this young girl?"

"Oh, listen to you! That's just a big old bucket of hogwash, Ira. Living out here like a monk in the middle of nowhere should cause you to thank your lucky stars for having that granddaughter of yours here with you. It'll give you a purpose in life and something to worry about other than stewing over getting your hay up on time or griping about the cattle prices. Now, I understand that Lillian was a difficult child to raise, but that doesn't mean Maggie will be the same way."

"I know, but without Audrey here to help, I just don't know what on earth to do with a twelve-year-old girl. I surely don't."

"Nonsense," Annie replied. "You need to come to grips with the fact that Audrey isn't here. And you're not so old and senile that you don't know how to love a grandchild, are you? Plus, I'm your neighbor and friend, and I'm always here to help. I know a thing or two about raising girls—I've got three of them, you know!"

I could almost feel Ira's relief sift through the screen of the open window at the offer of some support. "Did she bring anything else to wear besides those peddle-pushers she has on?" Annie asked.

"Well, she didn't have much in that garbage sack of a suitcase she brung, a pair of jeans and a few blouses, I think," Ira replied. "And I did see one of those hippie-looking dresses—don't think she has anything other than those tennis shoes she's wearin' for footwear."

"She's already way taller than me and any of my girls, but my sister is about Maggie's size. I'll see if she has some old work jeans and boots that she could spare. You know, you'll have to take her to Billings to do some school shopping before too long."

"I know, I know," said Ira hesitantly. "Could you please come with me and help? I wouldn't know what the heck to buy for her."

"I guess I better. I somehow can't see you browsing in the Junior Girls' department for underwear!" laughed Annie. I threw Whit a look of shock, mortified at the very thought of Ira shopping for my undergarments.

"I'll leave you with this advice," Annie continued. "You need to just relax and quit beating yourself up for how you handled Lillian all those years ago. Go ahead and let yourself be a grandpa—let her get to know you, too. She's never had a father in her life, so she could sure as heck use a grandpa. And don't be a darned old mute—that young gal needs you to talk to her. You'll be fine, Ira. And remember, I'm just down the road a piece should you need a helpin' hand."

So as not to be seen, Whit and I sneaked back to the front porch on our hands and knees. "We could sure use some cookies and lemonade," Whit announced as we barged into the kitchen. "We've been playing out in the barn and need us some treats."

Chapter 15

DRIVING OL' BLUE

Despite yearning for my old San Francisco life with my mom, after a couple of weeks of being at the ranch, I had to admit I was starting to like being around the farm animals. Except for the chickens, that is. I was still scared to death of the hens and roosters, and I dreaded every minute of the daily egg-gathering chore.

One thing was for certain in my new world at the Old Scarface ranch: Dimwit was my new best friend! He could hardly wait to see me every morning and was my constant outdoor companion. Even Betsy-Lou and I were getting along better, especially since my arm, shoulder, and hip soreness had finally gone away. I think pumping that stubborn well-handle made my muscles stronger, and I felt a sense of satisfaction in getting faster at completing my Betsy-Lou duties. She was still really rough with me when I was cleaning out her pen, but I wasn't afraid of her anymore. I realized she was just excited to see me once she figured out I was her new meal ticket. And Ol' Swayback seemed to like me, too, and the feeling was starting to become mutual. He was sweet as could be and seemed to love being brushed and petted.

"Come on, young lady," Ira shouted from the barn door as I was finishing up my chores one morning. "We need to go into Sandstone Springs for supplies and some tractor and baler parts. This is a good time to introduce you to the town where you'll be going to school this fall."

I hurriedly finished rinsing out Betsy-Lou's pail and raced to catch up with Ira as he strode toward the pickup truck parked in front of the house.

"You drive *Ol' Blue*," he said, motioning me to the driver's side of the pickup truck. "She's a '57 Chevy Stepside with some hard miles on her. Them there dents on the doors, fenders, and box come from more than one or two angry bulls and mamma cows butting into her over the years, but she's still as reliable as an August draught," he said, walking to the passenger side door while motioning for Dimwit to jump in the pickup bed.

Whatever was in *Ol' Blue's* troubled past, I sure as heck didn't expect to be chauffeuring Ira and Dimwit in her.

"Bu-but, Ira. I-I don't know how to drive. We didn't even have a car in San Francisco," I nervously explained. "And, I-I'm not even old enough to have a driver's license."

"Well, this ain't San Francisco. You see any policemen hidin' in the bushes just a-waitin' to give you a ticket for driving without a license?" he asked sarcastically. "Out here, drivin' is just a part of ranch life, and as far as learning how to drive goes, I reckon there's only one way to learn—just get to-drivin'. That driver's door sticks, so ya' gotta yank on the bugger to get 'er open."

He wasn't kidding about the door. I guess one of those bulls he was talking about had butted it because there was a big dent where the door met the frame. It was a good thing I was stronger from cranking on that pump handle and could jerk it open on the second try.

As I climbed into the driver's side seat, I noticed it had some kind of woven pad strapped to it. I could see through it well enough to see that both the original seat and backrest had big cracks in them. It was a good thing that I was tall for a twelve-year-old because I still had to stretch to see over the steering wheel.

"Okay, young lady," Ira began, "Ol' Blue is what they call a stick-shift. In other words, you gotta manually shift gears as you gain speed. You see the gear knob? It's a tad bit worn now, but you see the diagram on it? What's that tell you?"

"Well, it has 1 and 3 and R on the top, and then some lines connecting to 2 and 4 on the bottom," I replied hesitantly. "What does that mean?"

"It means there are four gears and a reverse. You shift into a different gear depending on how fast you are going—first gear for the slowest, fourth gear when you're cruising the fastest," he explained. "Now, there's three pedals down on the floor; the clutch is on your far left, the brake is in the middle, and the gas pedal is on the right. Push the clutch down all the way to the floor, that's right, all the way. Okay, work that stick back and forth in neutral—that's the part in the middle where you can wiggle the shifter back and forth. That's right, get used to that. Now go all the way to the left and slide it into the second gear slot…that's it. Since first is a very low gear and only used when pulling a heavy trailer or starting out in mud or ice, we're gonna start her off in second gear. When we've gathered enough speed, we have to shift to third."

The stick didn't seem to want to go into second gear, and I held my breath waiting for him to holler at me for doing it wrong. But he didn't say anything while I kept forcing the shifter into gear and making all the grinding noises. I breathed a sigh of relief when it went into place.

"Now, let's practice a little before we fire her up and try the real thing. What you've got to do is slowly let out the clutch at the same time you push down on the gas pedal—there you go. Do it again a few times until you get the hang of it, slower on releasing the clutch, or you'll kill the engine when we start her."

I can tell you this much: It's sure a lot easier to pretend you are driving and shifting when the pickup isn't running! When Ira showed me how to pull the choke knob and turn the key to start the engine, my first attempts at getting the vehicle moving forward were a disaster. I either pushed down on the gas too hard, let the clutch out too fast, or both. Ol' Blue would cough and lurch, belch and burp, and spit and sputter until the shuttering engine would finally quit. And we hadn't even moved forward a foot. I braced myself for a bawling-out, and sure enough, I didn't have to wait long for his criticism to begin.

"No, no, no! I told you not to drop that clutch all at once!" he snapped. "Ya' gotta let that clutch out smooth-like. And ya' gotta be given' her the gas at the same time. Now do it again—and do it right this time!"

"Quit yelling at me!" I screamed back, the spillover tears belying my promise not to cry. "I've never done any of this before, I've never driven anything, let alone a cranky old truck! And I've never fed calves or knocked chickens off their nests, either. I'm doing the best I can!"

Dear God! Did I just boil-over and sass back to Old Scarface? What's going to happen now? Am I going to be spanked like I was at the orphanage? Kicked out of the pickup and left at home?

I just sat there, gripping the steering wheel and fighting back more tears, waiting for the bomb to drop. After what seemed like five minutes of dead silence, Ira finally spoke. Thankfully, his tone wasn't angry, but it wasn't understanding or apologetic, either. "Well, are ya' gonna sit there and bawl and give up, or are ya' gonna buckle down and try again?"

I don't know if I was either too mad or just too scared to answer his question, but I wiped the tears from my eyes, reset my jaw, and tried again. And again. And again and again. After what seemed like fifty tries, I finally was able to time the release of the clutch with just the right amount of push on the gas pedal to get Ol' Blue moving forward without killing the engine. In my excitement of completing the first phase of driving, I forgot about still being angry for getting yelled at.

"I did it, Ira! I did it!" I shouted with joy. I was shocked when I glanced over and saw that lopsided grin slowly spread across my grandfather's face.

"Yes, you did it, but keep your eyes on the road and stay between the ditches, young lady," he warned when I got too close to a nearby ditch for comfort. "Okay, steadily give her the gas, and I'll tell you when you're going to have to shift into third."

I won't lie—I wish I could say I was shifting smoothly and doing a good job of driving Ol' Blue straight by the time we had gone seven miles and reached the outskirts of Sandstone Springs, but I'd be, well, I'd be lying. I thought it good that the gravel road into town was so narrow and bumpy that Ira had me go slow enough that I never did need to shift into fourth gear. But I had to go back into second gear a couple of times when going up hills, and I dang near killed the engine grinding the gears trying to shift from third gear into second. I got really shook-up when a pickup pulling a horse trailer came over the hill and was heading right for us.

"Okay, don't panic now. These county gravel roads are pretty narrow, so I want you to shift down into second gear and slow her down…that's it. Now, just ease over to the side of the road so you can give him room to pass by," Ira told me in a far more calm and reassuring voice than I was expecting to hear. "There you go, nice and easy, nice and slow."

You wouldn't believe how badly my hands were shaking on that steering wheel! But somehow, I stayed far enough over for the pickup and trailer rig to pass by and also managed to avoid going into the ditch. I have to tell you, I was totally wiped out by the time Ira had me pull over on the side of the gravel road to switch drivers when we reached the outskirts of town.

I was surprised—no, make that shocked—when Ira said, "Pretty decent job for your first time, young lady."

Chapter 16

MY INTRODUCTION TO SANDSTONE SPRINGS

As Ira drove us into Sandstone Springs, I think my mouth dropped open and got stuck there for a while. I mean, I knew from what Whit Whitfield had told me that the town would be small, but man-oh-man, I didn't figure on it being this small!

Ira just laughed when I asked him if there were any stoplights in town. "Nope, a couple of stop signs is the closest thing we have to a stoplight. We've got a dad-gum nice county courthouse over there," he pointed out as we drove by the two-story building that was built out of none other than—you guessed it—Sandstone.

Our first stop was at Percy's Grocery, where Ira introduced me to Myra, the store clerk. She had the warm, friendly face of a grandmother and laughed sweetly when I asked if she was Mrs. Percy.

"No, honey, but I am Percy Walker's mom. I fill in every Tuesday when Percy and my daughter-in-law run to Billings to pick up some items for the store that the supply truck doesn't deliver. Shame on you, Ira, for never telling me what a lovely young granddaughter you have."

When Ira just ignored her comment, Myra winked at me and led the way to the candy aisle. "We might be a small store in a small town, but we have the best selection of licorice and chocolates this side of the ol' Mississippi."

When we were far enough down the aisle to be out of earshot of Ira, Myra whispered. "I'm sorry to hear your mom is not a bit well, honey. I will be praying for her."

I must have looked surprised when she spoke of my mom's medical condition because she added with a chuckle, "It's just the way things work in a small town, Maggie. Most folks around Sandstone Springs will know before you do if you had Corn Flakes or Rice Krispies for breakfast! By the way, that mother of yours had some kind of singing voice in high school, she sure did. I know me and my husband Ralph always looked forward to hearing her sing carols at the Christmas concerts."

Our second stop was at the Sandstone Springs Feed store, where we picked up dog food, a couple of sacks of chicken feed, and some powdered milk for Betsy-Lou. When Ira explained to Mr. Restig, the store owner, that I was his granddaughter and was going into the seventh grade at Sandstone Springs in the fall, he seemed to give me the once over.

Why did he look at me like that? Could he possibly be my dad? He's about the right age. Do we look alike at all? Have the same chin? Nose? Complexion? I decided there really wasn't much resemblance, if any. Even though my mom zipped her lips every time I brought up the subject of my father, that doesn't mean I don't often wonder about who he might be. After all, it only stands to reason he most likely lived in or around Sandstone Springs.

Mr. Restig then led us back into a big warehouse room, where sacks of all kinds of feed were piled as high as the ceiling. He introduced me to a boy who was unloading sacks from a big truck trailer. "This here is my son Randy—Randy Restig. Even though he ain't near as tall as you, he's gonna be a freshman."

Randy didn't look at me, nor did he speak as he continued his work. I said "Hi" anyway, as it seemed like the polite thing to do. Maybe he was just shy, but when he gave his dad a glare, I figured he was more likely mad or embarrassed about his dad's remark about him being shorter than me. I was relieved that he didn't look anything like me, as I didn't want to have a rude stepbrother to deal with at school.

After stopping at Hoekstra Implement to get Ira's parts for his equipment, our last stop was at Dr. Rath's Veterinary Clinic. Doc, as I soon learned everyone called him, came into the waiting room when he heard the bell over the office door. "All on my own today, Ira. The missus is feeling poorly, so I'm all you get around here. Pray tell, who's this pretty young lady you're traveling with today?"

"This is my granddaughter, Maggie," Ira stated. "She's going to be staying with me for the school year."

"Well, what a pleasure to meet you, Maggie," said the kind-faced man that I guessed to be about the same age as Ira. "I have a granddaughter who will be in the eighth grade—her name is Ginny. What grade are you going to be in?"

"I'll be a seventh grader," I replied.

"Holy cow, you're taller than my Ginny," he exclaimed while glancing out the window to see Dimwit hanging over the edge of the pickup bed with his tongue hanging out. "So, how are you getting along with Dimwit? I see he made the trip to town with you." Reaching behind the counter for a dog bowl and a doggie treat, he said, "You fill this up with water from the outdoor spigot and take it to Dimwit. It's pretty darn hot out there, and he'll need a drink and a snack. Can you do that for me?"

"Yes, sir! Thank you, sir!" I said as I hurried out the door to tend to Dimwit. I immediately noticed the spigot handle was way easier to pump than the one at the ranch. I was filling up his water bowl for the second time when Ira came out of the clinic. I was kind of glad when he didn't say anything about me driving home. He must have been thinking along the same lines as me.

"You can practice driving Ol' Blue anytime you want to. Probably best to just drive in the yard and up the lane 'til you get the hang of getting it going and shifting. I'm gonna get you on the Ford 8N tractor, too—that'll help you work on your shifting. Don't worry, it takes a heap of practice to do it smooth-like. You did a good job for your first time."

"Thanks, Ira," I said, turning my head to the window to smile. *I'll be darned,* I thought to myself. *After being barked at for every little mistake I've made thus far, I think I actually just received a compliment!* I took it to mean he wasn't overly mad at me for talking back. But trust me, I had no intention of repeating that behavior anytime soon!

Chapter 17

CITY GIRL RANCH HAND

"**W**ell, young lady, it's high time you started learning to be a real ranch hand around here," Ira announced at the breakfast table on the morning of the 4th of July. "If we wasn't knee-deep in haying, we'd run into town for the parade and fireworks. Sandstone Springs has a right-fine celebration for a town its size, it surely does. But since we can work in the field, it's time for you to learn a new job."

Thinking of the 4th of July made me nostalgic for home. Cho and I had always gone to the annual celebration at Gable's Tavern. The police would block off the streets on either side of the Tavern, and hundreds of kids, including Cho and I, would bring our sparklers, firecrackers, and whatever other fireworks our parents would let us buy. As evening approached and the light show ended, my mom and the *Sterling Saint and the Satin Slippers* band would play from a stage that was erected on the street in front of Gable's. Cho and I would dance away until the streetlights came on, and Sun-Ju would round us up to go to their house.

"We're going to put your driving and shifting practice to use today," continued Ira. "You're gonna use the Farmall tractor to pull the hay rake and prepare the field of alfalfa I knocked down the other day for baling. Think you can handle that, young lady?"

Boy, oh boy, I thought to myself. *What if I mess up and get bawled out again?* "Well, ah, okay. Do you really think I can drive that tractor good enough to rake hay?"

"Only one way to find out, ain't there?" he said with a glint in his eye.

Anxious about Ira leaving me alone out in the middle of a hayfield to do a job I had never done before, I asked, "Where are you going to be? Will you be close by? Can Dimwit come with me?"

"Don't worry, I'll be baling in the field right next to you. And yes, Dimwit can go with you. I sure don't need that fool dog chasing my baler around." With Dimwit in tow, Ira had me drive Ol' Blue to the fields, taking the bumpy dirt trail at the end of the cow pasture that turned sharply toward Buffalo Butte. I was glad that we had to go slow so that I wouldn't have to shift into third gear.

When we finally reached the field, Ira showed me how to fill up the tractor with fuel and grease the moving parts by finding something called *zerks,* which are like little nubs where the grease goes. It's kind of fun to hook up the grease gun to the zerk and pump the slick and slimy stuff in there. I guess the grease lubricates the moving parts—like ball-bearing joints and that kind of thing.

"Go on now, git," Ira snarled at Dimwit, who kept sticking his nose in the way of the grease gun. With Dimwit trotting behind the rake, I rode next to Ira on the tractor as he made the first round on the field of freshly cut hay. The hay rake we were pulling was a sidewinder kind of thing with a bunch of wheels with spokes or spines on the ends. Don't ask me how, but the wheels spin around and around and somehow sweep the loose hay into a tidy row. Ira said it was called a "windrow," and it prepared the downed hay for baling. He started on the next round and showed me where I should keep the front wheel of the tractor in order to rake right next to the last windrow but not touch it. That was the scary part, staying close enough to the windrow so as to not leave any of the cut hay, yet not so close that you run the rake into the row and mess it up. He showed me what gear to be in and how fast I had to go to make the wheels spin the right amount.

I was nervous when I started out on my own, especially with Ira standing close by and giving me a watchful eye. I let the clutch out so fast that the front wheels jumped a little, scaring the dickens out of me.

"What is it with you and clutches? Don't let that clutch out so fast!" I heard Ira holler. That made me even more nervous to try again, but I clenched my teeth even harder, let the clutch out slower, and got started more smoothly the second time.

It took me most of the morning to really get the hang of it. I messed up a couple of times, either leaving too much of the mowed alfalfa grass between the far edge of the rake and the windrow or drifting close enough to take a swipe out of it. Even though I felt like I'd done a reasonably good job, I was prepared for another Ira scolding when he stopped by my field for lunch.

"Well, looks like you did okay for your first time raking, young lady," he said after taking a painstakingly long look at the result of my efforts. "But you gotta practice on keeping the edge of that rake a little closer to the windrow on this next field. We can't be a-leavin' loose hay in the field to just rot." I breathed a sigh of relief when it became apparent that was to be the extent of the critical review.

Other than swatting flies and sweating like crazy in the ninety-degree heat, the afternoon went better. Not that I didn't make a couple of mistakes, but they were fewer and less noticeable than the morning session.

"Ira, did my mom ever rake hay like I just did? Or do chores?" I asked as Ol' Blue bounced over the ruts on our way back to the house.

"Well, no, your mom was no ranch girl. She really had no interest in the ranch at all. Not in the animals, and certainly not in what you did today. She did help your grandmother around the house, I guess."

I waited for him to say more but was met with only the bumpy road and a wall of silence from my passenger.

As I pulled up in front of the shop, Ira said, "Let's grab a quick bite of vittles and head down to the pond. Been meaning to take you down there, but just haven't found the time. Have you ever fished before?"

"No, I've seen fishing boats out in the bay, but I've never actually tried to fish. Is it fun to catch one?"

"Yep, but we just have little brook trout in this pond. They put up a good fight, but I reckon it ain't nothing like catching some of those big ocean fish around San Francisco."

We picked up a couple of spinning rods at the shop before starting the quarter-mile hike down to the pond. Since this was the first time I had been all the way down to the water, I took a double-take when we approached, as I could see an old, two-seat wooden bench and a gravestone at the edge of the pond.

"I made that ol' bench there," Ira explained. "Built 'er in 1915, I believe it was. And that there is your grandma Audrey's resting place, God rest her soul," he said softly. "A finer woman the good Lord never made. Most folks nowadays bury their loved ones in a town or city cemetery, but many of us old-timers in these parts prefer their family plot to be on the farmstead. I know it might seem silly to some, but it gives me comfort to have her close by, you know, so I can see her every day."

I admit I was surprised and a little touched by his obvious devotion to Grandma Audrey. I moved closer to clearly read the words that were chiseled into the granite headstone:

AUDREY GRACE NOBLIT STONE

SEPT 24, 1902 – MAY 8, 1963

BELOVED WIFE, MOTHER, GRANDMOTHER,
FRIEND

Were Ira's eyes watering when he talked about my grandma. Was that why he turned his head to the side—to wipe away a tear? I wanted to ask Ira questions about my grandma, but he quickly moved our conversation to fishing.

Remember when I told you that I hated grasshoppers? Well, that's what we used for bait, sticking the hook right through the middle of the nasty bug. It took me quite a while to figure out how to cast that grasshopper where I wanted it to go, but Ira was unusually patient, and I finally got the hang of it.

Once we had our lines cast where we wanted, we sat back down on the bench. I was surprised that I felt oddly comfortable casting the fishing lines next to my grandma's headstone. I think I was only three or four the last time she came to see us in San Francisco, but I remember vividly how warm and kind she was. I also recall how comfortable and safe I felt sitting in her lap. My mom said she came to meet me shortly after I was born, but of course, I don't remember anything from that trip.

Enjoying the calm and relaxing sound of the water lapping the shoreline on the beautiful July evening, Ira began his nightly ritual of packing his pipe and having a smoke. I didn't mind the smell of the pipe; it was stronger than cigarettes but not as smelly as cigars. At least, I didn't think so.

"Your mom smoke?" Ira asked.

"A-ah, yes. She smokes too much, or at least I think she does," I replied.

"Figured as much. I used to smoke cigarettes—more than a pack a day. Your grandma didn't think much of that habit, I can tell you that. I finally made a deal with her 'bout five years before she passed. If I quit cigarettes, I could have one smoke a day on the pipe." Then with a flickering glint in those steel-blue eyes and a slight tug at the left corner of his mouth, he added, "She agreed, as long as I never smoked that 'awful thing' in the house!"

Ira replaced my bait-less hook with a fresh grasshopper and gave me some more helpful tips on casting my line. "You don't smoke, do you?" he asked in a hopeful tone.

"No," I said with a giggle. "I'm only twelve." I wasn't lying—I didn't smoke but thought better of it to tell him that there were all sorts of twelve-year-olds and even younger kids in my old San Francisco neighborhood who were sneaking cigarettes from their parents or older brothers and sisters.

After Ira hooked a fish and handed me his pole to experience the excitement of reeling the fighting and leaping brook trout into shore, we re-baited our hooks and cast our lines again. "So, did your mom partake in that there marijuana that all those hippies seem to smoke these days?" Ira asked in an almost accusatory tone.

"Ah, not that I know of," I responded hesitantly. I really don't know if she did or didn't. I mean, she never smoked it around me, but she could have when she was with the band guys. And I know what it smells like, too—after all, I come from San Francisco, the city that some would call the hippy capital of the world. Cho and I would always smell marijuana when it flowed out the open side door and into the alley when we were listening to the *Sterling Saint and the Satin Slipper* band at Gable's Tavern.

"How 'bout those other drugs, like that LSD stuff they claim can make you plum crazy? You don't think she's, well, you don't think she's in that mental institution because she's using them kind of chemicals, do you?"

"No, I'm sure she didn't do any hard drugs like LSD," I replied honestly. Even though I was just a kid, I'd seen people on the streets who were all weirded out on drugs like LSD and heroin. I was sure my mom had never used that kind of stuff. I was glad that Ira didn't ask any more questions, and we silently went back to enjoying our evening of fishing.

All of a sudden, we heard a howl in the distance, and Dimwit went from quietly lying at my feet to running toward the howl and barking like crazy. "Get back here, ya' stupid dog," hollered Ira. "Don't worry, it's just some coyotes out yonder somewhere.

Dimwit will come back soon enough. He ain't brave enough to chase after 'em."

Sure enough, Dimwit put on quite a show of bravery but was soon back at my feet. "I've been meaning to ask you if it's coyotes or wolves that I hear in the distance every night."

"Oh, that would be coyotes. Ain't been any wolves in Montana since a fella shot the last one in 1930—a great big white wolf that was killing sheep and cows over by Stanford in Judith Basin County. If we ever go to Great Falls, we will stop in Stanford, and I will show him to you. They have him mounted in the courthouse."

Ira didn't speak again and seemed perfectly content to chew on the stem of his pipe and cast his line. We didn't catch any more fish, but it was a beautiful night to watch the reddened summer sun slowly drop on the distant horizon.

Chapter 18

UNEXPECTED SLEEPOVER

"Yes, ma'am, this is Ira Stone again. That's right, I'm Lillian Stone's father," Ira said into the phone. "I'm wondering if there has been any change in Lillian's status over the last week."

I was standing right next to him, anxiously hoping to hear some kind of good news from the Psych Ward at San Francisco Memorial Hospital. This was the fourth Sunday in a row since I'd been at the ranch that we had called, and I squeezed my hands together in the hope that the nameless face on the other end of the phone would deliver more promising news.

"I see, I see," Ira muttered, the look on his face clearly telling me my mom was still in her *spell*. "Well, please let us know immediately if there is any change. Now, Dr. Drummond keeps you up-to-date on her condition, right? Uh-huh, very good. You have my number, right? Yes, that's correct, 406-537-2817. Unless we hear from you in the meantime, I'll call again next Sunday."

Ira hung up the phone and abruptly changed the subject. "I'm a-thinkin' that hayfield I knocked down over north is going to be ready to rake within the next hour or two, so you best get your raking rig fueled, greased, and ready to go," Ira instructed. "Oh, and remember how I showed you to check the oil level? Don't forget to add oil if she's low. I'll be baling just across the road from you if ya' need something. Weatherman says there's a good chance for thunderstorms in the late afternoon through the evening, so let's get to going and get as much hay raked and baled as we can in case we're hit with a doozy of a storm."

While I didn't want to think about going through another big lightning and thunderstorm, I was relieved when Ira informed me I would be spending the afternoon on the tractor. The need to concentrate and focus on the task at hand would mean I wouldn't have time to worry about why my mom was still in a *spell.*

Sure enough, the weatherman wasn't wrong in his storm prediction, as the swirling black storm clouds started to roll in by late afternoon. But it didn't rain, not then, anyway, only lightning, thunder, and wind. I won't lie, it scares the dickens out of me to be outside when the lightning starts flashing its light-up-the-sky daggers, but I just kept on raking since I could see that Ira was still spitting out bales in the next field over.

Even though we were able to finish raking and baling our respective fields without encountering any rain or hail, the mean-looking clouds continued to build and roll in from the western horizon. But it wasn't until much later that night that the sky opened its spigot in a big way. I was as scared as when the first storm hit. I don't want you to think that I'm a big wimp because I'm really not. I mean, I stayed alone in my house in San Francisco when I was only six or seven years old without being a fraidy cat, and like I've told you before, the neighborhood we lived in could be pretty darn scary. But a severe eastern Montana thunderstorm is a different kind of scary than what I'm used to.

The alarm clock on my nightstand said 2:15 a.m. (I don't know why I need an alarm clock in my room—after all, I have Ira) when the first bolt of lightning and crack of thunder brought me out of a deep sleep and onto the floor in a single bound. Even though Ira had told me that Montana wasn't in a tornado belt, I started to worry about it when the wind whipped in, and torrents of rain and hail began to blast against my window.

It didn't take me long to remember that Ira had told me Dimwit could sleep with me when a storm hit. I raced down the stairs to get him, almost jumping out of my pajamas when the whole first floor was lit up by a wide sheet of lightning. Poor Dimwit was whining loudly and scratching on the mudroom door as I raced to let him into the main house.

But instead of hurrying upstairs to my room like he did the first time, the silly dog took a right turn and bolted through Ira's closed-but-not-latched bedroom door, jumping up onto my grandpa's bed. I held my breath, fully expecting Ira's roar to be louder than the thunder and hail. But after a brief snort and slight change in position, he resumed his normal, rhythmic snoring.

I knew I should pick up Dimwit and take him to my bed upstairs, but when the next thunderbolt hit like a runaway steam engine, I jumped into bed next to the dog. I waited a few minutes to make sure Ira was still soundly asleep before carefully lifting Dimwit to the outside of the bed and settling in the middle between him and Ira. As the storm raged on, Dimwit snuggled into my back, and I nestled up nice and tight against Ira. I felt calm—well, maybe not calm—but safe. For the first time during a Montana thunderstorm, I did feel safe.

When I awoke, the first rays of the sunrise were like flickering candles, dancing through the bedroom window with just enough light for me to make out Ira standing by the bed and staring down at me and Dimwit. *Uh oh,* I thought, peering back up at him nervously. *This is not good—he is going to be really mad!*

"Good grief," he muttered as Dimwit awakened and started to stir. "Good thing this bed ain't any bigger, or next thing a guy knows, you'll be bringing in Betsy-Lou to bunk with us too!" Since that was about as close to a joke I had ever heard him say, I couldn't help but blurt out a giggle at the picture in my head of me, Dimwit, Betsy-Lou, and Ira all sleeping in the same bed.

To my relief and surprise, I saw my grandpa start to smile that crooked smile of his. Even in the early morning dimness, I could see the glint in those ocean-blue eyes. And this time, instead of that one-sided grin making me sad, it made me happy. *Maybe,* I thought, *just maybe he's starting to get used to having me around.*

Chapter 19

RIDING GUNSMOKE

"Phone's for you," said Ira as I was cleaning up the dishes after supper. I had been at the ranch for about a month and hadn't really met any kids that would be calling, other than Whit, that is. I had quickly learned that Ira wasn't a fan of either of us wasting time with idle phone chatter, so Whit and I had to limit our brief phone conversations to only once or twice a week.

"Hey there," said Whit in her usual outgoing and cheerful tone. "Since it rained hard this afternoon and will be too wet to work in the fields tomorrow, how 'bout you come over to our house tomorrow about noon? I have a surprise for you in the afternoon, and then let's have a sleepover at my house. My mom says it's okay with her, and for you to let her know if Ira is a grumpy-bear and gives you any static about staying over."

I was pretty excited when Ira said our plans for a sleepover were fine, as long as I did my morning chores before leaving. He even offered to do the evening Betsy-Lou bottle-feeding for me so that I wouldn't have to come back home after supper.

I chose to jog the two miles to the Whitfields, as my mom's old bike was just too small for me to ride comfortably for that distance. I was happy when Ira said Dimwit could come with me. My canine best friend and companion seemed extra perky to be invited to the sleepover, but the mid-summer heat quickly took its toll on both of us. We ended up slowing to a walk for the final half of the journey.

We picked up the pace again when we saw the Whitfields' dog, Hank, racing down the lane to meet us. While Dimwit and Hank exchanged sniffs and greetings, I saw Whit waving us over to the barn.

"So what's this big surprise you have for me?" I questioned, gratefully accepting a drink of water out of the garden-hose Whit was using to fill a bowl for the dogs.

"Well, all I can tell you now is that we're going to go to Buffalo Butte to see the Indian drawings on the rocks. It's really eerie to see something that was drawn or carved into the stone like one hundred years ago, but really neat at the same time. Close your eyes and don't you dare open them until I tell you to," Whit ordered, her hands on my shoulders and guiding me down a barn alleyway.

"Okay, you can look now."

It took my eyes a few seconds to adjust to the dim light at the far end of the alleyway, but then I saw a horse's black nose pressed between the bars of the stall gate right in front of me.

"Maggie, meet Gunsmoke. Gunsmoke, this here is Maggie," she said excitedly. "I learned to ride on this guy. He's like twenty-one years old now, so getting up there in years. But he's not as old as your Ol' Swayback."

"How long do horses usually live?" I asked, looking into the pen that held the smallish red-brown horse with a white stripe on both his nose and left front hoof.

"Well, Toots—that was my mom's horse—died just last year at twenty-nine, so I think Gunsmoke has got some good years ahead of him. Hayley Harris, she's a sophomore and a really good barrel-racer, has a seventeen-year-old mare named Molly that she still races at the rodeos, so he's only four years older than that. Anyway, Gunsmoke is really gentle and will be perfect for you to learn on!"

"You said he's a guy horse, right? And I get to ride him?" I asked, not sure whether I was scared or just anxious at the thought of actually riding a horse. "I mean, I've never ridden a horse before, what if he bucks me off?"

"To answer your first question; yes, he's a guy. Well, a gelding is actually what he is. That means he's like a steer. You know, he's had his you-know-what's removed. And second, Gunsmoke hasn't bucked in years. He's a really nice horse, perfect for you to learn to ride on. Besides, I'll be right next to you the whole time."

I won't lie—even though I had come to really like Ol' Swayback, I was feeling awfully anxious about the prospect of actually trying to ride a horse. I was put a little more at ease when Whit said, "After driving Ol' Blue and learning how to drive the tractor and rake hay, riding Gunsmoke should be a breeze. Besides, being a ranch girl myself, I can tell when a person is or isn't an animal person. And animals definitely take a liking to you."

After Whit showed me how to bridle him with something called a hackamore, a type of bridle that doesn't have a metal bit to insert into the horse's mouth, the next lesson was putting on the saddle. Whit's horse was named Pizza and she had me watch her saddle the tall, white-and-brown-painted mare several times before letting me try it on my own. I was a little nervous about getting kicked when reaching under Gunsmoke's belly to grab the cinch, but Whit assured me there was no reason to worry. I quickly learned that a horse puffs out their belly to make it harder to tighten the cinch, and that you have to really cinch up hard to get the saddle snugly secured. It also took me a couple of times to properly tie the leather strap knot after securing the cinch.

Whit's mom, Annie, came into the barn just as we finished saddling. "Looks like you gals are ready to head out to Buffalo Butte. Here's a couple of water canteens, a few sandwiches, and a bag of cookies. Make sure you start out in the big corral to teach Maggie how to use the reins, and don't head out into the pasture until she feels comfortable in the saddle, and don't go galloping about before Maggie is ready, either. It's already ninety degrees out, and that breeze is going to make it even hotter. Make sure you take plenty of time to water the horses, dogs, and yourselves when you cross Sage Creek. And don't trot too much in this heat."

I didn't have too much trouble mounting the saddle on Gunsmoke, as my long legs made it easier for me than the short-legged Whit to get my left foot up and into the stirrup. In addition to my longer legs, Gunsmoke was way shorter than Pizza. It didn't take long for me to realize that Whit was a good horsewoman, and she was a good and patient teacher in showing me how to use the reins to tell Gunsmoke to turn, stop, and go forward or backward.

Then came the hardest part—learning how to trot. Whit was right in comparing it to driving Ol' Blue as I bounced around like we were going over a trail full of potholes and mud ruts! It took some coaching from Whit to learn to rise up and sit back in the saddle in rhythm with Gunsmoke's gait.

"Heck, Maggie, you're a natural horsewoman if I ever saw one," said Whit with her ever-present smile.

"Not so sure about that," I laughed, pulling down my *Rath Vet Clinic* baseball cap to prevent it from flying off. "Do you think I'm ready to try a gallop?"

"Well, let's not rush it. For one thing, we need to be out from under my mom's watchful eye. You heard her, she doesn't think I should let you gallop until you've ridden a couple of times. Let's see how you do with trotting on the way over to Buffalo Butte. If that goes well, we can maybe try a bit of galloping on the way back."

Once I passed Whit's "within the confines of the corral" riding proficiency test, we rode out the gate and started the two-mile trek to Buffalo Butte. I was happy that Dimwit and Hank got to join us but relieved when they finally settled in behind us after their initial exuberance of barking and darting all over the place. We walked until Whit said we were out of Annie's line of sight, and then we broke into a trot. I definitely hadn't mastered the timing of Gunsmoke's rhythm, but I slowly started to get the hang of it. I was glad when we came to the creek and stopped to water the horses, the dogs, and ourselves. Since Dimwit was definitely slower than the fleet cow-dog Hank, he was the last of the group to reach the watering hole.

"My dad says Buffalo Butte was a sacred and special place for the Indians who roamed the prairies many years ago," said Whit as we approached the monstrous sandstone rock outcropping that rose abruptly from the level floor of the valley. It made me think of a single, lonely saguaro cactus reaching for the sky in the desert or a volcanic mountain rising above the ocean surface.

"There are all sorts of neat caves and stuff at the butte. The Indians carved drawings, called petroglyphs, into the sandstone. Most have faded over time, but since the inside of the caves is more protected from the elements, some of the drawings are still fairly distinct. You'll learn more about it this fall in seventh-grade history, as Buffalo Butte is an important landmark in our neck of the woods. In fact, it's why we're called the Sandstone Springs Buffaloes."

After riding around the wide circumference of the butte, we unsaddled the horses and tied them to a scrub-brush pine tree in the only shaded area we could find. "Okay, not trying to freak you out here, but have you seen a rattlesnake at your place yet?"

"No, thank God!" I replied. "But Ira has warned me about them. I might just die on the spot if I see one."

"Well, we have to really keep our eyes out for them here at the butte. They like hanging around these rocks and in the caves," warned Whit. "We'll have lunch in the best petroglyph cave. I'll check for snakes, and you follow with the saddlebags and water canteens."

Dear Lord! I can't wait to tell Mom and Cho I brought my lunch in a saddlebag and shared my sandwich and cookies with a den of rattlesnakes!

Chapter 20

WHO'S BROCK BOYCE?

"Now, if I remember my history lesson right," Whit began after declaring our lunch cave to be free of rattlesnakes, "these drawings were likely done by either the Crow or Gros Ventres Indians and maybe later by the Sioux. Nobody knows for sure, but these carvings were probably done in the early- to mid-1800s, so they are probably at least a hundred years old."

Although most of the pictographs were well-worn and faded, it was fascinating to see that a few drawings were still defined enough to recognize. My favorite was of a horse with a rider in a headdress closing in on a buffalo, arm raised and ready to launch his spear. There was another of two horses running side by side, and yet another of an Indian aiming his bow and arrow at a mighty-antlered buck deer, or was it a bull elk? I wasn't sure, but it was a cool drawing either way.

"So, have you met Brock Boyce yet?" Whit asked as we sat with our backs to the rock wall opposite the drawings. Although still stifling hot, the cave was at least out of the sun and a cooler spot to have our lunch. Both Dimwit and Hank settled in beside us, panting heavily to expel their body heat.

"Who's Brock Boyce?"

"Who's Brock Boyce? Only the coolest cat in all of Sandstone Springs, that's who Brock Boyce is!" Whit answered excitedly. "You San Franciscan's would no doubt say he's *groovy* or *boss*. He's only going to be a freshman this fall and is not only the most handsome kid in school, but the best athlete, too. Every girl from fourth to twelfth grade is in love with him, yours truly most definitely included. And to top it off, he's a really nice guy.

"I can't believe your grandpa hasn't told you that the Boyce place borders Ira's to the west—about three miles as the crow flies. And that every year Brock helps him pick up his hay bales off the field and stacks them next to your barn to feed the cows in the winter. And you, of all people, the California transplant, get to be the one girl in all of Sandstone Springs to work alongside him. I hate to tell you this, but every girl in school, especially me, already hates you for it!" Whit laughed. I knew by the tone of her voice that she was kidding, at least I think she was.

"Well, even if I was interested in boys, and I can truthfully tell you I'm not that interested at this point, isn't he a little old for me?"

"Good grief, he's only two years older than you. I mean, you'll be in high school together. He'll only be a junior when you're a freshman. It's pretty common in small schools like ours to see a two- or three-year age difference when dating. In fact, Brock is going steady with Tracy Rindal, and she is gonna be a junior. I mean, it's usually the guy that is the oldest, but in this case, it's that snotty Tracy."

"So, I take it the rest of the girls in Sandstone Springs don't like Tracy Rindal? What's the matter with her?" I asked.

"You've got that right; none of the other girls like her. As much as I can't stand her, I have to admit that she's very pretty and has a nice figure. But she's just a stuck-up snob. She thinks she's hot stuff because she's been the head cheerleader since she was a freshman. None of us girls can see why he puts up with the way she acts, you know, the way she is so jealous of anyone that comes near him. Anyway, didn't you have a boyfriend or two back in San Francisco?"

"Nope, the only reason I hung around boys was to play football, basketball, and baseball against them. I take it you have a boyfriend?"

"Yes, Dale Kimmel and I have been going out," Whit explained, removing her hat and feigning a fashion model pose by running her fingers through her hair. "We've even kissed, more than just a few times, too. But I'm only letting him hang around until Brock comes to his senses and realizes I'm the only girl for him!"

I think Whit was only half-joking with her statement about Brock discovering her as his true love. If nothing else, Whit was confident in herself, and I admired that trait my new friend possessed.

"So, even though you say you've never had a boyfriend, you've kissed a boy by now, right?" inquired Whit.

"Well, yes, not sure you could even call it a kiss. Dale Beckman tried to kiss me after school one day last spring, but it was more like a quick smooch than a real kiss," I admitted. "Let's just say my world wasn't rocked when he bumped his front teeth into mine."

After our *Brock and boys* discussion, we took our time exploring the other caves, although the cave where we had lunch was the only one with petroglyphs that weren't mostly faded beyond recognition. It was even hotter when we saddled up and headed back to the Whitfield place, the horses noticeably less interested in any pace other than a walk. It was even more difficult to get them moving after stopping for a long drink at the creek, and I totally understood Whit's reasoning when she said my first galloping lesson would have to come on a cooler day. Besides, poor Dimwit was lagging pretty far behind us as it was.

"Even though we didn't gallop, you should know that you're going to have a saddle butt tomorrow," Whit proclaimed.

"Okay, I'll bite, what's a saddle butt?"

"It means that your rear end is going to be sore as heck tomorrow," Whit explained with a sly grin. "Even though I ride frequently, today's trip to Buffalo Butte and back will probably give me a bit of the saddle butt, too."

It was almost dusk by the time we returned to the barn and unsaddled and brushed down our horses. I didn't realize how hungry I was until we went to the house to wash up for supper. The pleasing aroma of Annie's chicken casserole made my stomach rumble, as did the pan of freshly baked cookies. Although it made me homesick, the everybody-talking-at-once among the Whitfield sisters was a pleasant reminder of the many boisterous meals I shared with the six children at the Jeong residence.

Much to the dismay of the younger Whitfield girls, after doing the dishes, Whit and I retired to the tent that Mr. Whitfield had set up for us in the backyard. We were so exhausted from the long ride in the scorching heat that we just sat next to the tent without speaking, admiring the cloudless and glorious canvas that was the Montana sky. We soon retired to the tent and climbed into our sleeping bags. The symphony performed by the crickets and the soothing rhythm of a slowly flowing creek quickly pulled me into a deep slumber.

I awoke at dawn, knowing that I needed to get back for morning chores lest I get scolded by Ira for being tardy. And Whit was right, I knew from the very first movement getting out of my sleeping bag that I had a bad case of the saddle butt!

"I had a great time," I replied to Ira's inquiry about my sleepover at the Whitfield's. "Whit and I are becoming fast friends, and the whole Whitfield family is really nice to me. And guess what? I got to ride Gunsmoke over to Buffalo Butte with Whit, Dimwit, and Hank, and she showed me the Indian drawings in the caves. It was so cool, and we got to sleep outside in a tent and everything!"

"Yeah, they don't come any better than the Whitfields," Ira confirmed. "Best neighbors a guy could ever ask for, that's for sure. I'm glad you got to ride ol' Gunsmoke over to Buffalo Butte, been meanin' to take you over there to see the Indian drawings. Didn't run into any rattlesnakes, did ya?"

"No, thank goodness! But Whit warned me to be on the lookout," I exclaimed. Ira gave me a glimpse of his lopsided grin when I added, "And Whit was right when she said I'd have a sore backside today; I could barely get out of my sleeping bag and put my jeans on this morning!"

Chapter 21

DIMWIT PICKS
THE WRONG BATTLE

*I*was just picking up the breakfast dishes when Ira pulled his favorite grease-stained cowboy work hat from its hook on the mudroom wall. "When you finish with the dishes, fill up our lunch pails, would ya? Ham and cheese sandwiches for me and throw in some of them there chocolate chip cookies of Annie's. I'll fill up my water thermos and suggest you do the same, it's gonna be hotter than two goats in a pepper patch this afternoon, I'm a-thinkin'."

I chuckled to myself hearing another one of Ira's silly sayings and tried to decide what kind of sandwich I'd make for myself when I was done with the dishes.

"After I'm done fixin' that dad-gum baler knot tier for the thousandth time this summer, I'll be taking the Ford tractor and baler way over to that field next to the Boyce pasture, you know, the one that you raked up a couple of days ago. By the time you finish your chores and get your tractor fueled and the rake greased, you can head out for that field by the bull pasture that I mowed a few days ago. Ol' Blue will be here, so if you break down or otherwise need me, you can drive her over to get me.

"Now, make darn sure it's dried out enough before you start raking. You remember how I showed you to determine whether it's ready to rake, don't you?"

"Yes sir, I remember," I said confidently, almost patting myself on the back of the pale blue shirt that Annie's sister had given me, along with a couple of other work shirts, two pairs of jeans, and a pair of work boots. I don't want to brag, but I thought I was doing a pretty good job at learning how to become a ranch hand. Or at least as good as a San Francisco girl can be who didn't know the front from the back end of a cow only six weeks ago.

Since I hadn't been chewed out (or at least not too badly) for a couple of days and was finally starting to get a little more comfortable around Ira, I decided to take a chance on trying to joke with him.

"So, Ira, can I ask a question?"

"Yep, fire away."

"Just how hot are two goats in a pepper patch?" I asked, trying to keep a straight face.

"Well, I reckon 'bout as hot as Satan's house cat," Ira drolled, turning his head away from me in an attempt to hide the slight rise in the left corner of his mouth. I thought it was pretty clever when he followed with, "Shoulda knowed you San Fran folk would be more familiar with the devil than a goat."

Knowing that it would be late morning before the hay was dry enough to rake, Dimwit and I took our time doing chores and preparing the tractor and rake for the task ahead of us. Fortunately, the hayfield I needed to rake wasn't very far from our buildings, as I had to drive real slow on the rut-filled trail just to keep from bouncing all the way off the uncomfortable metal seat.

Once we reached the field and I determined it was dry enough to rake, I started carefully on the first lap around the perimeter of the barbed wire-fenced hayfield. I say carefully—very carefully—because I had to position the far edge of the rake only a couple of feet from the perimeter fence in order to sweep in all the felled grass. I sure didn't want to test Ira's patience by ramming the rake into a fencepost and smashing it to smithereens.

As he usually did when I was raking a field, Dimwit started out trotting next to the tractor, occasionally racing off to chase after a grouse, pheasant, or rabbit. I found it especially entertaining to watch him stalk a gopher mound, as he was always too slow-footed to catch the little ground squirrels (Ira hated gophers because some of the bigger mounds would clog up his mower-sickle!) before they scampered to a mound and disappeared down the hole. By the time I completed the first lap around the field, he was tired of the chase and gave me a "let me ride on the tractor" look. I came to a stop and let him hop up on the footrest where he sat on his haunches until he leaped off to give chase to a group of scampering gophers.

Dimwit saw it before I did. I even heard his deep-throated growl above the engine noise, which was pretty darn loud. He jumped clear of the tractor before I could stop, racing ahead faster than I'd ever seen him run. I'm not sure whether my heart stopped or simply jumped out of my chest when I saw what he was after. About twenty yards ahead of us and just to the side of the windrow I had made on the first round was a coiled-up rattlesnake!

I braked to a quick stop and shut down the motor, all the while watching Dimwit charge toward the deadly serpent.

"Dimwit!" I screamed at the top of my lungs. "Dimwit, you get back here! Get back here this very minute!"

But he paid no attention to my commands, instead crouching low and darting dangerously close to the snake before jumping back. He continued his attack and retreat, attack and retreat movements regardless of how much or how loud I screamed at him. I could see that the snake was on high alert and was furiously shaking its rattles, creating a scary buzzing noise that could even be heard over Dimwit's barking, yips, and growls. I leapt off the tractor and tried to get close enough to grab him and pull him out of harm's way, but he was far too close to the rattler for comfort, almost within striking distance.

Even the rattler tried to warn Dimwit to back off by launching several lightning-quick strikes that came up just short of its mark. Maybe Ira was right, Dimwit might not have much in the smarts department. Despite my continued pleading and screaming efforts to draw him away from the danger zone, he kept dashing ever closer to the recoiled serpent.

I knew it was coming, and I realized I was powerless to stop it. I couldn't scream, talk, or hardly breathe when it actually happened. Dimwit's final lunge and the resulting rapid-fire strike by the rattler happened in an instant, but to me, it was as if the sequence of events occurred in slow motion. I swear I not only saw, but heard the *thud* of the actual strike to Dimwit's right shoulder. Yelping loudly, Dimwit ran crazily in circles before retreating toward me and collapsing at my feet. With an eye on the offending snake to make certain it continued to slither away from us, I knelt down next to my whimpering dog to try to comfort him and inspect the bite. In between his constant licks of the wound, I could see blood oozing from the two fang marks.

"Oh, Dimwit," I whispered softly as I stroked his neck. "Why, why, why didn't you keep your distance from that snake? What are we going to do? Don't you even think about dying, Buster. Don't worry, I'm gonna get you some help, and you'll be good as new before you know it!"

This would be a good time to show up, Ira! I thought. *I didn't have a lot of experience with rattlesnake bites back in San Fran, and I could use some advice on what to do!*

Chapter 22

AN UNEXPECTED TRIP
TO DR. RATH'S

I won't lie—my mind was spinning, and I had no idea what to do. *Okay, calm down, Maggie. Think–think,* I told myself. I knew getting hysterical was not going to help matters, so I forced myself to try to think rationally through my tears of worry. I knew one thing for certain: I had to get Dimwit into Dr. Rath's clinic as quickly as possible. Since Ira was baling hay miles away from us, it would take far too much time to get Dimwit home and drive Ol' Blue across the bumpy trail to go find him. No, it was clear that I had to act swiftly—I needed to get back home and immediately drive my still cowering and whimpering dog to town.

Since we were less than a quarter mile from home, I decided it would be quicker and easier on Dimwit if I carried him rather than bouncing him through the rutted-trail on the tractor. Grunting, I stooped down and picked him up, wincing when he yelped, but I knew I had no choice but to move him. I tried to keep my movements as smooth as possible, but speed was of the essence. I was breathless and my arms and shoulders ached when we reached Ol' Blue, and I carefully laid my wounded dog on the old pickup's bench seat. I got into the driver's seat and Dimwit laid his head on my lap.

I was more than happy when the engine fired up after a couple of quick pumps of the choke lever and only the third turn of the key. To be honest, I was so focused on getting Dimwit to town as quickly as possible that I hardly remember the drive other than Dimwit's constant moaning from my lap. I lightly petted him, carefully avoiding the bite area on his right shoulder. Even though I was crying and my heart was racing with worry, I tried to compose myself and talk to Dimwit as calmly and reassuringly as I could. One thing I do remember was that I put Ol' Blue's petal-to-the-metal all the way to town. I even went so fast that I had to shift into fourth gear! Luckily, we didn't encounter any vehicles on the way to town.

With the vet clinic being on the opposite side of town from where I approached, I turned off main street and roared down the less traveled of the three east-to-west streets and sped into the clinic parking lot.

I was relieved when I saw that Dr. Rath's pickup truck was the only vehicle parked in front of the clinic, as I didn't want to wait in line behind any other animal patients not facing Dimwit's life-and-death situation. I tried to honk Ol' Blue's horn as I approached, only then remembering the horn had to be pressed in exactly the right spot to even produce a weak beep. Of course, I couldn't seem to find that magic spot, so I just hit the brakes and screeched to a stop right in front of the office door.

I'd never met Mrs. Rath, but assumed she was the older lady who rushed out of the office to meet me as soon as I opened the pickup door. "Dimwit got bit by a rattler!" I shouted, as she gingerly reached in to help lift the whimpering dog from my lap.

"Get the door for me, honey, let's get Dimwit to a treatment room right away," said Mrs. Rath.

I won't kid you—once I got Dimwit safely delivered to the clinic, I sort of fell apart again. I was so afraid that Dimwit was going to die that it took every ounce of reserve I had to keep from returning to a bawling and blubbering mess. Mrs. Rath laid Dimwit on the examination table, and we both lightly petted the whimpering dog until Dr. Rath came into the room. His soothing and reassuring presence helped reduce my river-raging tears to a slightly flowing stream. He calmly asked me where we were when Dimwit encountered the snake and the approximate time that he was bitten. He also questioned me as to why Ira wasn't with me.

After I explained he was baling hay way over by Boyce's, he said, "Maggie, you did the right thing in getting him here the fastest way possible. I know it's hard, and I know you're scared and worried about Dimwit, but you need to take a few deep breaths and try to settle down. You see, he senses that you're upset, and that causes him to be even more anxious than he already is. Now, I need to devote all my attention to treating Dimwit, so I want you to go out to the front office with Mrs. Rath. I'll be out as soon as I do a thorough exam and begin treatment."

I don't know what I would have done if Mrs. Rath hadn't been there to help me pass the time until Dr. Rath came out with his report of Dimwit's condition. Naiomi Rath looked about the same age as her husband, which meant she was like Ira—in her seventies. Remember when I told you that Mrs.

Walker down at Percy's Grocery was a grandmotherly type? Well, I immediately felt the same way with Mrs. Rath. I was glad there was no one else in the waiting area when we sat on the only bench among a few wooden chairs that adorned the small entry room of the clinic.

"Now, now, Maggie, take a few more deep breaths and try to calm down," she said in a soft and soothing voice. It felt comforting when she put her arm around me, and I easily settled into her shoulder as she wiped the tears from my eyes.

"Do you think Dimwit is going to be okay?" I asked anxiously while trying to compose myself. "I mean, he's really hurting. He just laid his head on my lap and cried and whimpered the whole way here. Have you ever seen any other dogs bitten by a rattler? They don't all die, do they?"

"Okay, slow down, Maggie—another deep breath, honey. There now, that's better, isn't it?" Mrs. Rath said in a consoling and reassuring tone. "Unfortunately, this Sandstone Springs area is rattlesnake country, and we see more than the occasional animal in our clinic who's been bitten by a rattler—dogs and horses especially. I'm going to be honest with you when I say rattlesnake venom can be lethal. That being said, not all animals die from snakebite. I'm not a veterinarian, I'm only Dr. Rath's assistant, but I've seen enough snake strikes on dogs come through this clinic over the years to tell you that there is one piece of good news about Dimwit's situation; the bite was to his shoulder and not to the face or neck. Bites to the face and neck usually cause swelling that tends to cause breathing difficulties."

"So, you don't think Dimwit will die?" I asked, trying hard not to start sniffling again.

"I can't guarantee anything at this point, Maggie. So, for now, let's just think on the positive side due to the bite occurring somewhere other than the head or neck. I'm sure Doc will be out to give us an update soon."

It reminded me of when Sun-Ju, Cho, and I were waiting to hear from the doctor about my mom in the Emergency Room at San Francisco General, as it seemed like we sat there on the edge of our seats forever. Thankfully, Mrs. Rath was able to ease my mind somewhat and help pass the time by chatting and gossiping about recent Sandstone Springs events and happenings.

Finally, after Mr. Jimmerson dropped off a lame horse and Mrs. Sluggett picked up her neutered cat, Doc Rath entered the waiting room and pulled up a chair next to me. Taking my hand in his, he began to talk in his kind and gentle tone.

"Okay, Maggie, here's the situation: I'm not going to sugar-coat this, you deserve to know how dangerous these snake bites can be. The bad news is that many dogs do not live through it. Rattlesnake bites are very poisonous, and although scientists are working on it, there currently isn't a shot or antidote to counteract their venom. For many dogs, even if they live through the poison, they often die from an infection that is secondary to the actual bite."

After Mrs. Rath gave me another Kleenex to wipe my nose, I interrupted and said, "You said this was the bad news, is there some good news? Mrs. Rath said it's better to get a bite in the shoulder than the neck or face. That's good news, isn't it?"

"Yes, honey, that is good news—or at least better news. Again, it's also good that you got him in here fairly soon after the bite. Dimwit isn't out of the woods yet, but I've cleaned up his wound and given him some medicine to help with the pain and swelling. I also gave him a pill to help him sleep. More importantly, I've started him on antibiotics to ward off the infection scenario I mentioned earlier. Dimwit will need to stay with us at the clinic for at least a couple of days so we can keep an eye on him. You and your grandpa can visit any time until he's healthy enough to go home."

As much as I hated leaving my canine friend, I knew I needed to get back to the ranch and my hay-raking job. After a final look at the now-sleeping Dimwit and expressing my gratitude by giving a big hug to both Dr. and Mrs. Rath, I started out the door toward Ol' Blue before being stopped by Dr. Rath.

"Maggie, I know you've driven Ol' Blue out on the gravel roads before, and I'm sure you're a capable driver, but with all the excitement and worry about Dimwit's snakebite, Mrs. Rath is going to follow you home, just to make sure you get home safely. Is that okay with you?"

I felt better about things when Mrs. Rath gave me another big hug before turning around and heading back to town. "Try not to worry, honey. We'll take very good care of Dimwit, and I have a good feeling that we'll be calling you to come pick him up in no time. In the meantime, I'll call you every evening with a report on how he's doing."

After Mrs. Rath left, I slowly drove Ol' Blue down the bumpy trail to the hayfield. You better believe me when I tell you my eyes were on high snake alert as I walked from the pickup to the tractor and rake! Fortunately, the snake that bit Dimwit must have crawled under a windrow somewhere, as I didn't see it or any other snakes for the rest of the three hours it took to finish raking the field. I worried about Dimwit so much that I made more raking mistakes than I should have, but I hoped that Ira would understand. I also hoped he wouldn't be mad at me for driving to town all by myself. Boy, did he know what he was talking about when he said that knowing how to drive was needed on a ranch! At least I'd have Dr. Rath on my side, as he clearly said it was quick thinking on my part to get Dimwit to him right away.

The phone was ringing when I walked in the door from raking, and I was happy to receive the "he's resting comfortably and doing as well as can be expected at this point" update from Mrs. Rath. Knowing that Ira would be back from baling soon, I should have started supper, but instead, I flopped into a chair in the living room and fell into a deep sleep. I guess the crazy events of the day were starting to catch up with me.

Chapter 23

A STERN
LETTER TO MOM

"**I**'m not one bit surprised that fool dog stuck his snout into a coiled rattler," Ira said disgustedly when I explained the details of my eventful afternoon. "I told ya' he's got mush for brains."

It was exactly the reaction I expected from Ira. It used to make me mad when he would talk bad about Dimwit, but I'd been at the ranch long enough now to just ignore what he said about my canine buddy and not let it get to me.

After apologizing for falling asleep instead of fixing dinner, I listened to a constant litany of his under-the-breath muttering. "I swear, that blankety-blank mutt ain't got a brain in his head." But just as I figured I was about to get in trouble for taking matters into my own hands and driving Ol' Blue into town by myself, Ira surprised me by saying, "Ya' did the right thing there, young lady, in taking that dumb dog into town right away. It's a dad-gum good thing I had you practice driving in Ol' Blue, ain't it? Doc says he probably wouldn't have made it if you'd taken the time to come and get me, being that I was way over by the Boyce's."

"You've already talked to Doc?" I asked anxiously, continuing on before he could answer. "How does he think Dimwit is doing? Is there any sign of infection? Is he breathing okay? Did he say when he can come home?"

"Whoa there, Nellie! Good Lord, can you ever talk fast! Well, Doc thinks that brainless dog of yours is doing pretty darn good, all things considered. No sign of infection, at least not yet. He wants to keep him at the clinic for at least another few days just to make sure nothing develops."

Since there was no felled hay left for me to rake the following morning, I had some time to kill after I completed my chores. Since I'd been putting it off for a couple of weeks while trying to decide whether it was time to take a different approach, I decided it was time to write to my mom. Even though I knew it was probably silly to have a heart-to-heart with someone in a coma, I was getting more and more upset with my mom. In fact, I was getting downright mad that we had lost everything because of her spell.

Dear Mother,

I hope you are doing okay and will come out of your spell soon. I know you need your alone time, and I don't want to put any pressure on you, but you've been in this spell for three months now. Yes, I've been counting the days and weeks. I think it's time for you to start thinking about waking up. Okay? I miss you. It's time to see if we can get our apartment back and go home. Because you stayed in your spell, we didn't have enough money to keep it. You should know I stayed with Sun-Ju and Cho when you didn't come out of your spell. It's time you also knew the Jeongs didn't have enough room or money to keep taking care of me so I had to go to St. Peter's orphanage until Ira came and took me to the ranch. Please wake up so we can try to go back to our normal life. Please??!!

Love you and miss you!
Maggie

I realized I hadn't answered Cho's last letter, so I dropped her a short line. I didn't tell her much more about my new friendship with Whit. I was afraid that Cho might feel bad if I made it sound like I had a new best friend, so I talked more about my animal friends. It was getting hot by the time I jogged the letters down to the mailbox, but I ran the whole way. It felt weird to not be looking back to see how far behind Dimwit was, but it was good to know he should be coming home in the next few days.

Chapter 24

MEETING BROCK BOYCE

"**Y**ou drive," said Ira as we climbed into Ol' Blue for the trip into Sandstone Springs. "Probably won't be ten minutes 'til that fool dog sticks his snout where it don't belong—yet again."

I can't even tell you how excited I was when Mrs. Rath called the night before with the news that Dimwit was ready to come home. I had been really worried about him and missed his ever-present companionship.

"Brock Boyce is going to come by at about 10:00, and we're going to start picking the bales off the hayfields, so we'll have to skedaddle right back home," Ira informed me as I concentrated on shifting back into second gear to go up the steepest of the inclines on the way to town. "I'm going to hook up the flatbed trailer to the Farmhall M—you'll drive while Brock throws the bales on the trailer, and I stack 'em. When we get a full load, we'll take the trailer back behind the barn, where we'll make our haystacks for winter feeding. You can help me throw the bales off the trailer, and Brock will stack them on the ground. He's a good hand, that boy is, strong as a corn-fed bull and a hard worker."

Hmm, I thought. *Wouldn't Whit and all the girls be jealous if they knew I was spending the day with the likes of Brock Boyce?* Again, I wasn't all that interested in boys at the moment but had to admit I was more than just a little curious to meet this Brock guy that Whit and all the girls in Sandstone Springs had been raving about.

I was happy to see Mrs. Rath behind the counter when we walked in, and she rushed out to give me a welcomed hug and squeeze. "Doc is already out on a ranch call, so he left Dimwit's instructions with me. You better listen to this too, Ira."

"Why? He ain't my dog, thank the good Lord," Ira said gruffly. "Best give your instructions to the young lady who takes care of him."

"Oh, for heaven's sake, pay him no mind," Mrs. Rath said with a wave of dismissal. "Okay, honey, he still has a bandage over the fang marks, and Doc would like you to keep that on for at least another few days. There are several more bandages in this sack, so you should change it again tomorrow. Remember to liberally apply the antibiotic ointment to the wound. Then, you need to give him one of these big antibiotic pills twice a day for another five days. Roll it up in a slice of cheese or mix it in with his dog food. He'll spit it out if you try to force him to swallow just the pill. Also, he's a little gimpy, and that's to be expected. He needs to take it easy for the next couple of weeks, so don't let him come with you if you are riding horses or back in the hayfields. I wrote out the instructions and put them in the sack, so if you forget anything just refer to that. And, of course, call us anytime if you have any questions or problems."

"I have a question for you, Naomi," Ira inquired.

"What is it?" asked Mrs. Rath.

"Any chance you will be getting any new dog brain shipments anytime soon?"

"Well, aren't you the funny one!" declared Mrs. Rath as Ira's crooked smile slowly appeared. He faked a big *ouch* when she playfully punched him in the arm.

Hard as it was, I stayed true to the instructions and locked Dimwit in the mudroom when we went out to the shop. Ira hooked the flatbed bale trailer to the tractor and gave me a quick lesson in how to make turns when pulling a trailer. Turning was a little tricky, so I was glad I'd be going slow enough to not have to change gears. After a few practice runs, Ira gave me a nod of approval.

Brock showed up at the scheduled time, and according to Ira's yard-gate thermometer, it was already 86 degrees. A hot wind blowing from the direction of Buffalo Butte made it feel even warmer.

Remember the Buffalo Butte horseback ride when I told Whit I wasn't yet very interested in boys? Well, based on the double skip beat of my heart when Brock stepped out of the truck, I think I might have spoken too soon. You know the old saying, "tall, dark, and handsome?" That definitely fits the bill when it comes to Brock Boyce. He was really tall for just a freshman, around 6'2", I would guess. His complexion was swarthy, no doubt made even darker by working in the sun all summer. His wavy, unruly black hair spilled out beneath his grease and sweat-stained cowboy hat. His hair was longish—not San Francisco shoulder-length long— but reaching far enough down on the back of the neck to cover the edge of his sleeveless T-shirt. Unlike most other freshmen I knew, he already had a thick black shadow of whiskers covering his face. And handsome? Oh my—handsome he was!

In his typical brusque fashion, Ira gave a brief introduction. "Brock, this here is my granddaughter, Maggie. Maggie, that there is Brock. He's our neighbor from over yonder."

"Hi Maggie, nice to meet you," greeted Brock with a warm and engaging smile that caused my heart to do yet another extra pitter-patter. "I heard you moved here from San Francisco. I'm sorry to hear about your mom. I hope she gets better soon."

"Thanks, Brock," I murmured, relieved when Ira abruptly interrupted our conversation with a *let's get to work* look. When we got to the field, Brock strapped on canvas chaps, explaining to me it was to protect his legs from the coarseness of the bales and any surprise rattlesnakes that didn't slither away in time to keep from being part of a bale. I must admit I couldn't help but notice, if not rudely stare, when he took off his shirt. I'm not kidding when I say he had muscles on top of muscles! It was hard to believe he was only going to be a freshman.

"This should help you get in shape for football this fall," Ira suggested as Brock hustled from one bale to another, picking them up by the strings and tossing them on the trailer for Ira to stack. When Ira had stacked six rows high, the full length of the trailer, we stopped and had a water break.

Okay, okay, I admit I kept sneaking looks at Brock. His skin was shiny from working up a sweat, which seemed to make his muscles look even bigger. When we finished our water break, Brock and Ira sat on the back of the trailer while I slowly started the lengthy trip back to the barn where Ira wanted the hay stacked.

"You're catching on quickly, Maggie," Brock said, complimenting me on picking up the knack of throwing the bales off the trailer and hitting the ground at just the right angle so as to roll over several times toward him.

"A good toss and roll saves Brock from having to do a bunch of extra movement to pick up a bale and return it to where he's stacking," Ira explained. I mean, I wasn't nearly as good at tossing as Ira, but I must admit it didn't take me too long to get the hang of it.

It took us until a little after 6 pm to clear the field. I don't even remember for sure how many trailer load runs we made, but it was quite a few. I do know we had built a sizable haystack and were all completely sweat-soaked, stinky, and dirty by day's end.

Brock stayed and had supper with us after we were done. I had to admit that Whit was right, Brock was really a nice guy. After he and Ira talked about the calf and hay crop compared to last year, he engaged me in the conversation. He asked a lot of questions about San Francisco, and I think he was really impressed when the conversation turned to sports. His eyes widened when I whipped off the names of Jerry Lucas, Al Attles, and Nate Thurmond of the San Francisco Warriors pro basketball team. He was further amazed when I told him that quarterback John Brody and wide receiver Gene Washington were my two favorite 49ers football players.

"So, did you ever go to any of the 49er or Warriors games?" asked Brock.

"Nah, my mom isn't a sports fan. Plus, we don't have enough spare money to buy tickets. But I always look at the papers to see how the 49ers, Warriors, and Giants are doing."

"Never met a girl that likes and knows her sports the way you do," stated Brock, wearing a look of admiration across his face.

"You oughta see her run," declared Ira. "She runs like a deer."

I was surprised Ira noticed that I ran at all, not to mention whether I was slow or fast. I think I might have blushed because Brock kindly changed the subject.

Brock had no sooner said his goodbyes and walked out the door when Whit called for a Brock update. I was truthful when Whit asked if he'd taken off his shirt, but I lied and said I didn't really notice his muscles. I also decided not to mention how long we talked about San Francisco and sports. I figured the less said would keep the jealous curiosity to a minimum.

"Well, whether he talked to you or not, I still hate you for getting to work side by side with him!" she said, her tone somewhere between serious and joking. "Give me a call if you decide to share any juicy details from your day with my man!"

Chapter 25

SANDSTONE SPRINGS COUNTY FAIR

"Whit's on the phone," Ira hollered to me in the yard, where I was carefully playing with the still sore and slow-moving Dimwit. Even if Ira hadn't said who was calling, I figured it was Whit. I mean, other than Brock (who had an eleventh-grade girlfriend), I hadn't really met and become friends with anyone but her—so who else could it be?

"Hey there," said my neighbor in her usual mile-a-minute manner of talking. "Has Ira told you about the Sandstone County Fair?" Before I could get a word out, she hurried on. "Well, it's by far the biggest event of the summer and is always held during the last week of July. Tonight is the first night of the Midway Carnival, so do you wanna come with me, my mom, and sisters to the fair tomorrow afternoon and evening?"

"Sure, that sounds fun! I'll have to ask Ira first, though," I said, lowering the phone and hollering at my grandfather. "Ira, can I go to the fair with the Whitfields tomorrow afternoon and evening? I only have a little bit of raking on that last field, and I should be able to finish it by noon."

"I guess so, long as you get your chores and the raking done, you can go."

"There's the Ferris wheel!" squealed Whit's youngest sister, Willow, as we topped the hill and started the last two miles of gentle decline into Sandstone Springs. I had been to an amusement park in San Francisco a few times, but never a county fair like this one. There were several big barns, sheds, and outbuildings that were full of all kinds of 4-H animals. I didn't know what 4-H was until Whit showed me her Sandstone Springs 4-H Club pig at the sleepover.

Whit explained it was a club where you could raise all kinds of different animals as a project. Both she and her sister, Wanda, raised pigs, but she said that you could choose a steer or a heifer (that's what they call a young girl cow), sheep, goats, chickens—or even a dog or a cat!

Whit also said that if you were raising steers, heifers, pigs, or sheep, you could make money by selling your animal at the 4-H sale auction. She said she cries every year when she sells her pig because she knows they are headed to slaughter, but that last sale check for a whopping sixty-two dollars made her feel a lot better about it.

We went to the pig barn first, where Whit and Wanda fed and watered their pigs, Hamatha and Hertha. The Whitfield girls had been taking care of their pigs since they were just little piglets, but now they each weighed about 240 pounds. I helped the girls clean out their pens and wash and scrub their prize hogs until their coats were all shiny.

"Me and Wanda show our pigs in front of the judges tomorrow. If you do a good job of handling your pig, you can win a Showmanship ribbon," Whit explained. "We'll have to spiff them up again before the show so they are sparkly clean—the judges like to see a freshly groomed pig."

After spending most of the afternoon helping the girls tend to their pigs, Annie agreed to let Whit and I go on the carnival rides and play at the game booths. Wanda and Willow were pretty mad when their mom said they were too young to come with us. It was 5 pm when Annie gave us the green light, giving us strict orders to meet her back at the entry gate at 8 pm. Ira had given me ten dollars to purchase ride tickets, so I was good to go.

As little as Sandstone Springs was, I guess I shouldn't have been surprised that Whit knew every kid and adult on the carnival grounds. It didn't take long for us to hook up with a group of Whit's friends, and we all did the rides and played the games together. Three of the five girls that joined us were either upcoming eighth graders or freshmen, but Laura Rife and Sandy Barnhart were going to be in my seventh-grade class. They were all nice to me, and we had so much fun on the rides and playing at all the game booths.

I couldn't help but notice the difference in dress from San Francisco to rural Montana. All the junior high and high school kids at the carnival, both boys and girls, dressed far differently. The long floral pattern dresses and bell-bottom pants of California were replaced with straight-legged Levi's and western shirts and blouses. Some of the Montana boys had longish hair, but not hanging down on the shoulders like the guys in San Francisco. Cowboy hats and boots were in favor of the headbands and shiny black disco shoes of the city. I was glad I wore Annie's sister's Western garb instead of the one hippy dress I brought from home. I would have stuck out like a sore thumb!

"Don't look now, but Brock is behind us," I heard Whit whisper to the other girls when I was trying to win a teddy bear for her at the basketball hoop.

"Yeah, and I see he's still with Tracy," confirmed eighth grader Betty Fordyce.

"Lucky-duck Tracy, I heard they're going steady now," added Laura Rife, curling her upper lip in disgust. "Oh my gosh, they're coming over here!"

I just kept shooting while all the other girls giggled nervously, pretending like they didn't see them approaching. I didn't realize the couple had moved right up behind me when I hit six out of the last seven shots to win another teddy bear.

"That's good shooting, neighbor," Brock said admiringly. "Took me about twenty games to finally win a prize, and I'm supposed to be a pretty good shot."

I'm sure I was a little flushed in the face when I turned and nodded a hello. I couldn't help but notice that he cleaned up nicely, his wavy black hair mostly tucked under a Saint Louis Cardinals baseball cap.

"Well, Brock, are you going to introduce me to your teddy bear-winning neighbor?" asked Tracy in a mocking tone.

"Sure. Maggie, meet Tracy. Tracy, meet Maggie. She's Ira Stone's granddaughter and came to us from San Francisco."

"Glad to see the scar didn't get passed down to the grandkid," spat Tracy before I could utter a hello.

"Ira's my friend, and don't you talk about him like that," snapped Brock. "Apologize to Maggie right now, or you can do the rest of the carnival without me."

"Sorry about that, Miss San Francisco," she snarled sarcastically, throwing me an evil grin when Brock wasn't looking.

"I knew you were a sports fan, but where did you learn to shoot a basketball like that? Must have been back in San Francisco?" asked Brock, obviously impressed at my accuracy.

"Yeah, I guess so," I said hesitantly, embarrassed by his making a big deal of it. "I used to play basketball and baseball with the boys during recess and after school." I didn't tell him I also played some football with the guys, whenever they would let me, that is.

"You should come over to my place some evening, and we'll play *HORSE*. I've got a pretty good setup, poured a concrete pad last summer, and attached a regulation-size metal backboard to the yard pole just yesterday."

"Let's go hit the midway, Brock," whined a bored-looking Tracy after I muttered a "that would be fun" response. "I think we've chatted long enough with these kindergarteners, don't you?" she snarled, giving us, especially me, a look of annoyance and disgust as she grabbed Brock's hand and pulled him away.

"Holy cow, I can't believe Brock came up and started talking to you like that!" exclaimed Betty as soon as Tracy and Brock were out of hearing range. "Just like that, came up and started talking!"

"No kidding!" swooned the rest of the girls in unison, everybody laughing when Sandy and Laura put a hand to their foreheads and staggered around as if they were about to faint. All but Whit, that is. She had turned her back and pretended to be watching a couple of grade school boys trying to win a teddy bear.

"I mean, I think he likes you, Maggie!" continued Betty. Then turning to the other girls, she added, "Did you see how mad Tracy got when Brock started paying all that attention to Maggie?"

"He doesn't like me in that way," I said quickly, trying to come up with a way to change the subject to anything but this. "Brock helps Ira with the hay stacking, so I met him a few days ago. We talked a bit about sports and stuff, that's all. I don't think Tracy has anything to worry about. Why would he be interested in a lowly seventh grader when he has an older girlfriend as pretty as Tracy?"

"I don't know about that," Betty reasoned. "Tell me if I'm wrong, girls, but I don't recall Brock asking any of the rest of us to come to his house and play HORSE, do you?"

"He sure didn't ask me," exclaimed Sandy.

"Nope, me either," confirmed Laura.

After deflecting a few more questions about the day I spent stacking hay with Brock Boyce, Betty asked, "So, did you have a boyfriend back in San Francisco?"

"Ah, no. No, I didn't. I'm really not all that crazy about boys, at least not yet," I answered. I tried to ignore the flip-flop my stomach did when I knew Brock was behind me.

"Well," said Laura Rife, tossing her hair back over her shoulder like Sally Fields sometimes does in the movies, "if you're not interested, you can send Brock over to our ranch to stack hay any old time he wants—I won't mind one bit!" Whit had rejoined us, and all the girls, including me, giggled at Laura's comment. *Did Whit's laugh seem forced? Is she jealous that Brock directed all his comments toward me and not her?* I decided I was just reading things wrong. She was too good of a friend to be jealous over something as innocent as that, wasn't she?

I felt better as the night went on, and Whit seemed to return to being her old self. In fact, we had so much fun that she pleaded with her mother to let us stay longer.

"Don't you dare argue with me, Whitney Whitfield," Annie scolded. "It's time to go home. We have a big day tomorrow in getting your pigs ready to show, not to mention the sale auction in the late afternoon."

I guess we were more tired than we thought, as both Whit and I fell asleep before we hit the outskirts of town.

Chapter 26

BIRTHDAY PLANS
EAVESDROPPING

As I watched Annie and Whit drive into our yard a few nights after we'd been to the fair, I couldn't help but reflect on how Whit and her family were lifesavers in helping me adapt to my sudden introduction to life on Ira Stone's ranch. Like her mother Annie, Whit was just one of those people you couldn't dislike no matter how hard you might try. We became instant friends, and I loved going over to their place to work, play, and go horseback riding. Spending time with Whit also made it easier for me to get used to not having my best friend Cho around.

Notice I said work. I quickly learned that kids who grow up on farms and ranches know how to work. As Ira had done with me, kids here were expected to do chores as just youngsters. Boys were driving tractors, combines, and stacking hay by the time they were ten years old. Girls were doing cooking, cleaning, gardening, and sewing at that age. With no boys in her family, Whit did all the same kinds of animal chores as I did, plus she could run the tractors and machinery that mow, rake, and bale the hay as well as any boy. She could even back a grain truck up to a hopper and auger a load of wheat into a bin!

I was becoming more and more impressed with her horsemanship, too. Thanks to Whit's expert tutelage, Gunsmoke and I were becoming quite the couple. I was surprised—no, make that shocked—when Ira said, "I know that Whit's a dang good rider, and I hear tell you and Gunsmoke are getting along pretty good, too. I'm a-thinkin' you and Whit can move them cows down to the late-summer pasture. You'll only need to push them a little over a mile, and we won't move all 125-head at once. I'll pen 'em up, and you gals can probably drive 'bout 40-head at a time. Think you two can handle that, or do I need to call Brock to bring a couple of buddies with him to do the job?"

"Heck no! Me, Gunsmoke, Whit, and Pizza can do it, for sure," I replied, trying to sound way more confident than I really was. I mean, I wasn't one bit worried about Whit being up to the task, but I was plenty nervous whether I had yet developed the necessary skills to chase down a stray cow or calf and return them to the main herd.

Stop that, don't be getting ahead of yourself, I scolded myself when I started worrying about what I'd do if the herd were to stampede—you know, like they do in the movies. On the positive side, I'd already had some practice at galloping Gunsmoke, as I was getting much more comfortable with controlling him with the reins. Still, I was nowhere near Whit's riding skills, nor was Gunsmoke as fast and nimble as her horse, Pizza. Pizza looked and ran like one of those Indian paint horses you see in the old westerns on television.

Speaking of TVs, Ira didn't have one. I didn't really miss it because my mom didn't have one either. I used to watch it all the time over at Cho's, though. We tried not to miss an episode of *The Brady Bunch*, *The Beverly Hillbillies*, or *Bonanza*. We especially liked *Bonanza* and would always pretend that Adam and Little Joe were our boyfriends.

As Whit and I came out of the barn after checking on Betsy-Lou, we could hear the muffled sounds of Annie and Ira drifting through the open kitchen window. Whit gave the hush signal by placing her index finger to her mouth, and we stealthily made our way to our hiding spot beneath the kitchen window. Just like the time before, we could clearly hear everything Ira and Annie were saying.

".......well, you're right about that," we heard Ira say. "I'm for dang sure an ornery old coot, and she's quite the young gal. I dare say she's plum easy to have around. Unlike her mother, she seems to take to the ranch and animals like she's been around them all her life. And by gosh, the animals sure enough seem to like her, too. She ain't no complainer neither, not about doing her chores or anything else I ask her to do. She ain't a daydreamer like Lillian was, leastwise not near as bad. She's a hard worker and everything like that, but that don't make it any easier in knowing what I'm supposed to be doing for a twelve-year-old girl."

"Oh, for heaven's sake!" Annie exclaimed. "So, tell me—what's got your shorts in a bunch this time?"

"Well, main thing is her birthday is coming up on the 7th of August—less than a week away. I don't know, Annie, I just don't know what kind of birthday present to get a thirteen-year-old girl. Should I have a party? And if I do have a party, who besides you and your family should I invite?"

Whit and I exchanged a pitying look. I mean, I was surprised he said all those nice things about me and felt bad that he was worrying so much about my birthday.

"I have all sorts of suggestions for gifts," Annie stated emphatically. "How about getting her a TV? Good grief, Ira—it is the 1960s. And the late 60s at that. Even that old miser Ezra Canfield has a TV, and he's in his late eighties!"

"Hrruumph! Don't need one of those idiot boxes clutterin' up my living room!"

"Well, we're not talking about getting a TV for you, are we?" said Annie sarcastically. "No, we're talking about getting one for Maggie. And don't give me that crap about how expensive they are. Don't you forget for one minute that I know more about your finances than you do. Remember, I do the books for your ranch, and who do you think helps you do your income tax preparation every year? Granted, nobody that farms and ranches out here in the boondocks is in any danger of becoming rich, but I do know you've had this ranch paid off since the good Lord was in diapers. You only have about 125 cows, but you've got a keen eye for good stock, and you take better care of them than most people do their kids or pets. You're no millionaire, but you sure as heck ain't broke either. You can afford the TV and the rest of what I'm going to suggest you get her."

Whit and I looked at each other with mouths shaped in an "O" and faked like we were clapping our hands. We were anxious to hear what else Whit's mom had in mind for my birthday presents.

"And we need to get her to Billings before harvest and school starts. Maggie's probably already worn out those hand-me-downs of my sister's, so she needs work and school clothes. And before you start sweating bullets worrying about a shopping trip, I'll take her with me and my girls to Billings this coming Tuesday. I'll pick her up first thing in the morning and make sure she gets what she needs."

"Great, great," answered Ira in a defeated voice. "S'pose I better go sell half my cowherd to cover all your crazy expenditures."

"Oh, don't give me that nonsense. And I'm not done yet. That girl needs a new bike. That old one of Lillian's is from the Dark Ages and is way too small for her. And second, you need to get her a horse. As you know, she and Whit have been riding quite a bit, and Whit says she's caught on quickly. Maggie has been riding Gunsmoke, and they're getting along just great. And before you start to gripe again about how broke you are, I can assure you that you have all you need and then some sitting in that rainy-day savings account of yours in the bank. Plus, Wyatt says the majority of our wheat won't be ripe enough to harvest until at least the tenth, so we can have her birthday party at my house on the seventh. That's this coming Thursday, if I've got my days right. I'll take care of all the decorations, cake, and ice cream. And lucky you, that part won't cost you a red nickel."

"Is that all?" asked Ira sarcastically. "Or do I need to buy her a new car or pickup too?" When we heard Annie roar in laughter at that remark, we charged through the door like we were just coming from the barn for cookies and lemonade.

Chapter 27

SCHOOL SHOPPING TRIP TO BILLINGS

"You sit in the front with me," Annie ordered when she picked me up for the school shopping trip to Billings. "I'll need someone to keep me company, 'cause Whit, Wanda, and Willow will be asleep before we pass your mailbox at the end of the lane. Never seen such a group of sleepyheads once they get in a vehicle."

I knew Annie was just messing with Ira when she said, "I'm sorry, Ira, I guess there's just not enough room for you to come with us." Although he tried to hide it, a look of joyous relief washed over his face. He quickly handed an envelope to Annie, which I assumed was my shopping allowance cash. We all giggled when he gave us a quick wave before high tailing it to the barn.

"Ain't that just like a man?" Annie questioned. "They'd rather take fifty lashes to their backsides than go on a shopping trip!"

Whit actually stayed awake and chatted with us before joining her two younger sisters in slumber as we went through Sandstone Springs. I was kind of glad they were asleep, as I had a lot of questions for Annie. I didn't wait for long before starting my inquiry.

"Annie, can I ask you some questions about Ira, my mom, and my grandma?"

"You can ask me anything you want, honey," she replied. "I might not have all the answers, but I'll tell you what I know. Or at least what I think I know."

"Okay," I began tentatively, "This has been really bugging me, how did Ira get that scar? I mean, I've wanted to ask him about it, but I guess I'm too much of a chicken."

"I don't blame you for being apprehensive to ask him that. Ira is an intimidating man," replied Annie. "First off, to understand Ira, you need to understand your grandpa's generation. Whit's grandpa Whitfield, my dad, and Ira were all cut from the same cloth, and they all homesteaded land in this area. My dad and Ira came here from Ohio as young men—no more than teenagers. They had nothing, Maggie, most folks migrating west in the early 1900s didn't have a heck of a lot, and trying to farm or ranch this country out west with basically horses, oxen, or mules pulling primitive equipment was downright hard work. They didn't have the big tractors and combines that we have now, so everything they did on the farm or ranch was done by back-breaking labor. Those men and women that settled this country were tougher than boot leather, I'll tell you that for sure. They went through World War I, endured the draughts of the late teens and early 1920s, suffered through the stock market crash of 1929, and the Depression and draughts of the 1930s. I don't know how those folks survived, I truly don't. Oh yeah, and let's throw in World

War II in the 1940s. You've heard the phrase *survival of the fittest?* Well, that's the world my dad, Whit's grandpa, and your Ira grew up and lived in.

"Sorry for the long lead in to answering your question, but I think Ira's history is important for you to know as you try to figure out what makes him tick. Both my dad and Ira fought in World War. I honestly don't know the details, but my dad told me that he and Ira were shipped out from New York to France in 1917. All I know for sure is that Ira was wounded on the battlefield—probably took either a bullet or a piece of shrapnel to the face. Sorry, honey, but that's the extent of what I know about the scar. As you know, Ira doesn't talk much about such things.

I had so many different things going through my head that it took me a moment to ask the next question. "Whit says you knew my mom. What was she like when she was living here? I know she got pregnant with me in high school, did Ira and my grandma not like her because of that? Is that why she ran away?"

"Whoa, Maggie! I know you have a lot of questions you want answered, but one at a time, okay?" laughed Annie, reaching over to pat me on the arm. "I did know your mom, but I was four years older and ran with an older crowd. But you're probably already learning the ways of a small town. Don't get me wrong, people in these rural communities are wonderful and supportive, but the one downside of living here is that everybody pretty much knows everybody else's business before they know it themselves. I'll be honest with you, I think your mom was a handful. She had a rebellious streak to her, and from what I remember, your grandpa and her butted heads frequently. I think your grandpa and grandma had quite the problem keeping her under control. I don't mean to imply that she was a bad kid, but as they would probably say in San Francisco, the word on the street was that she was a bit on the wild side. But I'll tell you one thing I remember for sure, that girl could sing!

"And I do think the main reason your mother ran away had to do with the circumstances around her getting pregnant. I wouldn't go so far as to say that your grandpa and grandma didn't like her because of it, but you have to remember that getting pregnant at fifteen in 1955 was quite the news item at the time, still is, for that matter. Especially in a small community like Sandstone Springs. I don't think your grandparents, especially Ira, knew how to deal with it. I'm not making excuses for him, but that's how it was in those days."

I let that information bounce around my brain a few times before continuing my questions. "Annie, my mom never talks to me about my dad. When I bring it up, she just says he's not a nice man and I'm better off never knowing him. I don't mean to put you on the spot or anything, b-but, do you know who he is? He must be from around here, right? He could still be living here, couldn't he?"

Annie gave me a "you poor thing" look as she reached over and squeezed my arm again. "I'm sorry, honey. I truly don't know who your father is. But I will tell you the rumor that was going around at the time: your mom, and apparently a few of her friends, used to frequently sneak off to Miles City and Glendive to meet up with boys. Now, I'm not saying that it is all that unusual for small-town kids to go to the nearby bigger towns looking to meet members of the opposite sex, grass being greener on the other side of the fence, and all that sort of thing. But your mom was pretty young to be running around like that, and the boys she was hanging around with were reportedly a pretty rough bunch. As you can imagine, that didn't sit well with Ira. Anyway, the word always was that your father was some unknown guy from either Miles City or Glendive. I'm guessing the only one that knows for sure is your mother, and apparently, she isn't talking."

I stayed silent for a while, mulling over this new information about my dad that I was hearing for the first time. *Maybe my mom is right. Maybe it's best for everyone if I never know who my father is,* I thought. Finally, I moved on to my next question.

"I know that my grandma came to San Francisco to see me and my mom when I was a baby and again when I was three or four years old," I said. "My mom said she died a year or so after the second visit. Do you know what she died from? What was she like?"

"Your grandma Audrey was a sweetheart. Unfortunately, she had a heart condition, something about a defective heart valve from having Rheumatic Fever as a child, if I'm remembering correctly. She was a skilled seamstress, I can tell you that. If anyone in all of Sandstone Springs County needed something stitched or altered, or a new shirt, skirt, or dress, they went to Audrey. Because she had such a big and kind heart, she never charged much more than just enough to cover the cost of the material or fabric," Annie explained in an admiring tone. "I'll tell you something else; Ira was devoted to her. She's been gone for six or seven years now, and I'm not sure he's gotten over her yet. Don't get me wrong, he wasn't the outgoing type even before she passed, but at least your grandma could get him out and about around town occasionally. They went to church every Sunday and had brunch down at the Café afterward. They were active in the community and went to many of the school events—football and basketball games, school concerts, and the like. He stopped doing all that after she died and has pretty much turned into an old hermit ever since."

Annie reached over and took my hand, giving me a squeeze and a comforting smile. We rode in silence for a few miles before she spoke again. "I can tell you this much for sure, Maggie: your grandma would be proud as a peacock of the fine young lady you've turned out to be!"

"Why do you think Ira never came to see us?" I blurted out. "Did he not like us because my mom got pregnant with me? I mean, do you think that he doesn't like me because of that? Why did he come and get me from the orphanage if he doesn't like me?"

"Whoa again, Maggie! To be fair to Ira, I think he was treading water in dealing with your mom long before the pregnancy situation came about. The pregnancy may have been the final rock that caused his boat to sink, so to speak. I'm not defending why he never visited you and your mom in San Francisco. That's a bit of a mystery to me as well.

"For what it's worth, this is my best guess: Remember what I said about Ira's generation of men being stubborn old coots? Well, that's part of it—when those ol' guys run into a situation they are uncomfortable with, they sometimes just shut down and crawl into their protective cocoon. My dad is the same way. They're really good at just avoiding a situation that they can't control. Doesn't make it right, but it is what it is.

"I know that you worry about your grandpa not liking you, but that's absolutely not true! After all, who in their right mind wouldn't like you after being around you for more than ten minutes? Was he apprehensive about going to San Francisco and bringing you back to the ranch? Heck, yes, he was. Was he confused and worried that he was too old and wasn't up to the task of raising a twelve-year-old girl again? You betcha he was—he was scared to death. Was he concerned that he wouldn't be a good grandparent to you? Definitely!

"But I will tell you this: you're the best thing that could have happened to Ira. I can already see that he has a renewed purpose in life and a bounce in his step. It might not be apparent to the average Joe who isn't looking closely, but I can see it plain as day. I know him better than anyone else, so trust me when I say he's warming up to the idea of having you around. It just takes these old fossils a little more time than the rest of the world to show their true feelings."

This time, I was the one who reached across the seat and grabbed Annie's hand for a squeeze. We rode for a few miles without speaking before I broke the silence again. "I really miss my mom, Annie. I think about her all the time. It's probably stupid, but I send her a letter almost every week. I tell her about what's been going on with Ira, Dimwit, Betsy-Lou, and me. I tell her about my new friends—you, Whit, and Gunsmoke. I know she's in a spell and can't read them. Do you think sending her letters when she can't read them is stupid? Do you think she will ever get better?"

"I know you miss her, honey. And no, there's nothing stupid at all about sending her letters. I wish I knew the answer as to whether she will ever get better, but I don't have the crystal ball for that question. Unfortunately, nobody does. But you keep praying and sending your love and positive thoughts through your letters. Worst thing any of us can do is give up hope."

"One more question?" I asked anxiously, figuring she was probably getting tired of them.

"Shoot," Annie replied.

"Do you know how Ira found out that my mom had a spell and didn't come out of it? Do you know how he knew I was in an orphanage?"

"I'm sorry, honey," Annie said, reaching for my hand again. "He did tell us that your mom was in a coma, and he was going to San Francisco to get you. He asked us to look after his ranch and do his chores. But he didn't offer any more details. As you are no doubt beginning to learn, Ira ain't exactly a blabbermouth when it comes to doling out information and details."

I found comfort in holding Annie's hand until we reached the outskirts of Billings. I realized how nice it was to have a grown-up like Annie to talk to, especially since Ira didn't talk much. I figured it must be sort of like having a favorite aunt living nearby. I wondered if maybe someday it would be all right to call her Aunt Annie, I hoped she wouldn't mind.

Chapter 28

MY THIRTEENTH
BIRTHDAY PARTY

Even though my August 7th birthday was my day to cook breakfast and do the dishes, Ira surprised me when he said, "Well there young lady, today bein' your birthday and all, I'll do the cooking and wash the dishes." Then he really shocked me when he pulled out an envelope addressed to *Maggie,* written in the flowing cursive penmanship-style that is common with folks of Ira's age. I smiled to myself when seeing that both the card and envelope were wrinkled and faded, indicating that he had probably taken it from Grandma Audrey's desk drawer full of blank birthday and sympathy cards.

As Ira buttered the toast and liberally spread Annie's homemade raspberry jam on his slice, he turned to me and said, "That Whit can gab and gossip with the best of 'em, I doubt she can keep a secret longer than five minutes, so might just as well tell ya' the Whitfields are going to have a surprise birthday party for you this evening. You'll need to act surprised as the dickens when we get there."

Even though Whit and I had overheard Annie mentioning a birthday party for me at their house, I was still pleasantly surprised she was actually following through with it. I hurried through my chores and used the spare time I had created to write to my mom. I was feeling bad for kind of bawling her out in the last letter, so I thought I should maybe take a little more understanding tone in this one.

Dear Mother,

Do you know that today is my birthday? I don't want to hurt your feelings or anything like that, but I think it's time you come out of your spell so you can celebrate my birthday. Do you know you have been in a spell for a whole four months? Since you have been in this spell for so long, you don't even have to worry about buying me a present. I know I might have come across as angry in my last letter. I know you can't help it when you go in a spell, but I really do think you've had plenty of sleep and you need to wake up. We'll need to find another apartment. You will need to see if you can get your old job back at Del's. Hopefully, the band hasn't found another singer yet to replace you. I'm getting worried you won't have your job at either place if you stay like this much longer. You can't expect them to wait on you forever.

I've been busy doing chores and working in the hayfields. Me and Whit moved Ira's cows to a different pasture. I rode Gunsmoke. I think I already told you about him. I love riding him because he is so sweet and gentle. I went to the county fair with Annie and Whit and her little sisters. I won a few teddy bears at that basketball shooting game. The Whitfields are having a birthday party for me tonight. I'll write you and let you know if I get any presents. Oh yeah, Annie took me and the three Whitfield girls to Billings to school shop. Ira didn't go, and I think he was glad to stay home. But he must have given Annie quite a bit of money because I got some new underwear, two pairs of jeans, a pair of black slacks, two blouses, a sweater, and a winter coat. I guess it gets cold up here in the winter, right? Oh yeah, and I got a pair of work boots, gym shoes, and some really groovy cowboy boots! I sure needed the clothes and shoes because I've grown quite a bit over the summer and nothing I had was fitting anymore.

Well, that's about all the news from Sandstone Springs. Okay, please listen to me about waking up from your spell. Like I said, you have been in your spell for way too long and it's high time to wake up and get moving. Okay, I better go. I love you and hope to hear soon that you've woken up.

Love, Maggie

Dimwit and I spent the rest of the day working in the yard and garden. My poor doggie was still walking with a bit of a limp, but he seemed to be slowly getting his energy back. He stayed glued to my side even more than before the snake bite. After doing the evening chores early, I hurried to take a bath and get ready for my party. I was excited to be going to the Whitfields, as I knew Annie and Whit would make it fun. Even Ira washed up and put on clean jeans, a nice button-down western shirt, and a vest to go with his Sunday-go-to-meeting cowboy hat. He even gave me one of his crooked smiles when I told him that he looked spiffy.

Annie had me open my presents before we sat down for cake and ice cream. I got a cool bracelet from Whit and the girls, and a new work jacket from Annie. I was surprised to get a present from Dr. and Mrs. Rath—a new collar for Dimwit! It even had his name and our phone number engraved on a nameplate.

I won't kid you—I was kind of sad when it became apparent that I wasn't going to get a present from Ira. I mean, I tried not to be too disappointed, I really did. Despite eavesdropping on the conversation when Annie indicated Ira had plenty of money to buy gifts, I tried to convince myself that maybe she was wrong, perhaps he really didn't have enough money to buy me a birthday present. But my mom didn't have any extra money to buy gifts with either, and she always gave me at least one present on my birthday and at Christmas, sometimes two. I tried to put it out of my mind by telling myself to quit being a spoiled brat by expecting to get a present from Ira. *Be grateful for the presents I did receive* was what I needed to concentrate on, I decided.

After cake and ice cream, Whit and I went out to finish her chores. Ira stuck his head in the barn door and said he and Wyatt were going out to check to see if Whitfield's wheat was ready to harvest and that he would be back to take me home in about an hour. I was looking forward to the Whitfield harvest because Ira always operated one of their two combines. Plus, Whit said I could ride with her in a grain truck if her dad didn't give me another job to do, that is.

The sun was just starting to drop below the saddle buttes in the distance when Ira and Wyatt pulled back into the yard.

After Wyatt reported they were still several days from the grain being ready to harvest, I said my goodbyes, gave all the Whitfields a hug and thanked them for the party and all the great presents. After I unloaded my presents and took them upstairs, I told Ira I was tired after a busy day and was going to hit the hay.

"Before you head to bed, would you run out to the barn and make sure I opened the gate so Betsy-Lou can get outside and into the corral?" Ira asked.

"Sure," I said, calling out for Dimwit to come with me.

What the heck? I thought as I walked into the dimly lit barn. *Am I seeing things?* I couldn't believe it when I found Gunsmoke in Betsy-Lou's pen. And to top it off, leaning up against the gate was a brand-new, shiny, blue bike! Both the bike and Gunsmoke were wearing red bows with "HAPPY BIRTHDAY MAGGIE" written on them!

"Ira didn't forget me, after all!" I said aloud to Dimwit. I must admit, I wasn't too surprised about getting Gunsmoke, but I wouldn't have dreamed I'd get both a horse and a bike! I didn't care one bit that he didn't take Annie's advice and get me a TV.

I think Ira was embarrassed when I raced into the house, jumped on his lap, and gave him a big smooch on the cheek. "Thank you, thank you, thank you!" I exclaimed, smothering him in yet a few more smooches. "How in the heck did you sneak Gunsmoke and that pretty new bike into the barn without me knowing?" I asked incredulously.

"Well, it weren't easy. Hard to slip anything by you, that's for dang sure. But last night, I had Wyatt sneak the bike and Gunsmoke to that old shed at the end of our bull pasture. After we checked his grain for harvest readiness this evening, we slipped over and moved 'em into the barn."

"Your plan sure worked. I didn't have a clue! Thanks again, Ira. This was the best birthday ever. The only way it could have been better is if Mom would have been here to share in the party and presents," I said sadly.

"We'll call her again next Sunday," Ira said softly. "She'll snap out of that trance soon, you'll see."

I won't lie, I was beginning to wonder if she would ever wake up.

Chapter 29

TROUBLE IN PARADISE

"Maggie, Brock's on the phone," Ira shouted from the bottom of the stairs.

"Who? Did you say Brock?" I hollered back, unable to imagine why Brock would be calling me. "What does he want?"

"Yes, it's Brock. How in the world would I know what he wants?"

I raced down the stairs and picked up the phone from where Ira had left it on the counter. "H-hello," I answered timidly, "this is Maggie speaking."

"Yeah, I figured that was you," Brock answered with a hearty laugh. "Hey, glad I caught you over the noon-hour. If Ira doesn't have you in the field or you're not yet helping the Whitfields harvest, why don't you hop on Gunsmoke and come over to my place later this afternoon? We need to break in my new metal backboard and rim with a few games of HORSE."

"Alright, okay. But how did you know that Gunsmoke is at our place? I just got him for my birthday yesterday."

"I have my ways," he said, changing his voice to sound like one of those detectives on a TV show.

"I'll bet you do," I laughed. "I have to ask Ira, but if it's okay with him, I'll be over."

Ira just grunted when I told him I'd been invited to shoot hoops with Brock. "Ya' riding Gunsmoke over there?" he asked in an almost accusatory tone. "Well, get home well before dark," he demanded when my head-nod indicated I'd be riding. "Don't need ol' Gunsmoke steppin' in a gopher or badger hole cause he can't see where he's going."

The afternoon took forever to pass, as a bunch of questions kept bouncing around my brain. *Why would Brock want to play basketball with a girl, and a seventh-grade girl at that? Is it only because we are neighbors, and his buddies are too busy working in the fields to come and shoot with him? Is it just because I'm a pretty good shooter, or does he maybe—just maybe—kind of like me?* Whenever I found my daydreaming to be getting out of hand, I would scold myself out loud, "Hey stupid, in case you haven't noticed, he already has a girlfriend."

I felt foolish about all my thoughts of a possible Brock romance as Gunsmoke and I approached the Boyce ranch. Even from a distance, I could see there were two people on the basketball pad, and my suspicions were confirmed as I rode closer. The second person on the court was, you guessed it, none other than Tracy Rindal.

"Please tell me you didn't invite this little seventh-grade brat over here to shoot baskets?" snarled Brock's stuck-up girlfriend when Gunsmoke and I were in earshot of the couple.

Brock didn't answer right away, instead doing a reverse pivot dribble to the corner of the cement pad before pulling up for a high-arching jump shot. After watching the ball swish through the net of the shiny, new orange rim and official-looking metal backboard, I debated whether I should just turn around and head back home.

"Yes, Tracy, I did invite her over to play a few games of HORSE," he answered tersely. "Go ahead and get down, Maggie. Why don't you tie Gunsmoke to the corral post over there—the one in the shade by the water trough. I'm guessing Gunsmoke could use a drink."

As I tended to my horse, I couldn't help but overhear the conversation at the basketball court.

"Why don't you ever ask me to shoot baskets with you?" asked Tracy in the same whiny voice she'd used at the fair.

"Because she's a much better shooter than you, and I need some competition. She's the only kid in the whole school besides Trent Moseman and Danny Danforth who can stay with me in a game of HORSE, and both of their ranches are so far away that we rarely get together during the summer."

I must admit, I silently giggled to myself as I watched her stomp over and sit on a hay bale by the barn. She was in full pout mode, her lower lip almost dragging in the dirt. *I hope somebody kicks me in the seat of the pants if I ever act like that,* I thought to myself.

I won't kid you, I was very nervous to go up against the best basketball shooter in town. But once I settled down and warmed up with some practice shots, I actually surprised myself by being a teeny bit competitive against the star high school athlete and heartthrob. I mean, I never really came close to winning a game, but I had him down "R" to "H" in the second match.

"Well, guess you're not such hot stuff after all," muttered Tracey after I'd lost the third straight game. "I probably could have done just as well as you."

I ignored her childish slam and had to turn my head to smile when Brock replied, "Don't flatter yourself, Tracy. It'd be a cold day in hell when you'd get me down R to H." I thought he'd run after her to apologize when she stormed off to her car, roaring out of the driveway with tires screeching and dust flying, but he didn't even glance her way as she sped out of the yard.

"Do you want me to leave so that your girlfriend can come back?" I asked, suddenly feeling bad for Brock that my presence created such an obvious problem for him and his sweetheart.

"No, I don't want you to go," he said firmly. "And that two-year-old fit we just witnessed? That's the last straw. As of right now, she's no longer my girlfriend. I'm getting real sick of her jealous and controlling behavior, I should have ended this charade months ago."

While clapping my hands and doing cartwheels in my mind, we played a few more games of HORSE before Brock kindly took the time to help me work on my crossover dribble. He also showed me how to use the backboard on short shots around the key.

We were so engrossed in our practice that I didn't even realize Mr. and Mrs. Boyce were sitting on the hay bales with cookies and lemonade. After Brock made the introductions, I gave Mr. Boyce the once over, you know, to see if there was anything about his looks or mannerisms to make me think he might be my dad. Happily, I didn't see any similarities. Since Brock and I are at least hoop-shooting friends now, it would be weird to have a crush on a guy who might be your half-sibling!

My stomach kept flipping as I cinched up Gunsmoke's saddle and rode for home against the reddened hue of a lazy, mid-summer sunset. *This has been the best day since I arrived in Sandstone Springs almost four months ago,* I thought as I swung off the saddle to open the gate separating the Boyce and Stone properties. *Are my days of not being interested in boys over? Would he, could he, maybe like me enough to be his girlfriend? Or does he just think of me as some punk kid to play some basketball with?*

"Did you see Tracy have her spoiled brat fit?" I asked Gunsmoke after I remounted and broke into a gentle gallop toward home. "And do you think Brock and Tracy will stay broken up?"

I took it from the way he cocked his ears that he thought they would.

Chapter 30

FRIENDS, OR SOMETHING MORE?

"Hmm, would this be Whit or Brock?" Ira asked sarcastically when we heard the phone as we approached the house from finishing afternoon chores. "Seems you been gettin' right popular on the gab and gossip line lately."

I think I've already told you Ira isn't a fan of idle blabbin' 'bout nothin' on the telephone. There were usually only three calls Ira would make: the hospital every Sunday to check on my mom; to Annie, Wyatt, or a few other neighbors for ranch-related matters, and to Dr. Rath for veterinary issues. If I was in the house and the phone rang, Ira had informed me I was to answer the phone, even if I was upstairs in my room. I had also been instructed to ask who was calling. If it was anyone besides the above mentioned, then I was supposed to say he was out in the shop and would call them back later. I had noticed there was one occasional caller that Ira never called back: Inez Braddock.

Whenever I would cover the mouthpiece and whisper, "It's Inez," Ira would make a disgusted face and emphatically point toward the shop.

"She's nothin' but a busybody and just 'cause," is all Ira would say when I asked who she was and why he never called her back. I finally got the lowdown when I asked Annie about it one day.

"Ha! She's still calling him, huh?" she asked, laughing. "Well, she is an elderly widow that lives up the road a fair piece. Lost her husband about the same time your grandma passed. Anyway, Ira didn't like her husband Art any better than he does Inez. All of us ladies think she might have, as you kids always say, a *crush* on Ira. But your grandpa will have none of it!"

I was glad that Ira had recently installed at least one modern day telephone accessory—a long cord. "There ya' go," he had grunted after replacing the shorter old one. "You can now stretch this cord all the way to the mudroom and give me a little peace and quiet to read the newspaper." I noticed the cord was the only upgrade he had made. Unlike the sporty red touch-tone phone that hung on the kitchen wall at the Whitfield residence, Ira still had the old rotary-dial phone unit that sat on a TV tray stand just inside the living room. If I had to guess, I'd bet Gunsmoke and my new bike that the ancient black phone was the first and only one that Ira has ever owned.

"Don't be gabbin' too long, young lady," Ira admonished as I pulled the phone cord all the way to the mudroom. "I 'spect Wyatt or Annie will be callin' to let us know if we're needed for harvest tomorrow."

"I heard that, I won't keep you long," chuckled Brock as I closed the door. This was the third straight night he'd called since my inaugural visit to shoot baskets at his place, and my heart skipped a beat when he said, "You think Ira would let you ride over right now so we could play some hoops?"

"I 'spose you can go, but don't you be thinkin' this is going to be an every evening thing," snapped Ira. "And you be back here before dark too, young lady. We'll no doubt need to get at the chores early tomorrow, 'cause we'll probably be headin' to Whitfield's right after."

I quickly saddled Gunsmoke, and he seemed to know where we were headed as soon as I pointed him west. We trotted down the hill, past the pond and on to the gate of the pasture that separated the Stone and Boyce ranches. I had to use all the muscles I'd built up during the eight weeks I'd been in Montana to open and close the four-wire gate, and only had to lightly squeeze my legs into Gunsmoke's sides after remounting to encourage him into a slow and comfortable lope. *Just like shifting Ol' Blue into third gear*, I thought to myself. *Nice and smooth into a higher gear.*

We had to gently weave our way through a few groups of Ira's cows and calves as we galloped across the mile-wide pasture. Most of the momma cows didn't pay us much attention, but I had to giggle at how rambunctious the calves were. They were running about and dancing to and fro like a bunch of first graders showing off at recess. I smiled thinking about Betsy-Lou joining the party soon, as Ira had said she had only a few more weeks of bottle-feeding before joining the cowherd. I mean, I really did enjoy feeding her and we had become best friends, but I was happy that she'd soon be foot-loose and fancy-free.

But neither dodging the cows nor reminiscing about Betsy-Lou could keep me from wondering what was really up with all the sudden attention I was getting from Brock. *Could he really like a lowly seventh grader when he could have his pick of any girl in high school? Does he only like me in a sisterly way because I love sports, can shoot a fairly decent basketball, and live just a short horse ride away? Am I being foolish in even slightly getting my hopes up that he might like me for more than a friend?*

The only thing I knew for sure as I approached the Boyce side of the pasture was that I was totally and completely confused as to the status of this new relationship with Brock. Was it that of just a friend? Or was it something more?

Brock was already out shooting baskets when Gunsmoke and I rode into the yard. I tied up Gunsmoke at the same spot by the barn. "Don't forget to loosen his saddle cinch, he'll be more comfortable that way," Brock suggested. "I filled the water trough for him, too."

We had barely gotten through our first game of HORSE (which I lost O-to-E) before the gentle evening breeze turned more sinister. "No sense fighting this severe crosswind," Brock declared. "I've got a hoop up in the barn hayloft, so let's finish our game there. We stacked a bunch of square bales up there this summer, but I left enough room around the basket to shoot at least 10 or 12 footers."

It was nice to get out of the wind, but the haystack made for close quarters. We were halfway through the next game when I took a shot from the free throw line straight away, and the ball careened hard off the side of the rim to my right. Not realizing Brock was going for the ball, too, I crashed into him and found myself in his arms when he took hold of me to keep me from falling.

I started to apologize for running into him when it happened: He pulled me closer and kissed me! It was so sudden, I was shocked. I was stunned. I didn't know what to think or do, but I guess due to pure reflex, I quickly pulled back away from him.

"I'm so sorry, Maggie. I shouldn't have done that, I'm so sorry," Brock said apologetically. "Please forgive me?"

"Ah, n-no. I mean yes, I-I mean there's nothing to forgive," I stammered. "I'm just surprised, is all, surprised that you would want to kiss me. You know, with me just being a seventh grader and all."

"So, you didn't mind it? The kiss, I mean?"

"No, I didn't mind," I replied sheepishly, embarrassed by the red blush I knew was washing over my cheeks. "Again, I'm just surprised you would want to kiss me when you could no doubt kiss and go out with any high school girl you wanted. I mean, I could tell from the night I was at the midway during the fair that there are lots of high school girls that are prettier than I am."

"Don't sell yourself short," Brock said firmly. "Trust me, you are as pretty as any of them, prettier than most, in fact. In addition to that, you are more mature as a seventh grader than most of the juniors and seniors at Sandstone Springs, and you're smarter, nicer, and more fun to hang around with, too."

Fearing that my neck and face were now a burning red hue, I tried to interject a little humor. "Well, I think you only like me because I let you beat me in HORSE."

"Haha! That's probably part of it," he laughed, taking my hands and pulling me in closer. "Do I have your permission to finish that kiss now?"

"Yes, but you should know, I've never really kissed before. Not a real kiss, anyway. I'm not sure I know what to do," I nervously explained as I wrapped my arms around him.

"Don't worry. I can teach you kissing just as good as I've been teaching you basketball shooting tips," he murmured, gently tilting my head to meet his approaching lips. I lost track of time, I really don't know how long or how many times we kissed, but we quickly separated and loudly began to resume our game when we heard the barn door open below.

"Sorry to interrupt your game, but Ira just called," Mrs. Boyce informed us when she reached the top step of the hayloft. "Maggie, he wants you to start for home before that wind blows in a storm."

Even though Gunsmoke was chomping at the bit to gallop, I held him to a walk on the way home. The wind was easing up, and I needed some time and fresh air to sort out the wave of emotions I'd just experienced in the Boyce barn hayloft. I was still flush with the realization that he didn't think of me as a snot-nosed seventh grader. And I couldn't quit smiling about him saying I was just as pretty as Tracy Rindall and all the other older girls at school, not to mention being smarter and more fun.

But it was the *kiss* I kept coming back to. So unexpected, yet so delightful. I laughed at my awkward, deeply uncomfortable tooth-bumping first and only kiss with Dale Beckman less than four months ago. To go from that to kissing Brock Boyce was like, I don't know, like going from the fires of hell to the welcoming arms of heaven.

Even though I had already decided the only person I would tell about this evening's events would maybe be in a letter to my comatose mother, I was glad when the last words Brock said to me before heading home was, "What do you say we keep what just happened in there between the two of us, at least for the time being."

"I couldn't agree more," I had said. "Best to keep what just happened between you and me, for sure."

Chapter 31

HARVEST AT
THE WHITFIELDS

"How long have you been helping the Whitfield's harvest their grain?" I asked Ira at breakfast after he informed me that we would be spending the next couple of weeks helping our neighbors get their crops in the bin.

"'Bout forever, I reckon. It goes back to when Whit's grandfather was on the place. Me and him go way back, homesteaded right next to each other, we did. He's been gone for some time now, but I continued to help when Wyatt took over. Since I don't raise any grain and am usually finished with haying by this time of year, it fits well into my work schedule to help them cut their wheat and barley. I drive one of their two combines."

"So, are you like a hired hand? I mean, do you get paid?" I asked.

"Well, yeah. They pay me a modest harvest wage, but only for the harvest end of things," Ira explained. "We help each other out for free on the livestock end—calving, branding, vaccinating, moving cows, and such. That's just what neighbors do out here in farm and ranch country."

"I don't know anything about harvesting grain," I admitted. "What kind of job do you think they'll have me do?"

"I 'spect you'll just ride with Whit. She's been driving a grain truck for several years now. She'll no doubt teach you what you can do to help her out, might even teach ya' how to drive the grain truck by the end of harvest."

Ira was right in that Whit sure could maneuver that truck around, even though she could barely reach the pedals or see over the steering wheel. I couldn't believe she was a good enough driver to snuggle that big truck up next to the combine's auger and load the box with grain on the go!

While I finally did get a chance to learn how to drive the truck, I wasn't near enough accomplished to try loading on the go. The few times they let me drive, I had to just park near the combine when the grain tank was full, and they would drive over to me and unload. And I never did get skilled enough to use the big truck mirrors and back into one of the many storage bins they had conveniently located around the farm. My only real job was to stand where Whit could see me through the mirror on the driver-side door and guide her to the right spot for unloading the grain into the hopper. I did try to make myself useful by jumping into the raised truck box and shoveling out the last bit of grain through the trap door.

I learned a lot about grain the very first day; like winter wheat is planted in the fall, and spring wheat is planted in the, well, in the spring. Barley is a grain that is also planted in the spring and is used for livestock feed and—get this—to make beer! I learned that winter wheat is usually the first to ripen, followed by spring wheat and barley. I also quickly figured out that I was probably allergic to barley, because as soon as we started cutting the barley, I became itchy all over. Even worse, my eyes swelled up and my nose ran like a river. Whit said most people, including her, have at least some allergy symptoms after being around barley.

We spent the next ten hot August days harvesting for the Whitfields. It had been a month since Dimwit was bitten, and he was almost back to his normal self. I say *almost* because he still had a slight limp. But he was well enough to jump all the way up on the grain truck seat with only a little boost from me.

I learned that hail was as bad of a word for grain farmers as it was for ranchers who put up hay. Storm clouds had gathered almost every evening, hovering just above us like huge black and gray army helicopters, shooting down daggers of lightning and stirring up the winds. On several occasions, the roiling black and gray sky monsters fired a heavy dose of driving rain on the Whitfield's grain fields, but fortunately, they weren't bombed with hail.

Whit explained that the main reason harvest took less time than usual this year was due to one of the earlier hailstorms totally wiping out two hundred acres of what would have been their best wheat. She also said her dad bought something called hail insurance, which would pay you if you got hail that damaged the wheat. Even so, Whit said the insurance never paid as much as you would get if your crop wouldn't have been hailed on.

As busy as harvest can get, there were still enough equipment breakdowns and weather-related delays to give Whit and I plenty of downtime to discuss the highlights of the summer. I figured the question was coming, but I tried to play dumb when she excitedly asked. "So, did you hear the big news about Brock and Tracy breaking up?"

"Yeah, I heard something about that," I said innocently, trying to avoid eye contact.

"Heard about it, did you? Hmm, well, I heard from a little birdie that you actually witnessed Tracy's tantrum firsthand. Something to do with you playing basketball at Brock's place, is that true?" asked Whit. I couldn't tell for sure from her tone if she was mad or just jealous.

"Well, yeah, I guess I did. We were playing HORSE, and she had a tizzy about Brock shooting with me and not her," I said, trying to make it sound like it wasn't a big deal.

"So, just how did you end up at Brock's in the first place? Did you just show up, or were you invited?" she asked, with an edge to her voice.

"No, I didn't just show up," I replied. "He invited me over to play HORSE on his new basketball pad. I guess he thinks I'm a better shot than Tracy, and that didn't sit too well with her. She went into a pout and squealed out of the yard like the little brat she is. Brock said he was sick of the way she acted and that he was going to break up with her."

"So, I suppose you think he's sweet on you now that he's broken up with Tracy? Are you two going out now, or what?" she asked. This time there was no mistake; her tone was a blend of jealousy and resentment. And to be honest, it ticked me off. I decided right there that I'd had enough of her petty spitefulness when it came to Brock paying attention to someone other than her. Especially when that someone was me. Scouts honor about keeping the kiss with Brock a secret or not, I wasn't about to divulge any of the hayloft happenings with my jealous so-called best friend. Instead, I played dumb, and with a bite to my voice, I out-and-out lied.

"Of course we're not going out. Why would a guy like Brock want to date a seventh grader like me? We're just neighbors who like to shoot baskets together, and that's all there is to it."

"Okay, okay, no reason to get all huffy. I was just curious about what happened with Brock and Tracy," Whit replied, backing off from her prior accusatory tone.

One thing I learned about Whit over the summer is that she's quick to get over any spat or disagreement we might have. It's like a snap of the fingers, one minute she's in a harumph over whatever, and the next minute everything is peachy keen.

"So, how are you feeling about starting school at Sandstone Springs?" she asked, abruptly changing the subject and back to her usual friendly self. "Just in case you forgot, the first day is Sept 3rd. That's next Wednesday, you know."

"Don't worry, I have that date circled on my calendar," I said. "Can't say I'm not nervous about entering a new school for the second time in the last four months, that's for sure."

"Well, look at it this way, couldn't be much worse than being sent off to the orphanage, right?" Whit suggested optimistically.

"I guess that's one way of looking at it," I replied.

"It'll be okay, really, it will," said Whit in an attempt to be convincing. She assured me that most of the kids were really nice, as were the teachers. "You'll get Mrs. Poser for your seventh-grade homeroom teacher. She's really cool, she's been my favorite teacher so far.

"I'll call you the night before and we can discuss what we're going to wear on the first day," Whit continued. "And don't wear that hippie dress I saw hanging in your closet," she said with a chuckle. "Even though we're slowly starting to get a little more hip out here in the country, Sandstone Springs probably isn't quite ready for the San Francisco wardrobe just yet!"

Chapter 32

FIRST DAY OF SCHOOL
AT SANDSTONE SPRINGS

Even though Whit had tried to ease my anxiety about starting at my third different school in five months, I had a mostly sleepless night worrying about the big day. I couldn't help but think about this being the first time ever my mom wasn't around for school shopping or to help pick out my wardrobe for the first day. Not that we could afford to purchase much of a selection of school clothes, but it was always fun to jointly choose which of the two or three options to wear. And even though I was slowly getting more comfortable being around Ira, he wasn't exactly the ideal person to help with the first day of school clothing choices. To his credit, he let me and Whit have a lengthy attire discussion without shooting me the usual *you've been on the phone long enough* scowl.

I was kind of hoping that Ira would walk with me the quarter mile down to meet the bus, but after breakfast, he simply said,

"Better head down the lane to the mailbox and catch the bus. Ol' Jimmy Bost has been the bus driver on this route for nigh on to fifty years, I reckon. He ain't one to dilly dally around waiting on a kid to get to the bus stop. He'll be there at 7:45 sharp, so you best get to hoof'n it down there. Good thing is, fast as you can run, you'll be there in a flash."

I must admit it had taken me all summer to get used to how Ira talked. No one in San Francisco talked like he did. *Country slang* was what Whit called the language spoken in the plains of eastern Montana. But I'd been at the ranch long enough to know that "dilly dally" meant the same as to "lollygag"—wasting time, or just plain goofing off. Trust me, Ira was not a fan of either dilly dallying or lollygagging. "Hoof'n it" meant you better hurry up and get somewhere fast. Ira didn't do all that much talking, but I heard him say "I reckon" often enough that I caught myself starting to say it, too.

"Could Dimwit come with me to the bus?" I asked hopefully.

"Better not," replied Ira. "He don't have sense enough to get out of the rain, so he's probably too dense to come home from the bus stop. He'd probably follow the bus all the way into Sandstone Springs instead." I used to get upset when Ira would talk bad about Dimwit, but I finally figured out he mostly did it to get under my skin. I just ignored him when he started on that kind of talk now.

Mr. Bost was pretty old all right, but he greeted me by name and welcomed me on the bus with a smile. There were only four kids on the bus; a boy who appeared to be a fifth or sixth grader, and Wanda, Willow, and Whit. I had to laugh at the sight of Whit, who was standing in the aisle waving her arms above her head and shouting, "Over here, Maggie, I saved you a seat!" Whit was so excited for school starting that I could barely get a word in edge wise. We chatted, or I should say Whit chatted, the entire seven miles to town. I noticed Mr. Bost stopped two more times to pick up another five students who lived closer to town.

Before she went to her own room, I thanked Whit for taking me to my seventh-grade classroom and introducing me to Mrs. Poser. She must have known that I was Ira's granddaughter because she informed me that Ira had forgotten to place several of the requested school supply items in my backpack. *Thanks Ira, just what I need to start off the first day.* I apologized profusely and told her he hadn't shown me the list of supplies I was supposed to bring.

"Don't worry about it, Maggie," she said as she put her arm around my shoulder. "It's been a long time since your grandfather had to worry about following the directions of a first-day-of-school supply list. I have extras of everything you're missing, and I'll make sure you see all correspondence that goes out to the parents, or grandparents, from here on out."

I was kind of embarrassed when Mrs. Poser had me stand up while she introduced me to the other eleven students. It was obvious I was the only new kid in the class, and Laura Rife and Sandy Barnhart were the only classmates I'd met during the summer. I knew the town and school were small, but after being used to the big city of San Francisco and the huge schools and classes I had gone to for grades one through six, twelve students in the whole grade seemed really, really small.

Although it wasn't unusual, the first thing I noticed was that I was taller, in some cases a lot taller, than all of my classmates, boys or girls. I was always the tallest girl in all my classes in San Francisco, too. Like I mentioned when I was at the fair, I was pretty darn athletic and had always played ball with the boys, whether it be baseball, basketball, or track and field. During my short stay at the orphanage, I even played football and laughed when one of the boys finally admitted to me, "You sure don't run or throw like a girl."

Again, I don't mean to toot my own horn, but I'm also a dang good student. I'm lucky that school has always come easy for me. If I don't get all A's, I get pretty upset. Except for Art, that is. I have always been so lousy in Art that I'm more than happy to get a B-.

Since seventh graders at Sandstone Springs no longer enjoyed a morning or afternoon recess, the first break was for lunch. The fifth and sixth graders were still in the cafeteria when the seventh and eighth-grade classes were released for lunch. It looked like each class only had between eight and twelve students. It was kind of like the orphanage, where there were so few students per class that the big kids ended up eating with the younger ones. I was happy when Whit's class came into the lunchroom right behind us, and she hurried over to sit with me. It wasn't like I was alone because Laura, Sandy, and another girl from class, Susan Metcalfe, were already sitting with me.

All three were really nice and had all sorts of questions about San Francisco, like if everyone there was a hippie and said *peace* or *peace out, man* all the time. I told them there were a lot of hippies in San Francisco but that I was sure you didn't have to be a hippie to live there. When Susan finally moved past her inquiries of all matters San Fran and came back to the happenings of Sandstone Springs, she blurted out that my grandpa Ira looked like a Halloween scary monster with that big scar. Both Laura and Whit told her that was a cruel thing to say and to shut her trap. I don't think she was trying to be mean or anything like that, after all, it was hard to deny that Ira's scar looked pretty spooky.

The most awkward moment of lunch occurred when Brock and the other freshman were entering the cafeteria as we were leaving. We made eye contact and exchanged a hello and a slight smile as we passed. I thought we were very subtle during our brief encounter, but I should have known better. "Hmm, so nothing going on between you two, huh?" said Whit sarcastically. "Yup, nothing at all. And I'm six foot tall and beautiful, and TEEN magazine is begging me to be their cover model next month!"

Walking up the lane after Mr. Bost and the bus dropped me off, I reviewed the first day in my mind. Although the tiny little town and school were far different from what I was used to, the day went by fairly smoothly and most everyone seemed nice and friendly. I decided I was actually looking forward to day two.

Ira was quite chatty at supper, at least by Ira Stone's standards. He seemed interested as to how my first day of school went and even asked a few questions. I didn't have the heart to tell him that I was the only kid in my class who didn't have all the items on the supplies list that Mrs. Poser had mailed out well in advance of the start of school. I didn't want to hurt his feelings or make him feel like he wasn't being a responsible grandpa.

Chapter 33

GO BUFFALOES

"We haven't been very good these last few years," Whit explained on the bus ride to school on the Friday morning of Sandstone Springs' first football game of the season. "I think our record was a lousy 3-5 last year, but this year will be different, your new beau Brock will be a difference maker. Even though he's just a freshman, he'll probably be one of the best players in the conference."

"He's not my beau, Whit," I sighed in exasperation, still in the mode of trying to hide the kiss from everyone. Especially from Whit.

"Yeah, right. And I'm being courted by both Ricky Nelson and Elvis," she replied, flipping back her imaginary long hair. "How will I ever choose?"

It had been almost a month since Brock and I made our pact to keep our special moment in the hayloft a secret. To be honest, I wasn't at all sure what the status of our relationship was supposed to be. I knew I liked him, and I was pretty sure he liked me, but it was awkward to pass in the hall and pretend not to notice each other. If we did talk in a group setting, it was hard to act like we were just friends.

I was quickly learning that high school activities, especially sports, were a big deal in small towns. "Think about it," Whit had explained. "Except for church, our school activities are about the only social thing for adults to do in these small communities. It's not the same as big cities like San Francisco, where you have all kinds of other things to do—museums, zoos, aquariums, operas, musicals, fancy restaurants—stuff like that."

Everyone in school was happy that most football games were played on Friday afternoons, meaning school was let out early so everyone could attend the game. I got my first taste of a pep rally when those of us junior high and high school band members were let out even earlier to warm up for the rally. I had only been practicing with the junior high band for a week, so I was surprised the band director would even let me play. Since I'd had a little bit of experience with the instrument back in the sixth grade, I had chosen the clarinet to play. But I was a beginner at best, and was nervous as heck to play before a crowd.

"No worries," declared Whit. "Here's the thing with small schools like ours; we have so few kids that our junior high and high school bands are combined. Just make sure you sit next to Alicia O'Reilly, she's a senior and a really good clarinet player. That way, she'll cover up most of your mistakes."

The band started off the pep rally with a bang, pounding out the school song to an enthusiastic audience. Fortunately for us, our music instructor was one heck of a trumpet player, so he was able to drown out some of the sour notes coming from those of us younger, less skilled band members. Then Mr. Beltran, the high school science teacher and head football coach, introduced his players and gave a fiery speech that had everyone standing and cheering at the hopeful prospect of beating the Garfield County Mustangs, one of Sandstone Springs' top rivals from, as folks in this country say, "down the road a fair piece."

Here's another thing I learned about living in a really small town: There's not enough students to field an eleven-man team. Sandstone Springs and all the towns of similar size in Montana played either six-man or eight-man football. The Buffaloes had twenty-two boys in high school, seventeen of which came out for football. Apparently, that was enough to field an eight-man team.

It was exciting to see all the activity down on the football field as game time approached. The entire circumference of the field was lined with cars, and soon the fans stood three-deep behind both sidelines. Except for the five football players who were in the band, the rest of us settled into the student bleachers to get ready to play the national anthem. I was pretty sure every kid from kindergarten through high school was there to fill the rest of the student bleachers.

As game time approached, I looked up and down the sideline to see if Ira had come. As if reading my mind, Whit offered, "I heard my mom and Ira on the phone the other day. She told him in no uncertain terms to quit being a hermit and come watch you in the band and Brock on the field, but I guess he's still being a stubborn old bugger."

I tried not to show my disappointment and thankfully forgot about it when the game started. It was an exciting back-and-forth game that was tied at the half and won by the good guys on a twenty-seven-yard touchdown run by Brock with less than a minute to go. I kind of lost track of how many touchdowns he made, but I think it was at least four. The final score was 52-46.

I decided the heck with avoiding Brock after the game and worked my way through the crowd of kids and adults surrounding him and the rest of the jubilant team. "You made some really great moves on that last touchdown run, that's for sure!"

He shocked me by pulling me in for a hug. "Oh, thanks, I was lucky to get so many great blocks, especially the one from Monte down on about the five-yard line. Our whole team played really great!"

Brock's embrace lingered a bit longer than what would be considered a friendly congratulatory gesture, and he kept an arm around me even after we broke the hug. We couldn't help but notice the icy glare from Tracy Rindal when she pranced by us and launched herself into the arms of her new boyfriend, quarterback Derek Daly.

"I guess that's supposed to make me wildly jealous and beg her to come back," Brock mumbled.

"So, is it working?" I asked.

"Definitely! Would you please move out of my way so I can crawl to her on my knees and beg for forgiveness?"

Okay, what's going on, Brock? The hug; the lingering arm wrapped around my waist; the snide comments about Tracy? The only thing I knew for sure was that I was more confused than ever about the status of our relationship.

Chapter 34

DIMWIT FINDS TROUBLE—AGAIN!

It was getting well past mid-September, and the days were getting shorter than the early sunrise, late evening sunset days of summer. After a good couple of weeks into the school year, I was getting well-rehearsed in my before-school routine; Ira would holler, "time to get up, Maggie" from the bottom of the stairs every morning at 5:45, not a minute sooner, not a minute later.

Ira and I had made an agreement (or more accurately, he had informed me) that when school started, I would drop a day of making breakfast and only cook on Monday and Wednesdays during the week. His main rule was to make eggs (sunny side up), bacon or sausage (on Sundays) and toast for him. I also continued to like the "whoever does the cooking doesn't have to wash dishes" part of the deal.

I was surprised one September morning when Ira put a box of Cheerios on the table. Since there wasn't any cereal in the cupboard before, I guess he must have remembered way back to when he first asked what I used to have for breakfast in San Francisco. "You can have your Cheerios as long as ya' have an egg and some bacon. Always good to have some protein, young lady."

Never one to chat much regardless of the time of day, he was usually particularly tight-lipped at breakfast. So, I was somewhat startled when he asked another question after the cereal discussion. "Well, been a couple weeks now since school has been in session. I reckon it's a bit different from the orphanage and your old school before that in San Francisco. So, how's things goin' for ya' so far?"

"Yes, it's a lot different, for sure," I confirmed. "I'm not used to the small classes, and it's weird that the school is so small that everybody knows everybody. But that's good in its own way. Plus, almost everybody is really nice, even most of the older high school kids. I think I already told you I really like most of the teachers, especially my homeroom teacher, Mrs. Poser."

I kept blabbing about all things school-related, and I guess I got a little carried away in answering this rare morning question from Ira. He finally had to interrupt me with, "Glad you're likin' things okay at school, I surely am. But you best get to gettin' at your chores, so ya' won't be havin' to sprint down the lane to catch the bus."

The rising sun was just starting to throw spears of light at the ranch as the almost fully recovered Dimwit joined me to head toward Betsy-Lou and the barn. My canine buddy started acting funny as soon as we went out the mudroom door. Instead of staying at my heels like he usually did, he started to bark and race back and forth between me and the chicken coop. It was like he was trying to tell me something, like he wanted me to hurry and follow him. I thought I also heard the chickens being unusually noisy, but it was hard to hear over Dimwit's constant yipping.

"Okay, little fella," I said. "Let's go see what's got you and those hens so worked up." He headed for the coop at a dead run, and I was only a step or two behind him when he burst through the open door and the skunk that was raiding the nests for eggs, threw up its tail and sprayed Dimwit with the powerful, distinctive odor that only a skunk can make!

But it didn't just hit Dimwit. I had the sense or feeling that someone had sprayed a mist of putrid skunk stink on me with a squirt gun. Except it wasn't someone squeezing the trigger, it was a real skunk doing the shooting!

All I remember is that I turned and ran back toward the barn, collapsing in the dirt of the driveway and crying hysterically.

Dimwit just ran in circles around me, yelping and whimpering like he'd done after the snakebite. Then I heard Ira; there were no darns, hecks, or dad-gummit's this time. He let loose a string of cuss words the likes I had never heard before, and I had heard plenty of bad language from the older boys at the orphanage.

"*BLANKETY-BLANK YOU,* Dimwit! How many times are you going to tear into a *BLANKETY-BLANK* skunk or stick your nose into a *BLANKETY-BLANK* porcupine or rattlesnake before you learn? You ain't got a *BLANKETY-BLANK* brain in that *BLANKETY-BLANK* head of yours!"

Dimwit had dropped to the dirt as soon as Ira started yelling at him and was rubbing his face with his paws like he was trying to wipe off the skunk smell. I didn't blame him; I wanted to try the same thing.

"Are you okay, Maggie?" Ira asked, keeping his distance while trying to get close enough to observe how I was holding up. I tried to be brave, but I think I was kind of in shock. I mean, who thinks they will ever get sprayed by a skunk? I wished for my mom, even though I knew there wasn't much she could do. She sure couldn't hug me, stinking the way I was.

"I th-think so," I answered, trying to keep my voice from breaking.

"Sit tight for a minute," Ira said. "I've got to call the school and tell them you won't be showing up for a few days, and I've got to call Annie and see if she can bring me some tomato juice."

I had no idea what the tomato juice would be for, so I just sat there and sobbed. Dimwit yelped in short bursts, scooting ever closer to me each time. I knew he had taken most of the spray and probably smelled way worse than me, but the skunk odor was so strong in my nostrils that I didn't notice much of a difference as he worked his way nearer.

I was really glad to see Annie pull into the driveway. "Don't believe that old wives' tale about taking a bath in tomato juice," she told Ira. "I brought some hydrogen peroxide to mix in with the water. Nothing is going to totally get rid of the skunk smell on the first bath, but this is the best remedy I've come across."

It was kind of embarrassing when I realized the bathtub I was going to use was an extra horse trough in the barn. "Might as well throw the partner-in-crime in the tub with her," Ira suggested to Annie, pointing at the sheepish-looking Dimwit. "Ya' got any dumb dog shampoo in your bag of tricks?"

"As a matter of fact, I do," Annie confirmed with a smile. Thankfully, Ira mumbled about having to check on something out in the corral, so I quickly disrobed, and Dimwit and I braved the teeth-chattering cold water of the horse tank. Using each of her dog and people shampoos, Annie scrubbed down the both of us and rinsed us off with a couple of buckets of cold well water as we exited the tub.

Annie told Ira that Dimwit and I were to have three hydrogen peroxide baths each day for the next two or three days. "You two stinkers will be bunkin' out here in the barn for a few days," Ira informed us as he rolled out a sleeping bag on top of the straw bed he made in an empty barn stall. "I've got some work to do, but I'll be back to fill up your outdoor bathtub and take your lunch and supper orders."

"It's gonna be a long few days, my furry friend," I said when suddenly Betsy-Lou, Dimwit, and I had the barn to ourselves. The sense of skunk was so strong in my nostrils that I didn't even notice that poor Dimwit carried the worst of the stench on his coat. "Good thing we've got each other, because I'm pretty sure our other friends are going to be scarce for a while."

I had five more hydrogen peroxide baths and slept in the stall for two nights before finally ridding myself of enough of the skunk smell to sleep in the house and go back to school. Poor Dimwit had to sleep in the barn for a whole week. Ira must have felt sorry for me, as he didn't even give me his usual glare when I talked to Whit on the phone. Brock and I had agreed it was probably best for him to only call occasionally to avoid Ira's suspicions, but I was happy to hear his voice when he called the first night I returned to the house.

"I suppose you'd really like to smell my new perfume and give me a big kiss right now, huh?" I giggle-whispered after I'd stretched the cord into the mudroom and shut the door. We joked back and forth for only a few minutes before deciding, just to be safe, to hang up.

I was grateful to Ira for taking over my chicken coop chores for the three days it took to catch the egg-robber skunk in Ira's live trap. I didn't ask, and Ira didn't tell, the eventual fate of the attacking skunk. But I had no doubt he made sure I'd never have another face-to-face meeting with that particular rascal ever again. However, his presence lingered for a long time, as the chicken coop continued to smell like skunk for, well, like forever.

And here's another thing I can tell you for certain: after three days of cold-water plunges in the horse trough, I was never so happy to take a hot bath in a real house bathtub!

DOUBLE TROUBLE
AT SCHOOL

Whit had warned me to be prepared. "Here's the thing about small schools, Maggie, everybody in the entire school knows you and Dimwit got sprayed by a skunk. Lucky for you that you have a good sense of humor because you're gonna be teased." I was getting pretty good at reading Whit's tone, and I couldn't help but notice she was enjoying the prospect of her best friend about to become the laughingstock of the school. After only being at the Sandstone Springs school for just three weeks, I admit I was embarrassed and was dreading having to face everybody. And to make matters worse, I still had the sense that the offending skunk was sitting on my upper lip and continuously spraying his wretched mist into my nose. Even though Ira, Annie, and Whit all told me I didn't smell of skunk anymore, that lingering scent embedded in my nostrils wouldn't allow me to believe them.

Although I consider myself to be a good sport and capable of giving, as well as receiving, a good amount of teasing, I braced myself for Whit's predicted onslaught of mockery. I was pleasantly surprised by how kind and concerned the girls in my class were. The boys? Not so much. Nothing mean-spirited, mind you, but I was the constant recipient of pointing, nose-plugging, and laughter.

But the well-intentioned poking-fun banter went in a far different direction during lunch in the cafeteria. What changed? And what in the world did I do that landed me in the principal's office?

Well, it all came about as a result of me sitting next to an eighth-grade girl in the lunchroom that day. I had noticed from the very first day that a girl named Doris Stucky was ignored by most of the kids, always off by herself in between classes and in the cafeteria. As we got a little further into the first few weeks of the school year, I could see that not only was she being left out by the vast majority of kids, but a few of them were being downright cruel and mean to her. Not all of them, but definitely a few.

Doris was one of those kids who didn't get dealt a very good hand in life. First off, she was very overweight. We're all different, and I wouldn't normally say this about anyone, but she was also quite homely. Her glasses were as thick as Coke bottles, which made her wandering left eye even more noticeable. To make matters worse for her, she had an unpleasant body odor.

I've always had a soft spot for kids who, through no fault of their own, find themselves as outcasts, always excluded by their classmates and peers. I think it was early in the second week of school when I began to go over and sit with Doris during lunch. Not every day, but often enough to notice that my efforts to include her seemed to tick off my friends. Even Whit acted irritated, like I was breaking some kind of school code by being nice to Doris.

Anyway, during the few lunch hours I spent with her, I found Doris to be really, really shy. I also learned she was very smart. Even though the word "stupid" tends to get thrown into the mix when kids are tossing around names like "fat" and "ugly," she was anything but stupid. In fact, when I finally got her to trust me enough to have a conversation, she told me the only subjects she ever received B's were in English and History. I thought maybe she had difficulty reading because of her poor vision, so I offered to help her in those subjects if she would return the favor in Art. She was a beautiful artist, and as I have already told you, I'm pretty lousy at that subject.

"I'm sorry you got sprayed by a skunk, Maggie. I freak out just seeing one cross the road in front of the car. I can't even imagine coming face-to-face with one," she said when I sat down across from her on the cafeteria table. As usual, she was off all by herself, and I appreciated her sincere concern about my unfortunate mishap. I was in the process of explaining how Dimwit had rushed ahead of me into the chicken coop when Dexter Decker and Jake Baxter strolled up to our table.

Now, let me first tell you a little something about Dexter: he is a wide-as-he-is-tall eighth grader with a reputation for being the nastiest bully in junior high. Jake, on the other hand, is a skinny freshman who wants everyone to think he's a tough guy. He definitely has a mean streak to him, but from what I had seen so far, he only mouthed off when hiding behind Dexter.

"Well, take a look at this, Jake—Miss hot-shot San Francisco has finally found a friend," Dexter snarled in a loud, threatening voice, leaning over the table far enough that his large, square head was firmly planted within our personal space. Lifting his head to take an exaggerated sniff of the air, he continued. "Can't even tell how bad our very own skunk-sprayed Miss San Francisco smells 'cause big, fat, ugly Doris Stinky forgot her deodorant again, and her pits smell even worse than Miss Skunky Francisco does, pee-eww!"

"Yeah, pee-eww," echoed Jake, poking his head out from behind Dexter. "Big, fat, ugly, stupid Doris stinks so bad a guy can hardly tell how bad Miss Skunky Francisco smells."

Doris started whimpering, and I jumped over to her side of the table, wrapping my arm around her and pulling her in close. As Doris sobbed into my shoulder, I looked for the hall monitor, but he was nowhere to be found. I glanced hopefully toward the cafeteria entrance to see if Brock and the other freshman were coming in for lunch, but the doorway was empty.

"Yup, not surprised," Dexter said, the sarcasm in his voice practically dripping from his mouth. I found his obvious delight in making Doris cry to be sickening, and my anger meter was rapidly climbing. "Sure enough figures that anybody who's weird enough to live with the scar-faced monster, Ira Stone, would be weird enough to hang out with big, fat, ugly Doris Stinky!"

The loud-mouthed, one-sided conversation between the two bullies was getting the attention of my seventh- and eighth-grade classmates across the room. I was sure they could hear every word, but the fear-of-Dexter-look that was plastered on their faces made it clear I was on my own. There'd be no help coming from either the boys or the girls.

With my anger turning to outright rage, I suddenly didn't care if I was left to confront these brutes all by myself. After all, I'd dealt with similar types back in San Francisco, both from my old neighborhood and at the orphanage.

Dexter had three inches and thirty or forty pounds on me, but I wasn't about to sit there like a frightened puppy and listen to those creeps say mean stuff about Doris and Ira. As I prepared to make my move, I remembered the advice I had received from the toughest older boy at the orphanage:

"Hey, Stone," he had said, calling me over after he'd just seen me in a scuffle with a boy who had backed me into a corner and was punching me. "Fighting boys is different from the scratching and slapping that goes on when girls are fighting girls. If you're in a brawl with a guy, the first thing you do is kick him in the balls—that'll bring his hands down, so your second punch can be an uppercut to the jaw or a whack to the nose."

So, that's exactly what I did. I'm sure Dexter wasn't expecting any of the junior high boys to challenge him, much less a seventh-grade girl, so I caught him by surprise when I launched a foot to his you-know-what's. I immediately followed with a right-hand uppercut to his jaw. He was so stocky and solid that I wasn't able to knock him down with my first two blows, but it did stagger him enough that I was able to tackle him to the floor. I tried hard to keep hitting him with my fists, but he was too strong. He bellowed like a bull as he flipped me over and pinned my arms to the floor. Just as I was sure I was about to get a punch in the face, Jerry Miller, the thick-built, no-nonsense elementary and junior high principal, pulled him off me. "What in the world is going on here?" he shouted loudly. "The three of you in my office, right now!"

I couldn't believe it when both Dexter and Jake claimed total innocence—just minding their own business when I suddenly attacked them for no reason, is what they said. Just defending themselves from that crazed girl from California. *Yeah, right.*

"I'll get to the bottom of this, you can count on that!" Mr. Miller declared, sending us back to our classrooms with the promise that two things were going to happen: First, our parents (or grandparent in my case) would be called in; and second, there would be a punishment that would fit the crime.

I won't lie to you, Ira was the last person I wanted to see when school let out, but there he was, waiting for me at the entrance to school. I couldn't really tell how mad he was from the expression on his face, but I figured I was in deep doo-doo for breaking the school "no fighting" rule. There was nothing but silence until we were halfway home, and I suddenly blurted out, "What did Mr. Miller say? Did he tell you what my punishment is going to be? There are rules about fighting... am I going to be suspended or expelled from school?"

Ira must have driven another mile before he finally answered. "Well, he told me what the kids in the cafeteria had seen and heard. He told me what Decker and Baxter were up to and what they were doing to that poor Stuckey girl. He told me what you did about it."

We were turning into the lane when I just had to find out more about what Mr. Miller had said. "Am I going to be expelled?"

He didn't speak until he pulled Ol' Blue into its parking spot in front of the shop, shut off the engine, and shifted in the seat so that he was facing me. "First off, Maggie, I'm gol-dang proud of you for sticking up for Doris. No kid or person should ever be subjected to such meanness and cruelty. No sir, by God, that kind of thing can't and shouldn't be tolerated, not by you, not by me, not by anybody. Mr. Miller told me the Decker kid has been nothing but trouble ever since he's been in school and that it was about time somebody had the guts to stand up to him." Ira reported. He paused for a moment before continuing with a chuckle, "He just didn't figure it would be a girl that would take him on.

"As far as punishment goes, you're going to get the least penalty there is in the school handbook for fighting—you'll miss your Phys Ed class tomorrow. Jake Baxter is suspended from school for two days; Decker is out for a week, plus he'll be swampin' out the latrines for another week when he gets back."

"Did Mr. Miller say anything else?" I asked anxiously.

"Yeah, he said you not only stuck up for Doris but for your grandpa, too," Ira said. Then, with that lopsided grin of his spreading across the left side of his face, he added, "He also wondered if it was me who taught you how to throw that wicked kick-punch combination…said you'll be the first call he makes if Sandstone Springs ever starts a boxing or a karate team!"

We were halfway through supper that night when he suddenly put down his fork and said, "You know, Maggie, you don't always have to call me Ira. I mean, Ira's fine and all, but you can call me Papa, not that you have to, just if you want to, you know, sometimes…."

Just like when I found Gunsmoke and the bike in the barn on my birthday, I think he was kind of embarrassed when I jumped up from my chair, gave him a smooch on the cheek, and whispered into his hearing aid. "Haha, okay Ira, I'll add Papa to my list. Mind you, I'm not gonna go cold turkey and totally quit using Ira, because I'm pretty used to that now. But, you should expect more than a few 'Papas' coming from me in the future!"

Chapter 36

THE WEEK AFTER DEXTER

"I can't even believe you kicked that big jerk in the nuts!" Whit exclaimed excitedly when most of the junior high kids gathered around me as I walked into school the morning after the fight. "Dexter and Jake are such jerks. I'm glad they both got suspended from school, especially Dexter."

"Yeah, especially Dexter," Laura Rife chimed in. "Jake is just his puppet. He's not such a bad kid when he's not around Dexter. Anyway, I can't believe you just ripped into him like that! I was shaking in my boots when he was saying all that mean stuff about you and Doris, and I was all the way across the room!"

Yeah, I couldn't help but notice how you all rushed over to defend me and Doris, I thought. I guess I really didn't expect the girls to start throwing haymakers at a guy twice their size and strength, but what about the boys? Where were they?

Junior high boys can be so weird, but I have to admit I laughed as loud as anyone when four or five of the boys walked in front of our group of girls. They were all bent over and holding both hands over their crotches as they shuffled by, muttering, "Don't kick us, Stone, please don't crush the family jewels!" I thought it was pretty clever when the last boy in the line, class-clown seventh grader Dean Padget, pulled his hands back to show that he was wearing one of those baseball catcher's protective cups over his privates.

"Joke as much as you want, but I must have missed it when you big, brave boys hustled over to help the damsels in distress," said Whit sarcastically. "I think the reason you all disappeared was to go change your pants. You were all so scared of Dexter, you just sat there and messed your pants, didn't you?"

"I was just getting ready to go help when Mr. Miller came in and stopped the fight," declared Randy Restig indignantly.

"Yeah, me too," eighth grader Steve Crowder chimed in. "If Mr. Miller wouldn't have come in when he did, us guys would have joined the fight for sure."

Randy and Steve's "we were just about to spring into action" story didn't sound very convincing, and all the girls laughed when Sandy Barnhart mocked them with, "Yeah, it was too bad all you boys got mysteriously glued to that bench. If not for that, I'm sure just the sight of you brave fighters would have had not only Dexter but Muhammad Ali himself quaking in their shoes!"

The boys soon realized they were losing the verbal volley with the girls, and quickly slunk away. But I was surprised at how many of the high school boys stopped and patted me on the back in the halls during class changes. I didn't hear much of anything from the high school girls. "They're just jealous that a seventh grader is getting all this attention from the high school boys," is how Whit explained it. I didn't know if she was right, but I'd learned not to question Whit when it came to the inner workings of the school dynamics.

"Thank you for sticking up for me," Doris said when I sat with her at lunch. As usual, she was off by herself at the far end of the cafeteria. As a tear leaked from the corner of her eye, she added. "Nobody has ever done that, especially when it comes to Dexter and Jake picking on me. You're the only friend I have in the whole world, and I appreciate you being nice to me. Thank you."

As I reached over to squeeze her hand, I teared up when I saw Whit, Sandy, Laura, and several other junior high girls walking toward us, lunch trays in hand. Maybe taking on Dexter wasn't the worst thing I could have done after all.

Chapter 37

HOMECOMING AND SHIPPING CALVES

"You should come to Homecoming on Friday, Papa," I said to Ira as the special weekend approached. "Our football team is undefeated, you know. We're 4-0 and tied with Circle, that's who we're playing. It should be a great game." Although I was usually careful about bringing up Brock's name in front of him, I couldn't help but encourage Ira to watch him play. "You should really go see Brock, he's very good, especially for a freshman!"

"Hmm, well, I wouldn't mind takin' that game in, but as you know, we ship calves on Sunday, and I've got a pile a work to get done. Just like harvest is the only payday of the year for a grain farmer, selling the calves is the annual payday for us cattle ranchers."

It was the time of year for shipping calves, and it seemed like Ira was scheduled to help his fellow ranching neighbors round up and ship calves to market about two or three days a week during the whole month of October.

"So who's going to be helping us?" I asked.

"Whitfields, of course. Brock and his dad, along with the Bergstrom brothers over on Badger Creek. Maybe a few others, depending on their own schedules."

"What will Whit and I get to do?"

"You two can help Brock and Wyatt herd the cows from their fall pasture to the corrals behind the barn on Saturday. We need to work them on Sunday, give them their vaccinations and doctor any sickly calves and the like. Then we'll sort them off into separate steer and heifer pens and load 'em onto me and Wyatt's semi-trailers and get them to the livestock yard in town."

For an early October game, Homecoming day turned out to be a balmy fifty-five degrees with little or no wind. Brock had told me that the Circle Wildcats were the Buffaloes biggest rivals and a force to be reckoned with, as they had won the district championship the last few years. They had a big guy by the name of Roscoe Schindler, a senior headed to college next year on a football scholarship. He was like 230 pounds and played running-back and linebacker. Coach Lucero had said at the pep rally that we'd have to find a way to slow him down to have a chance to win.

Unfortunately, all the fun and hype of the Homecoming festivities—Thursday night bonfire, Friday morning parade and pep rally—were all for naught, as Roscoe Schindler and the Wildcats were too much for the Buffaloes to handle. When the smoke finally cleared, Circle took home a convincing 42-26 victory. Not that I expected him to be there, but Ira was nowhere to be seen.

I felt sorry for Brock when he showed up to help move cows on Saturday. He was so bruised and battered that he could barely get on and off his horse.

"You must have met up with Schindler a few too many times, eh Brock?" Ira asked, proving that he followed Sandstone Springs sports a little more than he liked to let on. "Heard ya' had four touchdowns, though."

Whit and I had fun at the shipping. We got to man the sorting gates, and then Whit showed her experienced touch in using the vaccine gun. The weather turned on Sunday, but the rain didn't start in earnest until all the neighbor helpers had loaded the calves in the trailers and headed out to the sale barn.

I was so busy putting away all the vaccine guns and other shipping day supplies in the tack room that I didn't even hear Brock come up behind me. "Here's some more stuff that Ira wants you to put away," he said, setting the box on top of the storage cabinet. Taking a quick glance over his shoulder to confirm we were alone, he pulled me close and surprised me with a kiss. "I've been thinking about that first kiss a lot lately and wanted to make sure I wasn't just dreaming," he murmured before leaning in a second time.

"Ah, if that was a dream, I hope to have the same one tonight. And again every night," I whispered in his ear before breaking our embrace. "We better go back out before Whit comes looking for me."

"No kidding!" Brock said with a grin. "Can't you just hear her making an announcement over the main office loud-speaker at school? "Attention all grades, attention all grades—Brock Boyce and Maggie Stone were seen kissing! I repeat, I repeat—Brock Boyce and Maggie Stone were seen kissing!""

I was so exhausted after the busy Homecoming and shipping weekend that I thought I'd fall asleep immediately after hitting the pillow, but visions of kissing Brock Boyce kept dancing in my head. I must have finally drifted into a happy slumber, as I don't remember Ira returning home with an empty trailer and a full wallet.

Chapter 38

SECRETS REVEALED

"I don't know, maybe it's because Thanksgiving and Christmas holidays are just around the corner. Maybe that's why I'm kind of blue," I tried to explain to Whit as we were getting ready for bed. Ira was stuck in Broadus for the night, having to wait to get the results of a veterinarian test before bringing home a bull he had just purchased. I was glad he called Annie to ask if I could spend the night at the Whitfields. "I haven't seen my mom in so long, two hundred twenty-four days, to be exact. She went into her coma on April fourteenth, Whit. I mark off every day on my calendar, so I know it's been exactly two hundred twenty-four days."

"I'm so sorry, that must be hard to live with," Whit said softly as we climbed under the covers on the chilly, pre-Thanksgiving November evening. "As mad as I get at my mother for sticking her big nose into my business and bossing me around all the time, I can't even imagine not having my mom around."

This wasn't the first time over the last few weeks that Whit had mentioned I seemed down in the dumps. Part of it was no doubt the Brock situation, but I wasn't about to talk with Whit about that. However, I did feel I could talk about my mom's situation with her. After all, despite some of our ups and downs, she was definitely my best friend in Sandstone Springs. It didn't take too much convincing for me to open up and spill my guts.

"Do you know what scares me, Whit? Sometimes it seems as if April 14th was just yesterday. Other times it seems like years ago. On days when the memories seem recent, I can clearly see her face. I can see her smile and hear her laugh. I can hear her voice, especially her singing voice, strong and powerful, just like Cher, Mamma Cass, or Patsy Cline. But I can also see the other end of her mood swings; a face of pain and sadness, and reddened eyes from a silent cry she made sure I never saw. And worst of all, the lifeless look of when in a spell.

"Yet other days, all memories of her, both good and bad, are cloudy. It's like they fade in and out, never completely coming into focus. It frightens me when I can't really remember her face; her voice; her hair; her scent. Does that make any sense? I'm sorry, I know I'm rambling."

"Yes, you explained it very well, and I kind of get the part where sometimes the fourteenth of April can seem either near or far in your memory," Whit said in an understanding voice. "You mentioned your mom being sad. Was she sad a lot of the time? Do you think that's why she would go into those spells?"

"Well, as I look back now, she did seem sad quite a bit of the time," I answered thoughtfully. "Maybe she was depressed, or something like that. And the doctors did say it's possible her spells could be caused by her mind wanting to escape from a bad experience in her past, like maybe the whole pregnancy thing.

You know, whatever it was that happened to cause her to run away from home and have me in San Francisco. But again, I don't think anyone really knows for sure.

"All I really know is that my mom has been in a coma for two hundred twenty-four days. And that's really weird because none of her other spells even lasted twenty-four hours. So what's going to happen? Is she gonna just stay asleep until she dies of old age? And what is she going to be like if and when she ever wakes up? Will she even remember me or anything about our old life together?"

"Oh Maggie, I'm so sorry," said Whit, tears streaming down both of our cheeks as she comforted me with a hug. I don't know how long I sobbed into her shoulder before I finally got a grip on my emotional outburst. We lay quietly in bed for a time, each mulling our own thoughts until Whit asked, "Just tell me to shut up if I'm being too nosey, but do you ever wonder about your dad? I mean, you don't have any idea who your dad is, do you?"

Before I had time to respond, Whit kept on rolling. "Mom said she thought Lillian is the only one who truly knows who your father is. I can't imagine how hard it is not to have either a mom or a dad. I mean, I know you have a mom and a dad, but you know what I'm saying, you don't know who your dad is, and your mom isn't available to you right now."

"It's okay, you're not being too nosey," I replied honestly. I didn't say anything about Annie telling me on our shopping trip that my dad was probably some guy from Miles City or Glendive. "In fact, it feels pretty darn good to finally talk about all of this with someone. So, here's the deal, even though I'm obviously used to not having a dad in my life, it doesn't mean I don't wonder who he might be. And yes, I often think about what it must be like to have a real father. I mean, I admit it makes me jealous sometimes to see you and your sisters with your dad. I can see how much you all love each other, and it makes me sad to know I'll never have that," I professed, then added with a laugh, "I'm always eyeing men around Sandstone Springs that are of about the right age to possibly be my dad. Don't you even think about telling anybody else this, but I even took an extra close look at Mr. Restig and Mr. Boyce—just to see if they had any features that could maybe link them to me!"

We talked well into the night, and I felt so much better after getting a whole bunch of excess baggage off my chest. I even told Whit some of my other major concerns; like how guilty I felt about being mad at God for not waking up my mom and for not answering my prayers. I explained the horrible dream that was becoming more frequent. The one where the memories of my old life in San Francisco were loaded in the hull of a ship that was drifting further and further from shore, slowly disappearing into the distant swells of the sea.

"I've told you about Cho Jeong, my best friend in San Francisco, right? Well, we used to write to each other almost every week for the first few months after I moved here. Then it went to only a few times a month. I think the last letter I either wrote or received was way back in early October. Anyway, just another example of how my old life with my mom and friends seems to be getting further out of reach. Am I just being paranoid, or acting like a big baby over all this?"

"Now you stop that right now! Of course you're not being a baby. Your whole world has been turned upside down, and you've handled everything better than me or any other kid our age could have. I can't believe how well you've adapted to living here, with your mom's situation and you being a city girl and all. And being ticked off at God? That's only natural in a situation like yours. As the Minister at our church says, God works in mysterious ways, so I'd keep at it with the prayers and wouldn't give up on Him just yet. And the letters with Cho? Hey, you now live a thousand miles apart. You are in very different worlds, so it's just natural that you're not in touch as often. Doesn't mean she's not your friend anymore. And speaking of being jealous, everybody here likes you, and it kind of ticks me off that you can get sprayed by a skunk, get in trouble at school for kicking a guy in the nuts, and come out smelling like a rose. Not only that, but you've got the coolest guy in the whole school falling at your feet!"

I was glad the lights were out, as I'm sure my cheeks reddened with the reference to Brock. I lay back on my pillow, the mattress of the queen-size bed swallowing the weight of my exhausted body. *Whit certainly has a way of making one's problems seem more manageable* was the last thought I had before drifting into a deep slumber.

But my eyes opened wide when Whit brought up the one thing I didn't want to discuss. "And Maggie, I'm really sorry about the Brock situation, I know you guys had a thing going on, and I'm sure it hurts to see him holding hands with Amber Hartford every time you see them in the halls. How do you ever go back to dating a seventh or eighth grader after going out with the coolest guy in the whole school? Add all this to your situation with your mother. No wonder you've got the blues."

I didn't respond, and fortunately, Whit got the unspoken message to let sleeping dogs lie. But my much-needed sleep was delayed when the memories of the day after shipping calves came flooding back. Brock had left a note in my locker, asking me to meet him at his pickup after school. I could tell right away something was wrong by the look on his face.

"Ah, ah, Maggie, I really like you. I mean it, I really do, b-but I don't think we should go out just now. I mean, it's just that maybe I'm too old, or you're too young, however you want to look at it, but I think we should cool it for now. You know, just for a while, like for a year or two. And maybe, you know, maybe we should date other people in the meantime...."

After the initial jolt, I tried to act like it was something I'd also been thinking about. I tried to pretend the news he'd just delivered was no big deal. "I've been wondering about that very thing," I said, trying to suppress the surprise and disappointment in my voice. "W-with me only being in the seventh grade and all. Yeah, you're right. We should just cool it for a while and go out with other people."

How could I be so stupid? I thought, pulling my hand away when he tried to take it as I turned to leave. *I'm such an idiot! Why did I think he could really like a kid in seventh grade? Why would he like some junior high transfer from San Francisco when he could have the pick of the high school litter?*

And Whit was right; I was devastated when less than a week after our breakup, I passed the hand-holding Brock and Amber in the hall. I tried to hold back the tears as I envisioned something I wasn't yet ready to emotionally handle—the two of them kissing.

Chapter 39

HOLIDAYS IN SANDSTONE SPRINGS

As I had come to learn, Ira was always invited to the Whitfields for Thanksgiving and Christmas dinners. Both holidays came and went without any good news from San Francisco. Despite the disappointment of my prayers going unanswered yet again, I tried to look at the bright side of my first Christmas in Montana. Ira had surprised me one early December day by giving me fifteen dollars to buy Christmas gifts.

When Annie took Whit and I into Sandstone Springs to do a little shopping the next day, that was more than enough to get Ira a new pair of work gloves and a good set of earmuffs from the Sandstone Springs Mercantile. I had drawn Laura Rife in our seventh-grade class gift exchange and used what was left of my fifteen-dollar allowance to purchase Laura, Sandy and Whit a yummy selection of Percy's taffy candy.

Even Ira seemed to be in the Christmas spirit, showing up one evening with a Christmas tree he had purchased from the Sandstone Springs Boy Scouts Club. He even bought some new lights and tinsel for me and Whit to decorate with. One of the main town events of the season was the school Christmas Concert. Grades six through eight were combined to do a few Christmas numbers prior to the high school chorus program. Again, I'm no Lillian Stone when it comes to singing, and I was pretty nervous when the curtain rose and there wasn't an empty seat in the auditorium. I spotted Dr. and Mrs. Rath in the audience, and knew they were excited to watch their fine soprano granddaughter Ginny sing *Silent Night* in a duet with Doris Stuckey.

Mrs. Clifford, our junior high chorus teacher, had come to me several weeks prior to ask for assistance in convincing Doris to share her beautiful voice with the community. I think I did a heck of a sales job, as Doris was so self-conscious of her appearance that she was extremely reluctant to have the spotlight focused on her in a duet. I think Doris felt more comfortable when Ginny, Whit and I brought in beautician Betty Delany to do her hair and makeup.

Speaking of Doris, here's the thing I'm most proud of since starting school at Sandstone Springs: Ever since I stood up for Doris by taking on the school bullies Dexter Decker and Jake Baxter, I've noticed a good number of the students being nice to her and including her in activities. Even Mrs. Clifford mentioned it. I guess that's why she thought I'd have the best chance convincing Doris to sing the duet.

I continued to search the audience and found Mrs. Walker sitting near the Raths. She gave me a little wave when we made eye contact. But I wasn't prepared for the biggest surprise guest of the night. I almost fell over backward when my eyes adjusted to the light, and I spotted none other than Mr. Ira Stone sitting with Annie in the back row. I probably don't have to tell you that I was touched to see his presence; good thing we had to change gears and start singing or I might have started to cry. I found it interesting when, after the program, both Mrs. Rath and Mrs. Walker mentioned how nice it was to see Ira attending school and community events again.

I was excited to wake up on Christmas morning to see that "Santa" had dropped off some gifts. Ira was just as generous as he was on my birthday, giving me a pretty Navajo saddle blanket for Gunsmoke, as well as an insulated pair of coveralls and boots to keep me warm while doing chores. He seemed to like the practical gifts I had chosen for him (if there's one thing Ira is, it's practical!).

Just like on Thanksgiving Day, we took our Christmas meal over at the Whitfields. We had a wonderful day filled with fun and laughter. I felt guilty about all the presents I got from our nearest neighbors: A stocking hat and mittens from Whit, a colorful winter sweater from Annie, and a new chew bone for Dimwit from the younger Whitfield girls.

But the levity of the day vanished when Ira called me into the living room upon returning from the shop. "Maggie, I hate to bring this up on Christmas Day, but I've been wantin' to talk to you about this for quite some time now. I know you been a-hopin' and praying for some good news from San Francisco about your mom. Now don't get me wrong, I don't ever want you to give up hope or quit praying for your mother to come out of this spell, but she's been in this coma for 'bout eight or nine months now. As much as I hate to even suggest it, I think the time has come for you to consider the possibility that she might not wake up anytime soon, maybe not for months. Maybe not for years. And God forbid, maybe not ever."

I couldn't help it; the tears started to stream down my face when he stood up from his chair and, for the first time, initiated a long hug. I knew he was right about the need to face up to the real possibility that my mom might not wake for a long time, or, as he said, maybe never. Unfortunately, knowing he was right and actually accepting the realities of his message were two different things entirely.

"Life can be hard and cruel sometimes," he said as he continued to softly pat me on the back. "Again, I don't want you to give up hope, but I'm just suggesting you might want to prepare yourself for this spell to continue for some time."

Chapter 40

THE CALL I'VE BEEN WAITING FOR

7:52 am, Saturday, January 17, 1970—271 days

I'll never forget the time, day, date and the number of days my mom had been in a coma when the phone rang that cold January morning. I had just helped Ira feed the cows their daily ration of hay by pulling the trailer of hay bales with the tractor. Luckily, we fed the hay in a flat and level pasture just behind the barn corrals, so I only had to worry about driving slowly in wide circles while Ira cut the bale-strings and threw out the hay from the trailer. We had just finished the feeding and had wiggled out of our insulated coveralls and were slipping into our comfy X-mas moccasins when we heard the phone ring from the mudroom.

"Now which one of your knot head friends would be calling this early on a Saturday morning?" Ira gruffly asked.

"I don't know. I'm not expecting a call from anyone," I replied, trying to pull on the second slipper as I opened the door and hopped to the phone.

"Is this the Stone residence?" came the stern and important sounding female voice on the other end of the line.

"Ah, yes, this is the Stone residence, Maggie Stone speaking.

"Hello. This is Andrea from Dr. Drummond's office at San Francisco General. I wish to speak to Mr. Ira Stone. Is he by chance available?"

"It's for you! It's a lady from Dr. Drummond's office!" I said excitedly in a loud whisper while cupping the speaker end of the phone with my hand.

Ira pulled my kitchen table chair next to his and motioned for me to sit. With our heads close together and holding the phone between us so I could better listen in, he said. "This is Ira Stone. With whom am I speaking?"

"This is Andrea from Dr. Drummond's office. Dr. Drummond would like to speak with you. Could you please hold for a moment?

I had to lean in even closer to hear the soft-spoken doctor, but I quietly clapped my hands in joy when I heard him say, "I have some news on Lillian. I was alerted just a few hours ago by one of our nurses on the floor that Lillian has regained consciousness, at least to some degree. I just completed an evaluation, to include some testing. She is somewhat responsive to standard neurological tests, pupils are responsive, reflexes seem to be intact, and she responds at least partially to most sensory stimuli. In addition, we're seeing an uptick in brain wave activity."

I was about to scream for joy and turn a cartwheel and had a million questions to ask, but Ira sternly shushed me with a finger to his lip. "I see," said Ira. "That sounds like encouraging news, especially considerin' she's been in that spell for 'bout nine months now."

"Can we go see her?" I mouthed, unable to sit still and stay quiet. "Ask him if we can go see her!"

After shushing me again, Ira turned the phone so I could listen to the doctor's response. "While this awakening is indeed encouraging, I urge you not to get overly optimistic yet. While Lillian is awake and responding to certain stimuli, she is not overly alert and has not yet spoken. She's not able to feed herself, so we've had to continue with tube feedings. Until she speaks, we don't have any way to gauge the level of her mental status; things like memory retention and whether she would be capable of recognizing family and friends. And if she does possess some degree of recognition, we have no way of knowing at this point how much of the relationship history she might recall. I'm also sorry to report that she has little to no awareness of her immediate surroundings.

"I don't mean to be discouraging, Mr. Stone, but I want to be honest and forthright about this change in her condition. Is it possible she could fully snap out of this and, at some point down the line, return to her old self? Possible? Yes. Probable? Likely not, as the data on these kinds of conditions would suggest a full mental recovery to be less than five percent. Is it also possible she could, at any time, lapse back into a coma for another extended period of time. Unfortunately, the odds of that are much higher than that of a full recovery."

"Well, I dang sure appreciate you being square with us and givin' us the truthful lowdown," Ira said, using one of his rough and calloused forefingers to wipe away the tears that were beginning to leak from my eyes. "But here's the thing, Doc. I got my thirteen-year-old granddaughter Maggie—Lillian's girl—sitting here pretty dad-gum excited about her mom coming out of her spell. I know Lillian ain't anywhere near back to her normal self, but is there any reason why we couldn't hop on a plane and come down to see her?"

My tears dried up quickly when I heard Dr. Drummond's response. "No reason whatsoever, Mr. Stone. In fact, I was about to suggest that. The data also shows a better chance of recovery when a loved one comes to visit. Good day, Mr. Stone. We'll tell Lillian you're coming, and I look forward to seeing you and young Maggie soon."

Chapter 41

THE TRIP TO
SAN FRANCISCO

I won't lie, I was shaking in my boots as the pilot taxied the big old rattly plane out to the runway for take-off. As I've told you previously, I'm not usually a scaredy-cat about trying something new, but my first ride on an airplane? Definitely a scaredy-cat!

At first, I felt somewhat comforted by sitting next to Ira until I noticed his gnarly, sun-darkened knuckles were as white as Bugs Bunny's two front teeth from the death grip he was putting on the armrests. He had confessed to me earlier that he definitely preferred dirt to air under his boots.

"Didn't care much for traveling on the water either," he had declared on our trip to the Billings airport, referring to when he and his fellow soldiers were shipped to France during WWI. "Only been on one plane ride before this, and that was when I flew your grandmother back to Knoxville, Tennessee for her sister's funeral. I can already tell I'm not gonna like this trip any better."

"Ohhh, dear God," I hissed under my breath. I pried Ira's hand off the armrest and squeezed it with both hands as the rapidly increasing ground speed of the plane pressed our backs against the seats. With our legs stretched out and stiff as boards, we braced ourselves as we gradually rose from the runway to the sky. I'm not sure either of us breathed until the old bird had shaken, shimmied, and rattled its way to flying altitude.

"You can give me my hand back now," Ira suggested when it became apparent we had survived the take-off.

"Oops, sorry about that," I muttered, kneading my hands in an effort to work some blood back into my fingers and hands. I was already dreading the landing at Salt Lake City, not to mention going through the whole process again on the second leg of the trip to San Francisco. At least the stewardesses were creating a diversion for us fly-fearful passengers by working their way down the aisle with peanuts, pretzels, and pop.

"Don't want ya' to get your hopes up too much about your mom, Maggie," Ira said quietly. "Like the Doc said, she might not be any more aware of things than she was when they called us a few days back. I think you need to prepare yourself; she might not recognize you. She might not be talking yet. I hope I'm wrong, but again, I don't want ya' to be disappointed if she ain't like you remember."

"I know, I know. But I don't think it hurts to hope for the best either," I replied, knowing deep down inside that he was giving me solid advice. Other than ordering our snacks and drinks, neither of us spoke for a long time. Maybe Ira's suggestion got me thinking, as I used the silence of the remaining trip to grapple with a thought that had been tugging at my mind for the two days since we received the call from the hospital.

What if mom's awake when we get there? What if she's acting like her normal self, just like she used to be after coming out of a spell? What if the doctors say she can leave the hospital? What if she wants me to stay in San Francisco, find a new apartment, and go back to my old school?

I knew I would be ecstatic if that was really what we found when we got to the hospital, but something kept gnawing at me. Something was causing me to hesitate, and I knew I needed to address it in my own mind. And I needed to get it sorted out before we arrived in San Francisco.

After mulling everything over, the truth of the matter was that I was confused over my internal reaction to the mom-wakes-up-and-everything-goes-back-to-normal scenario. I realized the more time spent in living my new life, the further my old life got pushed to the back of the line. After all, I hadn't lived my previous life for nine whole months now—278 days, to be exact. To look at it another way, I'd been living my new life for the last 278 days. And if I was being completely honest with myself, I was starting to enjoy my new life. After some really rough patches in those first few months with Ira, things seemed to be smoothing out. It took a good while, but Ira and I were not only getting used to each other, we were actually developing a real grandfather/granddaughter relationship. While the ranch, the animals, the school, the people, the town of Sandstone Springs, and the whole Montana thing was frightfully new and foreign at first, I have come to feel that I am maybe—just maybe—starting to fit in. I've found I not only enjoy working with the animals on the ranch but seem to have a natural knack for it. I have made new besties in Dimwit and Whit and now have many other friends at school.

In the unlikely event that Mom totally snaps out of her spell and we return to our old life, it would not only be sad but gut-wrenching to leave Whit and the rest of my new friends, whether they be human or animal. And Ira? It would be especially hard to leave Ira. I'd worry about him being all alone. I think he's gotten used to having me around and would miss me if I wasn't there. I would have never said that a few months ago, but now I believe it's true.

But what about Mom? She would need me for sure, probably more than Ira would. She had become quite dependent on me leading up to the last spell, and who knows how long or how often we might have to deal with similar lapses going forward. Yes, she'd definitely need me more than ever, especially since I'm almost a full year older now and capable of taking on even more household responsibilities.

But what if my mom only partially recovered from the coma? What if she improved enough to not have to stay in the hospital, but not be well enough to go back to work and live our normal life? What if she needed a lot of care? Would Ira be okay with bringing her to the ranch to live with us?

There was only one way to find out. He was deep in thought when I squeezed his forearm and anxiously asked, "Ira, what if mom only improves enough to get out of the hospital, but isn't well enough to go back to our old life… you know, work at Del's or sing with the band? What if she needs a place to live and someone to take care of her? If that happens, could we bring her to the ranch with us? Could we?"

I can't even tell you how relieved I was when he turned toward me and replied, "Of course, Maggie. We could dang-sure bring her home with us. I've actually been thinkin' about that scenario, too. To be honest, it's more likely to happen than a complete recovery."

"We're going to have a little turbulence as we make our descent into San Francisco," the pilot announced after the third big jolt of the last few minutes had me clutching Ira's hand again. "Please keep your seatbelts fastened and avoid moving about the cabin."

I didn't give Ira's hand back until the wheels finally bounced off the runway and we started to slowly taxi into the terminal. I was glad I'd just had that little chat with myself and Ira, and I recognized that a potential dilemma could develop with my living situation. If it came to it, I would, of course, be happy for my mom to come out of her spell and have a complete recovery. I would also know the proper thing for me to do would be to go back to San Francisco and be there for my mother, even if I would rather be in Montana. Even if I'd be worried about leaving Ira. And I was thrilled to hear Ira would be okay with Mom coming home to the ranch should that be her level of recovery.

As we came to a stuttering stop at our gate, I decided to take Ira's advice from back when I was constantly fretting about whether Dimwit would go after another rattlesnake again: "Ain't no sense worrying yourself sick over somethin' that may or may not happen down the road. Best to just cross that bridge when ya' come to it."

Chapter 42

ANOTHER VISIT
TO THE PSYCH WARD

It seemed like we were waiting forever on the tarmac before deboarding the plane in San Francisco, and I was getting antsy and super excited to see not only my mom but to reunite with Cho for the first time in months.

"Sun-Ju said they were going to stop by the motel and have dinner with us tonight, right Papa?" I asked anxiously.

"Nothin' I know of has changed since ya' asked me that two minutes ago, so yes, I reckon they'll be waitin' for us at the motel," Ira said, obviously getting annoyed at my frequent repeat questions.

"It's been almost nine months since I've seen you—you've grown so much!" I exclaimed to Cho after answering the knock on our motel room door and exchanging a bear hug. "I'm sorry I haven't written to you as often as I should have."

"I know, I know, I should have sent more letters, too. And yes, I've grown at least two inches since I saw you last, but I see I'm still a good six inches shorter than you," she laughed, raising up on her tiptoes in an attempt to appear taller. "You look stronger—must be from all those chores you've been doing at the ranch. I've gotten stronger from lugging all those dishes around at Del's, too. Did I tell you that Del is letting me do some waitressing? It's especially good because you get more tips than busing tables. I wanted to call and tell you about it, but my parents wouldn't let me. They say they can't afford the long-distance phone charges."

"Yeah, same here," I said, lowering my voice so that Ira couldn't hear what we were saying. "Ira doesn't even like it when I make local calls. The only long-distance calls Grandpa allows is to the hospital to check on my mom."

We had so much news to catch up on that Cho and I huddled together and blabbered the entire dinner. We were so absorbed in our own conversation that I almost didn't notice how little Ira and Sun-Ju had to say to each other. I had always wondered how much my mom had told Sun-Ju about her icy relationship with Ira.

"Maggie honey, I saw your mother this morning and you need to prepare yourself," Sun-Ju said to me as we walked back from the restaurant to our motel room. "She is conscious, but only barely. If you are expecting her to look like she used to be after coming out of a spell, well, it's nothing like that. She is thin… to be truthful, she's actually quite frail. I'm telling you this because I don't want you to go in there with an unrealistic expectation."

Even with Sun-Ju's warning from the night before, I wasn't prepared for what we saw when we entered the hospital room. After the nurse left the room and left us to ourselves, Ira reached out and gently pulled me to his side. As we cautiously moved closer to the bed, I heard him gasp. I couldn't shut off the spigot of tears as I looked down at what was supposed to be my mother. I wasn't even sure it was her ghost. Although she was always small and thin, whatever and whoever it was that lay before me was nothing more than skin and bone.

She had a tube down her throat, and more tubes came from a plastic bag hooked to a stand above her head. Those tubes were connected to needles stuck in her arms, mainly on the black-and-blue inside of her elbows. Wires were clipped to patches that were glued to the bare spots between what few straggly strands of hair remained. I assumed the wires were used to measure the brain waves that Dr. Drummond had mentioned on the phone. Her eyes were open, but I could tell they did not see. Sad eyes—sunken deep within the eye sockets—fixed and motionless, staring vacantly at some unknown point in the distance.

I don't know how long we stood there staring and crying before I remembered to talk to her, like Sun-Ju had first taught me when the spells began. "Uh-uh, hi Mom," I stammered, glancing up at Ira for some sign of support. He looked about as comfortable as a mouse in a room full of cats, so I just forged ahead, knowing I'd get no help from him. "Grandpa is here, Mom. Like I told you in the letters, he came and got me from the orphanage when you didn't come out of your spell. We've been at the ranch in Montana, haven't we, Papa? Papa and I love you, and we are hoping and praying that you will come all the way out of this spell real soon."

I stole a quick look at Ira. He was as stiff as the Tin Man in the Wizard of Oz but nodded, so I continued on. "I'm doing well in school at Sandstone Springs. Everyone in town still remembers how good of a singer you are, don't they, Papa? As you know, I can't sing like you, but I am playing the clarinet in the band. I'm not very good at it—I'm better at shooting baskets than playing the clarinet, that's for sure."

For the first time since we'd been in the room, Ira thawed just enough to shuffle his feet and stutter, "Yup, Maggie is a doggone good basketball shooter, that's for sure. Shoots better than most of the boys in high school already, at least that's what Brock Boyce says. And considerin' she's a beginner, she's doing just fine on that clarinet, too. She does real darn good with all the animals, too. Especially Dimwit… he's the ranch dog."

We paused for a moment, both Ira and I searching for even the slightest indication that she might be processing any of the one-sided conversation. Seeing no response, I continued, "Here's the thing, Mom. Papa and I have talked about this already, and we think if you came out of this spell enough to be… well, what I mean is, get well enough to get out of the hospital, that way you could come to the ranch and we could take care of you until you're back to your old self, right Papa?"

"Yep, we dang-sure could," replied Ira softly, nodding his head in agreement. "We could have your room all ready for you in no time."

We searched again for a reaction, but her eyes didn't blink, and she continued to stare lifelessly toward something in the far distance. It was almost a relief when we heard a knock on the door. Dr. Drummond entered, shook Ira's hand, and gave me a kind pat on the shoulder before speaking.

"I wish I could say there has been improvement since I talked to you this past Saturday, but I'm afraid her condition has remained unchanged. I also wish I had a crystal ball, but as I've said before, there simply isn't any way of knowing if she'll stay the same, get better, or fall back into the same deep coma she's been in for the past nine months."

"I understand, we understand," said Ira softly, glancing at me for confirmation. "If I could ask a question; she looks so thin, so weak and gaunt. I mean, I ain't no doctor, but you sure she don't have some kind of cancer or one of those brain tumors?"

"We've just run all the tests and taken all the appropriate X-rays to check for such things, and there's still no evidence of brain tumors or cancer at this time. All we can do now is to keep her here, where she can continue to get the high level of continuous care that her current condition requires."

"I see. I figure this is where she best be, at least for now," agreed Ira. "That being the case, we'll most likely be headin' back to Montana tomorrow, so I trust you'll keep us updated if there is any change, one way or the other, in her condition?"

"Yes sir, we most certainly will," replied the doctor. Then, handing me a Kleenex to wipe the tears from my cheek, he said in his kind, soft voice. "Maggie, I'm so very sorry. I know this must be hard for you to see your mother like this. But you need to stay strong for your mother, and for your grandpa too, okay?"

The plane ride home was long, especially since a heavy fog hung over San Francisco, delaying our scheduled departure to Billings by two hours. I used the hustle and bustle of the airport to distract me from thinking about my mom, or rather, what was left of her.

Ira only spoke to complain about the prices of everything in the airport shops. "Good Lord. Never thought I'd see the day it would cost a guy dang near a buck to grab a cup of java and a newspaper. And a buck-seventy-five for a measly burger and a few greasy fries? Highway robbery, if ya' ask me."

When you factor in the almost four-hour drive from Billings to the ranch, we spent the whole day traveling back from San Francisco. I was mentally and physically exhausted by the time we got home but didn't climb in bed until I retrieved all the rag dolls from my mom's room. I needed something, anything from my mom's past, to help erase the stubborn ghost-like vision of her in the hospital bed, hooked up to all those tubes and aimlessly staring off into space.

Chapter 43

BROCK EXPLAINS
THE BREAKUP

"**G**uess what, Ira?" I shouted excitedly as I entered the shop, then forging ahead before giving him a chance to respond. "We have district tournaments coming up this week, and guess what the halftime entertainment will be for our game with Richey on Thursday afternoon? Go ahead and guess!"

"Even if you stopped talking long enough to take a breath of air and give me a chance to answer, I ain't got no idea whatsoever of what the halftime entertainment will be for the Richey game," he said with a sigh and a look of exasperation. "But I'm a-thinkin' I'm about to find out."

It had been a month since the trip to San Francisco, and there had been no change in my mom's situation. "Still semi-conscious and responding to some neurological stimuli, but otherwise no notable improvement or deterioration in her condition" was the usual broken-record weekly report. I admit to being down in the dumps for the first few weeks after the trip. Even Ira seemed unusually quiet and reserved and never spoke of the awful day we had spent at the hospital. Whit and my friends at school tried their best to cheer me up, but it took a chat with Annie a week or so after returning from San Francisco to get me back on track.

"Maggie, I know it's hard to see your mom like this, especially when there's really no end in sight to her current condition. But here's the thing—she wouldn't want you moping around being sad and always worrying about her. She would want you to live your life to the fullest. She would want you to immerse yourself in your studies and school activities. So, honey, as hard as it might be, it's time to get living again. I'm reminded of what your grandpa wisely advised a number of years ago when I was worrying myself sick over my dad's failing health, and I quote: 'Ain't nothin' good can come of frettin' 'over what ya' can't control.' Easier said than done, but I found that actively engaging in living life was far preferable to being sad and depressed."

"Okay Papa, here's the deal; Natalie Niswanger, she's a junior, you know, cornered me in the hall and said the Sandstone Springs and Richey high school girls get to play a ten-minute basketball game at the halftime of our boys' game. And guess what else? She asked me to play on their team! I'll be the only junior high girl on either team. Can you believe that? I'm so excited I can hardly stand it!"

"Imagine that, Maggie Stone being excited by something. Will wonders ever cease?" he deadpanned, quickly pulling back as I stepped toward him to throw a playful punch. "So how are those high school gals dealing with having a punk seventh grader on their team?"

"Tracy Rindal didn't take the news very well, I can tell you that for sure," I confirmed. "Like Whit said, she'd rather pass a kidney stone than pass the basketball to me. Anyway, Mr. Miller has agreed to be our coach, and we are going to practice during the eighth period tomorrow and Wednesday. And do you know what else Brock and Mr. Miller told me?"

"Nope, no idea whatsoever."

"You sure aren't one for guessing, are you?" I said teasingly. "Anyway, they both say that our district might be playing girls' basketball as soon as my freshman year, so I'll be able to play all four years of high school! Can you believe that? And Brock says he'll help me practice and improve my game. Oh yeah, one more thing, Mr. Miller says the Montana High School Association is also considering bringing on volleyball as a sanctioned sport for girls. Wouldn't that be groovy?"

"Yep, girls getting to play sports like basketball and volleyball is, well, groooovyy," Ira commented, dragging out my hippie word.

After having our first official practice, I was pretty skeptical of our team's chances against the Richey girls. Including me, we only had five girls sign up. Brock's new girlfriend, Amber Hartford, was the lone senior, and Tracy Rindal and Natalie Niswanger were the juniors. Sophomore Liz Landers and yours truly filled out the roster. Mr. Miller rolled his eyes when realizing Amber and I were the only two who wouldn't dribble the ball off our feet in a lay-up drill. I think his shiny bald head turned even redder in frustration when I was the only player to actually make a basket during the lay-up exercise.

Speaking of Brock, the pain of the breakup sucker punch was somewhat eased the day after we returned from visiting my mom in San Francisco General. As was his method of contact, he left another "meet me at my pickup in the parking lot after school" note in my locker.

There were more than a few moments of awkward silence after I climbed in the passenger door, but Brock finally broke the ice. "I heard your mother has regained consciousness. Sorry to hear she's not had a complete recovery. And I'm sorry she's not able to talk or eat without the feeding tube. I imagine you were hoping she would be more alert?"

I was curious as to where he'd heard such detailed information but didn't ask. I didn't want to tear up, but the faucet just turned on. "Th-thanks, Brock. Yes, it's kind of a double-edged sword. It's good that she's conscious, but sh-she looks horrible. She is so ungodly thin—I-I didn't hardly recognize her!"

He reached out his arms, and that was all it took. At that moment, I didn't care that he'd tossed me aside for Amber. I didn't care that I'd sworn never to embarrass myself again by letting him hold me. I just collapsed into his arms and openly wept on his chest. "It's okay, Maggie. Let it all out, it's okay," he softly whispered. I don't know how long he held me until I finally quit sobbing, and we separated.

"I'm so sorry for bawling all over your sweater," I said, feeling embarrassed and trying to make light of it at the same time.

"No worries, I just feel so bad for you. I can't even imagine if I had to see my mother like that."

We chatted about my mom's situation for quite some time before Brock placed his hands on my shoulders and said, "Maggie, I have something to tell you. I've wanted to tell you every day since I dropped the bombshell on you, but I just couldn't. I had to wait until I was sure, sure that everything was good with you and Ira."

"What is it? What about Ira? What are you talking about?" I asked, curiosity getting the best of me.

"Well, the reason I broke things off with us was, ah-ah, was because of Ira. Remember that night at your shipping when we were alone in the tack room? When we kissed?"

"Trust me, I remember," I said sarcastically.

"As it turns out, we weren't alone. Ira had to come back to the barn to pick up something. He saw us, Maggie. He saw us kissing."

"You're kidding me, right?

"I wish I was. Anyway, he called me a couple of days later and asked to meet at our mailbox. That's when he told me he'd seen us kissing. You know how he gets sometimes. I mean, he wasn't exactly mad, but he told me in no uncertain terms that I was too old, and you were too young. He told me he liked me and that you were a wonderful girl, and if we were two years older, he'd be fine with us dating. But I was ordered to break off 'whatever it is that's a-goin' on between the two of ya's' immediately. He said he didn't want to see either me or my puckered lips sneaking around the Stone place until you were a freshman!"

"I am so embarrassed! I can't believe he saw us! Why didn't you tell me?"

"I wasn't sure just how you and Ira were getting along," Brock confessed. "I was afraid you'd be mad at him, and it would mess up whatever relationship you two had started to build. I thought it best for you to be mad at me instead."

He opened his arms to me again, and I quickly scooted next to him and asked, "Do you have any intention of bringing your puckered lips to my front door in September of 1971, or will you still be the property of Amber Hartford?"

"Yes, you can bet my puckered lips I will be there!" Brock exclaimed. "And you don't have to worry one bit about Amber. She's no match for Maggie Stone come her freshman year!

Chapter 44

DISTRICT TOURNAMENTS

"Your old girlfriend hasn't improved her game much," I said when Brock quizzed me about how the team was shaping up. "At least your new girlfriend Amber can dribble fairly well, but the rest of them either travel or double dribble every time they get the ball. I sure hope the refs go easy and don't call every little thing, otherwise, it'll be a long ten minutes." I must say I enjoyed it when Brock acted like his hearing had failed when I mentioned his current girlfriend.

My first district tournament experience was a blast! Circle and Sandstone Springs had the best and largest capacity gymnasiums in the conference, and the two schools hosted the tournament on alternate years. This year it was Circle's turn, so after a big school and community pep rally, the team and the rest of the high school and junior high kids filled the buses for the fourteen-mile trip.

I won't lie, I was so excited to play at halftime that my stomach was doing backflips the whole first half of the boys' game against Richey. I got even more anxious when I saw Ira, Wyatt, and Annie enter the gym just in time for the Richey band to play the national anthem.

The Buffaloes 14-9 first-quarter lead was quickly squandered when their 6'2" center, Trent Moseman, came down on an opponent's foot and collapsed on the floor in pain. The resulting ankle sprain was severe, and it was apparent Trent would be out for the rest of the game, if not the rest of the tournament. Without Trent's steady play in the post, Brock would have to pick up the slack. Realizing that, the Richey coach started to double-team Brock every time he got the ball. This coaching strategy was effective, as Richey held a 23-19 lead when our girl's team filed into the Home Economics room to change for our halftime entertainment game.

At 5'8", I was the tallest girl on our team. Unfortunately, I had to guard their 6'0" senior post player. She was not only tall and wide, but could get up and down the court quite well for a girl of her size. Furthermore, she was a pretty good shot. The ten-minute running-clock contest seemed to fly by, and I had a tough time stopping my taller opponent from scoring when her teammates were able to get her the ball inside the key. But when I was fouled on a driving lay-up and made the free throw to complete a three-point play, we were only down 8-7 with twelve seconds to go. When I was able to steal their inbound pass, Mr. Miller hollered at me to call a time out.

"Okay, Amber will take the ball out, they'll be trying to deny the entry pass to Maggie, so Amber will pass it to Tracy. Maggie, you go get the ball from Tracy as soon as she gets it, and you'll have about ten seconds to go one-on-one and take the final shot. Everybody got it? Okay, let's go win this thing!"

Brock caught up with me as I was walking out of the gym after the boys' game was finished. "We had just come back to the court for the second half when I saw that last out-of-bounds play you gals ran. Let me guess; Mr. Miller used you as a decoy so Amber could get the pass into Tracy. Then you were supposed to come and get the ball from Tracy and try to score. Am I right?"

"Yes, that was how Mr. Miller drew it up," I answered in a shivering voice.

"Don't need to be a genius to figure out what would happen next," said Brock disgustedly. "No way was Tracy going to pass you the ball and watch you be the hero. Nope, she decided she had the talent to do it herself. I guess she did manage to make a couple of dribbles before getting the ball stolen and losing any chance to win the game. Go figure."

"Well, no guarantee I would have been able to score the winning basket if she would have passed it to me," I offered.

"I would have bet on you to score. After all, you had all seven of your team's points."

"And I'm sorry about your game, Brock," I said as I patted him on the arm. "I knew it would be tough sledding when Trent went down. I think you guys did a heck of a job keeping it close after that. I mean, to only lose by five is pretty darn good. By the way, you had a season-high 27 points—not bad, considering they double-teamed you after Trent went out."

Since Ira left after our halftime performance to check on a sick cow, Annie and Whit brought me home after the game. Ira had already gone to bed, and I smiled happily when reading the note he'd left on the kitchen table: *good game you run like a deer you are a deadeye shooter.*

Chapter 45

INTERNING WITH
DR. RATH

I almost leapt from my chair and did cartwheels down the hall when Mrs. Poser passed out the spring quarter internship assignments! Yes, there I was, third on the internship list, right behind Sandy and Laura:

MRS. POSER'S SEVENTH GRADE
INTERNSHIP ASSIGNMENTS

Sandy Barnhart - Buffalo Jump Café, Jeanie Knox
Laura Rife - County Treasurer's Office, Kathy Bailey
Maggie Stone - Rath Veterinary Clinic, Dr. Richard Rath

Whit had told me months ago about Mrs. Poser's popular and long-standing internship program with the local businesses in and around Sandstone Springs. Each spring quarter her students would submit, in order of preference, their top three business choices along with a detailed explanation as to their interest in those selections. After carefully reviewing the applications and attempting to find appropriate student/business matches, Mrs. Poser would issue her assignments.

"The way you like animals, I just know you're going to put Dr. Rath at the top of your list," Whit said. "But let me warn you ahead of time, every year he's the most requested internship of the bunch. He was number one on my list, but I ended up getting my third choice, the Sandstone Springs Mercantile. So don't go into this expecting to get the first on your list."

Ira was happy with my assignment, too. With the hint of a crooked smile forming at the left corner of his mouth, he declared, "It would sure be handy to have an in-house vet to fix up ol' Dimwit every time he sticks his nose into a rattler, skunk, or porcupine, that's for dang sure!"

Dr. Rath was out on a calving emergency ranch call when I arrived for my first after-school appointment the following afternoon. Between phone call interruptions and customer foot traffic, Mrs. Rath was able to conduct the initial interview. Since the vet clinic had participated in Mrs. Poser's seventh-grade business internship program for a good number of years, she showed me the schedule outline they usually used for their student helpers.

"As you can see, Maggie, we like to have you come in for an hour or so twice a week after school," Mrs. Rath explained. "We want to give the students a good look at all sides of our business here at the clinic, from helping me do the less-glamorous tasks out in the front office to observing the doctor treat his patients here in the clinic. We also try to get you out with Dr. Rath on a house call or two, as that's a big part of a country veterinarian's work. He probably treats more animals on location than here in the clinic. For example, when a momma cow is down and having trouble birthing naturally—like when the calf isn't turned the right way—it's obviously difficult for the rancher to bring the cow to the clinic. In those types of situations, Dr. Rath goes wherever the patient is.

"If that all sounds good to you, we might as well get started. The next phone call is yours. Better to be thrown to the wolves sooner than later," my favorite grandmother figure said with a laugh.

"Rath Vet Clinic, Maggie speaking. How can I help you?" I answered, reading from Mrs. Rath's phone protocol sheet. I must have repeated that fifty times in the two hours I was there, as the phone rang almost nonstop. With Mrs. Rath's help, I scheduled appointments for two cats to be spayed or neutered, two sick dogs, and a horse with a suspected broken leg from stepping in a badger hole. After writing down at least three messages from ranchers wanting Doc to call them back concerning calving questions or problems, I took a call that had me stumped.

"Who did you say this is?" the caller asked.

"A-ah, this is Maggie Stone. I'm a student helper here at the clinic."

"Would ya' be ol' Ira's granddaughter?"

"Y-yes sir, that's correct," I answered.

"I see. Okay, this here is Marvin Sinclair. Would you please tell the Doc that Horace has come up plum lame? He ain't even walkin' good enough for me to get him in the horse trailer, so Doc's gonna have to come out to the ranch."

Mrs. Rath was watching and listening and smiled broadly when I covered the mouthpiece with my hand and whispered, "It's Marvin Sinclair, who the heck is Horace?"

"Horace is his mule, he's older than Methuselah. What's wrong with him now?"

"He's lame, and Marvin says he wants Dr. Rath to come to the ranch to see him," I reported. "What should I tell him?"

"Tell him Doc will call him back later today."

Between numerous phone interruptions and trying to listen to the many ailments of 94-year-old Hazel Holzer's bulldog, the rest of my session at the clinic flew by quickly. Although I was disappointed that Dr. Rath didn't return during my shift, I actually enjoyed my time learning how to work at the front office. Hectic as it was, I was glad I got to spend some time with Hazel and Erma, the bulldog. Both of them were pretty darned cute!

Chapter 46

FROM BETSY-LOU TO CINDY-SUE

After living through my first winter on the Stone Ranch, I had come to appreciate the hardiness of the men and women who earned their livelihood on the wind and snow-swept plains of eastern Montana. "Tougher than boot leather, that's what these farmers and ranchers are in these parts," Ira would always say. I had come to greatly admire Ira's love of his land and the livestock it fed and nurtured. And despite the often bitter-cold winter mornings, I enjoyed helping my grandpa load the trailer from the same haystack behind the barn that Ira, Brock, and I had built by picking the bales from the various hayfields. Most of all, I enjoyed the look of satisfaction Ira wore on his face after feeding his beloved cowherd and returning to the warmth of the kitchen and already-made hot coffee on the stove.

But now we were into the month of March, and while that certainly didn't mean we were past the days of cold snaps or heavy snowstorms, it did mean spring would be trying to rise from its long winter nap. March also meant calving season for Ira and his ranching neighbors. "Shouldn't run cattle if you don't like getting up every few hours in the middle of the night to check the cows. Nothing worse than oversleeping and losing a calf because of operator negligence," Ira would always say.

Even though I had yet to go on a calving ranch call with Dr. Rath, I was already getting some experience on the Stone Ranch. Some folks might find the calving experience to be gross, but I thought quite the opposite when I witnessed my first birth that didn't require any assistance from Ira. And it was neater yet when the second calf born needed our help. Ira had some of the same looking chains and "cranking" type tools that I'd packed in Dr. Rath's ranch-call bag, and it was pretty tense when Papa had to hook the chains to the calf's feet and assist the momma cow in delivering the baby calf. But everything worked out well, as both were soon on their feet with Ira helping the calf locate where breakfast was being served.

But calving wasn't always a bed of roses. I found out the hard way when, after school one day, I went to the clinic for my next internship session. "I'm sorry Myles, he's stitching up a horse that lost a fight with a barbed wire fence, but he should be done shortly," said Mrs. Rath to the phone caller. "You say you've got a first-calf heifer that's having a rough go of it? I see, I see, I'll send him out as soon as he's done."

"Can I go?" I asked anxiously. "Sorry to eavesdrop, but that sounded like a calving problem, am I right?"

"Right you are, young lady. And yes, I don't see any reason why you couldn't go on this ranch call. Myles Eppers lives about five miles past your place, so Doc can just drop you off on his way back to town."

After making double sure I had all the medicines and supplies in Dr. Rath's bag, we headed out for the Eppers Ranch. "You probably haven't talked to your grandpa since you left for school this morning, but he had a rough day. He called me out to your ranch about noon today as one of his older cows was having a tough time calving. To make a long story short, the cow made it through, but I got there too late to save the calf. Anyway, nothing a rancher, especially Ira, hates worse than losing a calf or a cow. Just a fair warning, your grandpa will probably be a tad grouchy when you get home tonight."

Being a rookie vet helper on my first ranch call, I didn't have any experience other than the few deliveries I'd witnessed at Ira's, but I was pretty sure Myles Epper's heifer and her yet-unborn calf were in a world of trouble. Dr. Rath worked feverishly for what seemed like an hour or more, but only the calf survived the ordeal.

"You got another cow to draft this little gal on?" Dr. Rath asked.

"Nope, haven't lost any calves yet."

"I'll bet Ira will buy this pretty little lady from you—one of his cows lost her calf just this morning."

Since it was approaching dark and a cold wind was pushing across the plains, Dr. Rath put the calf on my lap and turned up the heater. She was fidgety at first, but settled down as I petted her and talked gibberish in the calmest voice I could muster.

"You sure have a way with the animals, Maggie," the vet said admiringly. "I don't think Mrs. Poser could have made a better match in hooking us up together for this internship."

Doc was right; Ira was in a foul mood when we pulled up to our barn, but his demeanor improved when he saw what I was holding on my lap. "Your granddaughter is a good helper, Ira. She just might be the first woman vet in Sandstone Springs County if she keeps up the good work. I have another call, or I'd stay and help make sure your cow takes on this calf."

"Yep, my Maggie is right-good ranch hand, that's for darn sure. And thanks, but we'll be fine in introducing these two bovines to one another."

I think I allowed myself a quick blush from Ira's rare compliment, and then we immediately put the two together in a pen in the barn. The cow didn't seem too agreeable at first, even kicking at the hungry little calf when she tried to suck. But eventually she gave in, and Ira seemed confident the two had formed a bond.

"I 'spose you'll have to name this one, too?" Ira asked.

"Yep, I will. Now, can you guess what I'm going to name her?"

"Oh, so I have to play this guessing game with you again, is that it?"

"That's exactly right. So, get to guessing," I replied with a chuckle.

"I'm gonna go out on a limb here, hmm, could it be Cindy-Sue? Don't pretend that's not it—I know it's Cindy-Sue!"

"You got it!" I squealed. "How'd you know?"

With the familiar tug beginning to raise the left corner of his mouth, he said, "Where there's a Betsy-Lou, a Cindy-Sue is never far behind."

Chapter 47

BAD MOON RISING

I'm not sure I was any more relaxed than the first plane trip when the pilot turned up the throttle to charge down the runway for take-off. One glimpse at Ira's colorless knuckles confirmed that he wasn't exactly comfortable either. At least Ira let me take the window seat, and unlike the first trip in January, the sky was cloudless. I almost forgot how nervous I was as we slowly climbed above the sandstone rims that held and protected the city of Billings, then further rising to an altitude sufficient to clear the mass of magnificent Montana and Wyoming mountain ranges.

"Beartooths and Absarokas, I reckon those must be," said Ira when I asked the name of the mountain ranges we were passing over. I noticed he avoided looking toward the window.

The reason for this trip was similar to the first one, both a result of a phone call from Dr. Drummond. Like the January call, I'll never forget the time, day, date, and number of days:

5:56 pm, Tuesday, April 14, 1970—365 days.

Ira and I sat close together on the same two kitchen chairs as we did on the last call, Ira holding the phone between us so that we both could hear. "Mr. Stone, Miss Maggie, I'm so sorry to inform you that Lillian Stone passed away at 2:45 p.m. this afternoon," Dr. Drummond informed us in his usual compassionate tone. "We've been trying to get a hold of you ever since she passed. We were able to connect earlier with your San Francisco contact, Sun-Ju Seong, and she said she would be in touch with you soon."

I don't remember much about what he said next other than something about Lillian no longer having to suffer. I do vividly remember this revelation: My mom died one year after she went into this final spell. Exactly. To the day.

"This is not the reason I expected to meet again, Maggie," said a tearful Sun-Ju, hugging me as soon as we exited the tunnel from the plane and onto the concourse. "Cho is still at school, so she said to give you extra loves from her. She'll see you tonight, I'm sure."

As I look back, those next few days were a blur. We stayed in a motel near the mortuary that Sun-Ju had suggested for final arrangements. Sun-Ju and Ira had several long talks before sitting down with me and explaining their plans.

"Maggie, both Sun-Ju and I agree that your mom should be cremated," Ira explained, accompanied by a confirming nod from Sun-Ju. "The question is, where should her remains go? We think you should weigh in on this decision. Would you like her to be buried here in San Francisco? Or would you want to bring her to be with you, ah, us, and she could be buried next to your grandma at the ranch?"

"I want to bring her home to the ranch," I said, squeezing Cho's hand as I spoke. "I mean, I feel she's kind of been with me anyway. You know, with her old room being next to mine and all. Yes, I think we should bring her home and let her rest next to Grandma Audrey."

"I think she'd like that," Ira said softly. "And I know Audrey would appreciate the company."

Ira and Sun-Ju didn't waste any time making the arrangements, and we had a small service at the mortuary two days later. Besides the Jeong family, I was happy to see my mom's old band members in attendance.

"We finally did find a new female vocalist," one of them told me after the service. "But she sure can't sing like your mother did."

I guess some people might think it weird to be flying on an airplane with an urn among your baggage items, but I didn't care, I found it comforting. Besides, I knew for certain she'd be welcome back at the Stone Ranch.

Still, I pretty much cried the whole car ride from Billings to the ranch. Poor Ira, I don't think he knew what to do or say, so he mostly stayed quiet the entire way until we turned onto the lane at the mailbox.

"We'll need to have a gravestone made before we bury your mom down by Audrey. I'm a-thinkin you're the one who should decide on the words, so best to be giving that some thought. In the meantime, what do you say we put the urn in her old room?"

It didn't take me long to ponder that suggestion. "Yes, that sounds good. That's the perfect place until the gravestone is completed."

It took me a long time to get to sleep as I kept tossing, turning and going over in my mind the same questions I'd been pondering for the past year. *Why did she suddenly enter a spell she would never completely escape from? What was different about this spell than the old ones?* Peering through the window from my bed, I searched the blinking stars for answers to my questions. Finding none, I finally fell into a restless slumber about the time birds began chirping and the roosters started crowing.

Chapter 48

THE DREAM

"**Y**ou're pretty quiet there this morning, Maggie," observed Ira as he skillfully used his spatula to flip a pancake directly from the skillet to my plate on the kitchen table. "Anything in particular ya' want to yap about?"

While the vivid dream I had the night before was still fresh in my mind, I forged ahead. "Have you ever had a dream that felt so real you actually thought, well, you know, that maybe it really happened?"

"Yeah, I think most everybody can say they've had a dream like that ever now and again," Ira admitted. "Ain't had one like that recently, but I'm a-guessin' you just had yourself one last night?"

"Yes. Yes, I did," I confirmed. I hesitated for a moment as I gathered my thoughts and then started firing questions. "So, Ira, have you ever talked to God? Do you believe a dead person can talk to a living person? I don't mean like speaking to a ghost, but actually talking to a dead person who looks like a real live person.

I mean, a dead person that looks like they did when they were alive? Do you think that's possible?"

"Whoa there, Nellie, let's slow down a tad and let me try to answer your questions one at a time. First off, you've no doubt figured out I'm not a churchgoer, least-wise not since your grandma passed on. But that don't mean I don't chat with the Man Upstairs from time to time. But near as I can recall, all of them visits were one-sided, don't reckon I ever recall Him joining in on the conversation.

"As far as talkin' with dead people? Call me crazy, but I do that all the time with your grandma darn near every day down at her headstone. Now, I surely do understand what you're sayin' about your dream and how it can seem like somebody is really standin' right there. It don't happen near as much now that ten years have passed by, but I remember seein' my Audrey in dreams back then, and seeing her clear as a bell, too, just like you're sayin'. But kind of like the visits I was tellin' you 'bout with God, she ain't ever chatted back. But I can feel her presence, even to this day. I find comfort in having her close by, I surely do. Well, enough about that. Tell me about your dream."

"Okay," I started, trying to remember every detail and explain it precisely as it happened. "First thing I remember, Dimwit and I were in the barn checking on Cindy-Sue when Mom suddenly appeared and started walking toward me. And Papa, she didn't look anything like she did when we saw her in the hospital back in January; not like when she was hooked up to all those tubes, not all skin and bone and staring into the distance with sad eyes. She looked like she used to when she came off the stage at The Gables after playing a set. Still small and thin, but healthy looking. Smiling, laughing, and pretty as a picture!

"Anyway, we hugged for what seemed like forever before I brought over a straw bale for us to sit on. We laughed when Dimwit kept trying to jump up and wiggle in between us. I was surprised when Mom called him by name. She said she was glad I liked all the animals on the ranch, but the only thing she liked was the cats, not the dog, not the cows or even the horses. I told her I loved all the animals, except for the chickens, that is.

"Then it was sad because she started crying. She said she was so sorry for staying in her spell when I was at the age where I needed her the most. She said she tried and tried to wake up from her spell and come home to me, but her eyelids were so heavy she couldn't open them. Worse yet, when she tried to get up and rescue me from the orphanage, it was like she was buried up to her waist in quicksand.

"But she said she was okay now, even though she was dead. She said not to worry about her because she was happier than she'd ever been—except for not being able to be with me. She said that right after she died, God met her at heaven's gate and said that one of His bands was in need of a female vocalist. Next thing she knew, she was singing away in heaven! Can you believe that?

"So Papa, do you think it was really Mom talking to me, or was it a dream? And do you think maybe God finally answered my prayers? I mean, not the prayers I sent about waking up from her spell, but the prayers I sent after she died, asking Him to bring her into heaven?"

"Well, here's what I do believe," said Ira, reaching for my hands and pulling me into a hug for only the second time. "Whether it was real or just a dream don't matter. What matters is your ma found a way to tell you she tried to get out of that darn spell and come back to you. And more important than that, she let you know that she's okay now that God brought her into heaven. And she's doin' what she likes to do best, and that's a singin' with the angels.

"And here's what I'm a-thinkin' 'bout your prayers: I think God answered your prayers for Lillian to go to heaven instead of the prayers for her to wake up from the spell for a reason, 'cause He knew she'd be happier in heaven."

I leaned in for another hug before pulling back and agreeing with what Ira had just said. "I think you're right! I think God knew her life would be hard if she stayed here on earth. He knew she'd keep struggling with her spells and not be awake often enough to be with me or to sing with the band down at Gable's."

"Yep, that's exactly it. I know she misses you somethin' horrible, but I feel better knowing she's happy now up there in heaven singin' away," Ira said, squeezing my hand hard. "Far as I'm concerned, heaven sure beats layin' in some hospital bed hooked up to all those tubes; it darn sure does."

"I feel better knowing she's happy now, too," I confirmed. "I hated seeing her like she was, just wasting away to nothing. I think God made the right choice in taking her with Him. Like you say, He really did answer the right prayers."

Chapter 49

MOM COMES HOME

"Chores and ranch work don't get done by themselves," I announced, repeating one of Ira's favorite sayings as I headed out the door to do morning chores with my sidekick Dimwit. I thought I caught a small smile tug on the left corner of his mouth, confirming that he knew I was making a little bit of fun.

"I have to run into town for some tractor parts, so I'll be gone when you get back from chores," Ira replied. "Check on the cow and the orphan calf, would you? Make sure the momma is still lettin' that little gal suck."

I was happy that Ira had given me the responsibility of keeping an eye on Cindy-Sue and her new mother. "I was an orphan for a while too, Cindy-Sue," I explained as she hungrily found her meal ticket. "Really, it's not so bad; you found a new home a lot faster than I did. Don't worry; your new mom seems to have welcomed you to the family."

While Ira and I were in San Francisco tending to the details of my mom's passing, Ira had Whit come over and do my chores. In addition to looking in on how Cindy-Sue and her new mother were getting along, the eggs needed to be gathered and the hen house cleaned. I was glad Whit was taking care of things for me. I knew she'd take special care of Gunsmoke, Ol' Swayback, and Dimwit, too. I thought of how thankful I was to have such friends as Cho and Whit but wished Cho was living in Sandstone Springs instead of San Francisco. I knew her and Whit would hit it off as well.

When I finished my chores and returned to the house, I noticed an envelope propped up on the kitchen table. Upon closer inspection, I saw that "Maggie" was written on the envelope in Ira's sweeping cursive handwriting. *What in the world? Am I in some kind of trouble?* I anxiously tore open the envelope and began to read the letter.

Dear Maggie,

I know you're wondering why I'd write when I could say what I have to say face-to-face. As you know I ain't much of a talker. My words get all jumbled when I have some-thing important to say. Ain't much of a writer neither, only took schooling through eighth grade but can write down what needs to be said better than saying it. Here goes. First thing is your mom. I didn't do good dealing with your mom. your gma did better. I had a hard time with her. She wasn't like you. She hated the ranch. She was stubborn and hard to raise. When she got pregnant with you, I didn't handle it well. I've spent years trying to make excuses for myself to wash away the guilt and shame of how I handled the situation. Fact is I run her off. Instead of being supporting like your gma, I wasn't. She was only 15 and I should have done things differently. She needed support and understanding and got none of it from me. Whats worse is never coming to see you after you was born. no excuse for that. The only right thing I ever did was come and get you from orphanage. I know I was hard on you at first, too. I'm old and crabby and set in my ways, but want you to know I think having you here is my gift from God. I ain't good at saying it but I love you so much. You make my life worth living. Annie says I've got spring to my step since you been here. Anyway, I want you to know how sorry I am for the way I treated your mom and not coming with gma Audrey to see you when you was little. I'm so glad you're here now and hope you like it ok living here.

Love,
Ira (Papa)

PS Don't be mad at Brock for not coming around more. I know you two are sweet on each other. I was afraid you were too young and worried about that pregnant thing like your mom when she was a teenager. Told Brock he couldn't date you till you was a freshman. So blame me not him.

I was making ham sandwiches for our lunch when Ira came into the kitchen. Although he returned my greeting, he looked sheepish and wouldn't make eye contact. I finished putting the mayo and pickles on our sandwiches and went to him, grabbing his hand and leading him to his favorite chair in the living room.

"Sit down," I ordered, leaning over and taking his face in my hands so that we were eye to eye. "Papa, thank you for the letter. I know how hard that must have been for you to write. I understand how you feel guilty about not ever coming to see my mom and me in San Francisco, and I admit I wondered if you didn't visit because you didn't like us. But you should know that Mom never, ever said anything bad about you. Granted, she didn't talk about you at all. She did talk about Grandma a lot, she really loved her.

"I'm so, so happy that you like having me here, and I love you, too. And I love that you think I make your life better. I confess that at first, I wondered why you brought me here. I mean, why come for me when you didn't even visit me for the twelve years of my life? And then I thought, at least for the first few months I was here, that you didn't like me very much. But then we started getting used to each other. Remember? I think you've turned me into a pretty fair ranch hand, and I'd say we're a pretty good team now, wouldn't you?"

Ira nodded a yes, and I leaned in and gave him a smooch on the cheek. He wrapped his arms around me and pulled me in tight, our faces close enough that I could feel the wetness from his cheek. When I pulled back to look at him, I could tell he was embarrassed for me to see him cry. He wiped off the tears from his left cheek, but when I watched a large teardrop slide down from his right eye and shimmy and shake at the top edge of the wide scar before breaking loose and flowing into the deep crevice, I was reminded that he had no feeling on the right side of his face. He didn't wipe that tear because he had no idea it was there. Cupping his face with both hands as a diversionary tactic, I quickly brushed away the right-side remnants of his crying.

After completing the evening chores, Dimwit and I took a stroll down to the pond. It was surprisingly warm and pleasant for an early May day in Montana. I stood in front of the recently placed gravestone of my mom and read with pride the words I had chosen to be chiseled into the stone.

LILLIAN MARIE STONE

SEPTEMBER 6, 1940–APRIL 14, 1970

BELOVED MOTHER AND DAUGHTER

"SHE SANG LIKE AN ANGEL"

It felt weird striking up a conversation with a grave, but I took note that Ira had been visiting almost daily with Grandma Audrey for years. I took a deep breath and began to speak.

"Well, Mom, I'm still surprised that you chose to both enter your spell and die exactly one year to the day, but I guess you must have your reasons. I know you might not have the best memories of your days here at the ranch, but I'm really glad you're here now. I thought you'd like to be where I am, so I hope you don't mind. I know you didn't get along with Ira, and though he never said as much to me, I'm guessing you were pretty mad at him. Can't say as I blame you. But you know, Ira has changed since you were here, really, he has. If you don't believe me, listen to this."

Taking Ira's letter from my pocket, I slowly read it to her. I cried a few times as I went along, but figured Mom would understand.

When I had finished, I continued, "So, you can tell from what I just read you that Ira deeply regrets what happened between you two back then. I admit, I didn't like him very much when I first got here, either. It took a long time to get to this point, but I feel like this ranch is home now. You can see from the letter that Ira and I are in a good place. We're finally a family now—Papa, Grandma, you, and me—just like it should be. It's not how either of us would have envisioned the way we'd be together a year or so ago, but I find it peaceful knowing that you're here now next to Grandma, just down the hill at the pond.

"I promise I'll stop by every day and visit you. After all, you're only a stone's throw away! I'll tell you all about everything I'm doing at school and here at the ranch. I promise I'll even fill you in on the Brock situation that Ira mentioned in his letter. It's a pretty long and interesting story, so it'll probably take me a week's worth of visits to get you up to speed.

"Speaking of Ira, he's anxious to till the garden and get ready for planting at the end of the month. I better go see if I can give him a hand, so that's all for now. Don't worry, Dimwit and I will be back for another visit tomorrow."

Hearing his name, Dimwit cocked his head and looked up at me with a who-the-heck-have-you-been-talking-to look on his face. I gave him a pat on the head, and we jogged the hundred yards up the incline to meet Ira in the garden.

Knowing that I had just come from the pond, he said. "I'm glad your mom and my Audrey are together again, Maggie. And I like what you had them engrave on Lillian's headstone."

"Thanks, Papa. I'm happy they're together, too. I bet if we listen close enough on one of those calm and quiet evenings, we'll hear Mom singing from heaven. She sings like an angel, you know."

ABOUT THE ARTIST

*T*he renowned pencil sketch artist, Don Greytak drew the book cover, as well as the sketches scattered throughout the book.

Greytak, working from his Old Library Gallery in Havre, Montana, is noted worldwide for his multi-dimensional subject matter, to include decades-past farm and ranch settings so rich in detail that the observer is immediately pulled into the story the sketch is telling. Don is a master at incorporating era-specific vehicles and machinery into his art, and he is blessed with the extraordinary ability to capture what is real and find the humor in down-to-earth situations.

For more information or to view Greytak prints, go to: dongreytak.com

ABOUT THE AUTHOR

 *A* native of Big Sky country, Wayne Edwards spent his 30-plus-year banking career in his hometown of Denton, a rural small town located in the heart of Montana's expansive wheat and cattle country. Edwards began writing upon his retirement in 2019 and published both a children's book *Buster the Bridger Mountain Bear* and a fictional novel *Pacer Coulee Chronicles* in 2021.

Wayne and Lorinda, his wife of 49 years, spend their time between their homes in Bozeman, Montana, and Cave Creek, Arizona, surrounded by their children and grandchildren.

Wayne can be reached at WayneEdwardsBooks.com.